The River
Runs South

Audrey Ingram

The River Runs South

◆ *A NOVEL* ◆

AUDREY INGRAM

alcove
press

Published in the United States by Alcove Press, an imprint of The Quick Brown Fox & Company LLC.

Alcove Press and its logo are trademarks of The Quick Brown Fox & Company LLC.

Library of Congress Catalog-in-Publication data available upon request.

ISBN (paperback): 978-1-63910-457-4
ISBN (ebook): 978-1-63910-458-1

Cover design by Sarah Brody

Printed in the United States.

www.alcovepress.com

Alcove Press
34 West 27th St., 10th Floor
New York, NY 10001

First Edition: September 2023

10 9 8 7 6 5 4 3 2 1

To Mom, who told me to chase my dreams

And to Meredith, who told me this one was possible

CAMILLE THOUGHT THEY HAD a lifetime of love ahead, so she didn't linger in bed despite the tangle of Ben's long limbs clutching her waist. Ben liked a lazy start to the day, but Camille's brain spun with too many checklists to waste wakeful moments. She lifted her husband's arm like a lever in a parking garage, gently releasing it onto her pillow.

Camille padded softly into the bathroom, carefully closing the door so she wouldn't wake Ben. She sighed as she turned on the shower, her mind churning with thoughts of her morning meeting and all she needed to do. She efficiently lined up the brushes and bottles that comprised her morning beauty routine, trying to be diligent about the daily collagen supplements and creams the twenty-year-old at Sephora had told her were "must-haves." Yet Camille looked in the mirror and saw new lines and felt less confidence. Sometimes she wondered if all the energy she put into looking younger was actually making her older. She didn't appreciate the privilege of aging.

Camille stepped into the shower, carefully twisting her hair and piling it on top of her head. Left alone, deep-red tendrils exploded in wild chaos down her back. It was hair more suited to music festivals or protest marches than to courtrooms in Washington, DC. So every week Camille spent ninety minutes in the salon, having her hair pulled and straightened and smoothed so that she could fit in, or at least look the part.

After her shower, she unwound her hair and touched it up with a straightening iron, smoothing every unruly strand until it behaved, falling like a waterfall down her back. Then she dressed and tiptoed downstairs.

Camille hung their daughter's backpack on a hook by the door. Willa's water bottle and lunch box were already packed in the fridge, part of Camille's nightly routine. Camille jotted a note to Ben, reminding him of Willa's checkup and listing the questions he should ask the pediatrician. She placed the paper on the kitchen counter, finding a message Ben must have written the night before. Ben frequently left hidden notes listing things he liked about Camille. In this case, it was a love note to Camille's legs. She laughed, wondering how her sleeping husband could make her blush before the sun was even up.

Ben knew she was nervous about her morning meeting. The night before, he had patiently sat on the edge of their bed as she rehearsed her presentation. Camille wished Ben could sit in the back of every meeting, his playful grins putting her at ease. Ben always found ways to moderate Camille's intensity.

She walked toward the door and hesitated. It was overkill, but with Ben, there was no such thing as too many reminders. Camille sent him a quick text: *Don't forget Willa's appointment with the pediatrician.*

Ben must have heard the ding from bed, because as Camille closed the door, she glanced at her phone and saw a response. *Got it. Knock 'em dead.*

Camille grinned as she walked down Sixteenth Street toward her office, the sun beginning to rise. She loved this weather, the leaves yellowing, the crisp air entwined with the scent of burnt wood. Camille replayed Ben's pep talk from the night before, finding her anxiety easing and her confidence rising with every step. Ben told her that she worried unnecessarily because no one was as prepared as Camille, which was mostly true, except Camille was completely unprepared for Ben's death.

Camille sat through the meeting, unaware that her life was shattering. By the end of the presentation, Camille thought the morning had gone as smoothly as possible, confirmed by the client's tentative praise as he was leaving. Camille gathered her papers, reaching for her phone to update Ben on the success. But then she saw three missed calls from the pediatrician's office. Her initial reaction wasn't concern. She was annoyed. Despite her reminders, Ben must have missed the appointment.

Camille's secretary walked into the meeting and said there was an emergency.

Camille shook her head. "It's not an emergency. My husband forgot to bring our daughter to the doctor's office."

Camille stuffed binders and handouts into her bag, frustration building with every jerky motion. Her mind spun with the tasks she needed to finish before lunch. Now she added rescheduling the pediatrician to the list. The juggle between clients and motherhood was never-ending. And yet, somehow, Camille always made the appointments. She also signed Willa up for ballet lessons, color-coded grocery lists, and organized play dates. She did these things while also reminding Ben of the things he was supposed to do. At the moment, Ben's forgetfulness was no longer a charming quirk.

Camille's secretary repeated that there was an emergency. Camille looked around the room at the stoic faces. There were tears in her secretary's eyes. Camille slung her bag over her shoulder and walked to the door. Then Camille noticed two uniformed police officers waiting in the hallway.

Camille would relive that morning over and over again. She wished she had stayed in bed a few minutes longer. She wished she had called Ben on her way in to work so she could hear his voice again. She wished she hadn't spent a single moment assuming the worst of the person she loved most.

Mostly, she wished she had been home. Because when a seemingly healthy, funny, forty-year-old man collapses in his kitchen while toasting bagels for his six-year-old, his wife should be there to call 911. Instead, their daughter sat on the couch, watching cartoons, unaware of the tragedy until the weekly cleaning service arrived and found Ben on the floor. By then it was too late. Ben was gone.

♦ 2 ♦

CAMILLE COULDN'T REMEMBER HOW she got home. The officers told her Ben had suffered a heart attack, which made no sense because he ran three miles every day. Ben ran the same loop around Meridian Hill Park and back down Sixteenth Street every morning, even in the rain, which Camille found ridiculous. A man that ran seven days a week didn't die of a heart attack at forty.

Camille remembered people crying and people hugging her, which had never happened in the ten years she had worked at the law firm. Camille told someone she had to go home, and someone got her there.

She wanted to see Willa and Ben and put this nightmare misunderstanding behind her. She wanted to slide back into bed and crawl back under Ben's solid arm. She wanted to wipe muffin crumbs off Willa's lips and sneak a kiss with Ben in the kitchen.

But when she walked in the front door, Willa was sitting on the floor, sorting the collection of bottle caps she had collected from their neighborhood playgrounds. Camille hated that collection. It was dirty and slightly inappropriate for a six-year-old to squeal with pride when she found "a Corona, just like Daddy drinks." Ben found it charming. Everything about

Willa charmed Ben. Once, after a particularly challenging day of parenting that included Willa sitting in the garden fountain of their favorite taco shop, Ben laughed and said, "Willa is kind of like a tiny, drunk Camille." Camille had feigned offense, but it was pretty accurate.

Camille saw Willa with the bottle caps, and she immediately looked for Ben. For Ben to shrug his shoulders and say, "It brings her joy, Cam. Let it be."

Camille didn't see Ben. She saw their neighbor staring off into space. She saw a kitchen chair overturned and their couch pushed across the room. She saw Ben's backpack hanging on the entry hook and his shoes by the door.

Willa looked up and said so softly Camille could barely hear, "Momma, Daddy got hurt."

Camille scooped up her daughter and felt Willa's small legs wrap tightly around her waist. She smelled the crook of Willa's neck and felt the salty wetness of tears. Camille didn't realize she was crying until her sobs were so loud she could hear nothing else.

Later that evening, Camille's parents, Marion and Sam, appeared in her bedroom. Camille didn't remember calling them or telling them the news. All she knew was that her parents were there, wrapping her in a quilt, cleaning, and preparing food. Sam appeared to be on a stepladder changing lightbulbs and Marion was ironing cloth napkins. They were busying themselves with pointless tasks because no one wanted to sit still and let the reality of the day settle. Camille kept looking for Ben, so they could lock eyes and have secret silent conversations about her parents and their odd yet predictable routines. But Ben wasn't there.

Marion and Sam must have gotten a flight, because there was no way they could have driven from Alabama so quickly.

Camille couldn't process the details. She knew Willa was at her side, and her parents would take care of the rest.

At some point, Marion insisted on giving Willa a bath. Marion brought her sleepy granddaughter back to Camille's bed, while Sam made a fire in Camille's bedroom. Willa wrapped herself around Camille, and the only sound in the room was the crackle of burning wood. They lay there, each staring into different spaces, fingers entwined.

Willa turned to Camille, her small voice piercing the silence. "Momma, when is Daddy coming home?"

Silent tears began streaming down Camille's face. Camille wasn't prepared to explain the unexplainable. She couldn't research the right words to say. She was certain she was going to mess up, so she held Willa close and explained it as simply as she could.

"Daddy isn't coming home. Daddy's heart was sick, and it stopped working."

Camille expected questions, but Willa sat in silence. Camille knew there was much more to say, but for the moment, she welcomed the quiet. She brought Willa closer, feeling her daughter's leg curl around her hip, their chests rising and falling together.

Willa looked up at her mother and over to her grandparents, sighing deeply. She whispered, "We are all very sad."

★ ★ ★

In the days that followed, Camille refused to leave her bed. Willa spent most of the day beside her mother watching too many hours of cartoons and eating cheddar crackers, the organic kind, because organic snacks minimize a mother's guilt. They rarely left each other's side. Camille knew there had been people coming and going, voices and conversations swirling through the house, but she shut everything out.

Camille would not let anyone wash the sheets or touch Ben's clothes, but after four days, even Camille admitted that she needed a shower. On the morning of Ben's funeral, she pulled herself out of bed and made her way to the bathroom. She managed to wet her hair, and that was about it. Marion laid a navy dress on the bed, and Camille put it on.

Being the daughter of the perfect Marion Graves, Camille was expected to look a certain way. When she first started dating Ben, Camille had kept to a makeup routine that transformed her from barefaced to beauty pageant contestant in twelve minutes. Ben would watch Camille get ready, commenting on the magic and efficiency of the whole process. Camille dismissed him, explaining, "When your mother takes you to the Clinique counter at ten, you should be fast. I've been doing this for over a decade."

Ben had kissed her hard and said, "But I like your face underneath all that stuff. I'm going to reform you, homecoming queen." Whenever Ben caught Camille without makeup, hairs astray, he would bring his wife close and praise his hard work at chipping away her beauty queen persona. He loved "the real Camille," he'd say. Over the years, motherhood and work and exhaustion had delivered Ben's victory: Camille became a well-loved, stripped-down version of her former self.

Ben would have said he loved her simple look that morning, but he couldn't. He wasn't there to look at her, to hold her hand, to sit next to her and tell her that everything would be okay. The person best equipped to help Camille through her pain was gone. Camille wanted Ben's advice. She wanted to lie next to him, her head on his chest, and ask him how she was supposed to be a single parent. She wanted him to tell her how to manage her job and her daughter and a life all alone. She wanted Ben to tell her how to fix the empty hole in her heart.

Willa was waiting in the hallway, and Camille took her hand as they made their way downstairs.

Ben's parents were there, and the devastation on their faces made Camille shake. She couldn't imagine losing a child, their only child. Ben called his mother every Wednesday morning on his walk to work. He played golf with his father the third Sunday of every month. Camille wanted to say that she would learn to play and she would make those calls and she would do everything she could to take their pain away. But she couldn't say any of those things. She looked at them and saw their matching red-rimmed eyes and knew there were no words that could make anything better.

Camille stood, immobile, until her mother appeared at her side. Marion whispered, "One foot in front of the other. That's all you have to do," and Camille nodded.

Standing next to Marion was Camille's father, Sam. Camille looked at her parents. Marion's silver hair was cut in a perfect bob, her cranberry lips lined smoothly, her petite frame contrasting with Sam's towering figure. Sam's leathered skin, from too many days in the South Alabama sun, looked uncharacteristically pale. Sam was a fixer. He changed his own oil and he could rewire a lamp, but everything around him now was broken and there was nothing he could do. Camille watched as the sad lot of them made their way out the door.

The funeral was painful and beautiful. Throughout the day, Camille kept thinking, *Ben's missing this. He would love this so much. He would love seeing these guys.* She needed to look across the room and roll her eyes with Ben when his uncle started talking about genealogy research. She craved the familiar stories that poured out of the room, about Ben's days on the college soccer team, the pranks he played on colleagues at the architecture firm, the puppet shows he would put on for the kids at preschool pickup. She sat in the front pew of the church, flanked by her daughter and mother, proud of herself for holding it together.

Their neighbor walked to the front and began telling a story about how Ben had made flyers when Willa lost her toy stroller. Willa had pushed the stroller up and down the side-walk of their street, then left it outside the coffee shop, where it was taken. Ben made flyers and put them in every door along the block, on every car windshield. The next day, the toy stroller reappeared outside the coffee shop.

Camille had been away on a business trip. She'd had no idea. Hearing a new story about Ben made him come alive momentarily. The excruciating moment was too much for her to handle.

Camille cried and bent her body in half. She couldn't stop. She knew Willa was right there, but she couldn't contain the animal screams coming from her body.

Camille's father stood and picked Camille up as if she were a small child. He carried her out of the church, rocking and shushing his daughter, feeling the unbearable pain of knowing this damage was beyond repair.

♦ 3 ♦

THE DAY AFTER BEN's funeral, Camille pulled herself out of bed around ten. She spent five minutes staring at the floor, wondering what she was supposed to do next. She couldn't remember the last time she had spent five minutes sitting. She couldn't remember the last time she had stayed in bed until ten. She momentarily wished for the busyness of the past, before realizing none of it mattered without Ben.

Eventually, she did what she always did in the morning—she grabbed her phone and opened her email. It had been five days since Ben died, and it was the first time Camille had checked in with the office.

Camille's email habits used to drive Ben crazy. Every morning, Camille's hand would reach for her phone, her eyes opening to the blue screen and the urgency of international clients. She should have rolled over and nuzzled into the nook of Ben's arm, or kissed him gently, or taken a deep breath, but those were never the things she did to start her day. Instead, she responded to emails. Nighttime was worse, because the last thing she did before falling asleep was check her email. Ben used to threaten to ban the phone from the bedroom. He joked that there were so many better ways to end the night than with a phone in her hand, but Camille would roll her eyes, wishing he understood the pressures of her career. It had taken Ben's death to break Camille's habit.

She groaned at her in-box—576 unread messages. This was what happened when she didn't check her email regularly: the inescapable avalanche after five days of neglect. There were words like *urgent* and *emergency*, and Camille felt her stomach turn. It was too much to triage on her phone; she needed to go in to the office.

She trudged into the shower, deciding that shampoo and soap were a necessity at this point. She quickly dressed, throwing on a black cashmere sweater and gray pants.

Her hair was still wet when she went downstairs. The house was quiet, despite the bodies cluttering the living room. Camille's parents and Ben's parents lingered, not sure how to leave or what to do. Everyone's grief mixed in the air, sticky and thick, suffocating the ability to talk. There were flower arrangements covering the dining table and baked goods littering the kitchen counters. No one was eating and yet more food kept appearing. The adults were milling around, dusting surfaces that had no dust and fluffing cushions that hadn't been sat on. Willa seemed to be the only person with any appetite, and she savored her unlimited access to pies and cookies. No adult felt like being responsible, and it certainly wasn't the time anyone was going to tell the child no.

Camille walked toward the door, cleared her throat, and tentatively said, "I have to go in to the office for a few hours."

No one spoke, nervous glances whipping around the room. Eventually, Camille's mother walked forward, shaking her head. "No one expects you to be working right now. Why don't you sit down, and I'll fix you a plate of food?"

Camille grabbed her coat. "I'm not hungry. I won't be gone long, but I need to take care of a few things. None of my clients' lives stopped."

Ben's mother inhaled sharply, and Camille immediately regretted the comment. She needed to be more careful, especially around Ben's parents. Grief was a tiptoe up the stairs, but Camille was clomping on every creaky board. She should be sitting on the couch, crying with Ben's mother, because that was the right way to act after your husband died. But Camille couldn't cry anymore. All the tears had drained out of her body. Grieving Ben's death seemed like an impossible task, and Camille had no idea how to do it. Fixing a few client emergencies seemed like something she could handle. She needed to escape the sad house full of probing eyes and return to a world where she could pretend her husband's heart hadn't stopped.

Camille's father knew her better than almost anyone. Sam put a firm hand on his wife's shoulder and nodded his head. "Of course, Cammy. We'll be here. You take all the time you need."

Willa went back to eating cookies; the adults went back to their fidgeting. They all let Camille leave, not sure whether there was any point in insisting she stay.

It was an eerie feeling walking to the office. Everything was the same—the coffee shop on the corner was still open, the buses were still driving down Sixteenth Street, the children were still squealing on playgrounds. It was as if the world remained unchanged even though Camille's life had shattered. Camille couldn't decide if she was relieved or angry.

Camille kept her head down as she walked into her office. She didn't want eye contact or conversations. There were no condolences that could bring Camille any comfort, so she preferred silence.

She turned on her computer and started making lists—
the clients with real emergencies; the clients with an absurd
definition of emergency that could be handled with a reassur-
ing email; and all the other mess that could be forwarded to
an associate. Camille's life was a well-organized, constantly
updated to-do list. The familiarity of making lists allowed
Camille to temporarily push aside the fact that she had no idea
how to take a microscopic step forward in a life without Ben.

She'd made a sizable dent when she heard her office door
swing open and a familiar voice ask, "What the fuck are you
doing here?"

Only one person at the firm barged into her office without
knocking, and only one person could tease the hint of a smile
out of Camille on a day like this.

"You're going to get another letter from HR if you use
language like that," Camille said.

The woman standing in Camille's office smirked. "Apol-
ogies. What the holy fucking hell are you doing here? Is that
better?"

Camille nervously bit her lip. "I'm working, Paige. What
does it look like?"

Paige closed the door and crossed her arms, glaring as her
blonde hair spilled across the deep V neck of a dress that strad-
dled the line of acceptable office attire.

Camille and Paige had started at the law firm together a
decade ago, forming an instant friendship. In their first month
at the firm, Paige was sent home twice for clothing that was
deemed "inappropriate" by the middle-aged HR director.
Instead of being embarrassed or changing her outfit, Paige was
unfazed, claiming there was no way she was going to sacrifice
fashion for a job. Paige was always unabashedly herself, which
she could get away with because she was brilliant. Camille and

Paige had come up through the trenches together, both eventually making partner. There were more times than Camille could count that she had relied on Paige for support—an emergency coffee run, a rant about how to deal with the male partners, a much-needed cocktail after a long day.

Camille looked across the desk at her friend and sighed deeply. "My email was out of control. I needed to come in to the office."

Paige rolled her eyes. "That's the stupidest thing I've ever heard. Stop emailing. Go home."

Camille shook her head.

Paige leaned forward as she said, "Cam, the funeral was yesterday. Take some time. Go home to Willa. There is nothing here that can't be handled later."

"I can't sit in that house anymore. It's full of Ben, and Ben's parents, and . . ." Camille trailed off in a hiccupping breath.

"Okay, okay. Not home. But not here. You shouldn't be working right now."

"I don't know what else to do, Paige. I don't know how to live our life when Ben isn't here to live it with us." Camille swallowed hard. She wasn't going to cry, so she shook away the tears. "I know how to do this job. This is the one thing, maybe the only thing, I think I can do right now."

Paige nodded her head. "Fine. Then I'm going to do it with you. I'll grab my laptop, and we'll sit across from each other while you email. You are not sitting in this office by yourself. You are not alone."

Camille looked up, knowing Paige was right. She had a houseful of family and an army of friends who had called and written notes and stood next to her at the funeral and sent food and played with Willa. She was surrounded by people, but none of them was Ben.

✦ 4 ✦

AFTER THREE WEEKS OF taking shifts, Camille's and Ben's parents left. Camille convinced them that she was okay, that she could take care of her daughter and take care of herself. Willa made it easier. A six-year-old's life didn't stop, even when she was surrounded by grief. Death was difficult for Willa to grasp, whereas it was all Camille could think about. Willa still had questions about why the leaves were falling, and do birds get cold, and could they eat chocolate ice cream for dinner every night? Camille's love for Willa forced her to find a way to get up every day and do all the things her daughter needed her to do.

In some ways, it was easy for Camille to fall back into the routine of their lives, because for so long everything had been constantly busy and precisely scheduled. For years, Camille had gone to sleep thinking about everything she needed to do the next morning: initial the homework sheet, unload the dishwasher, check in with counsel in London, finalize the report for the client, pick up dry cleaning before the firm fundraiser. The programming of her life allowed her to go through the motions. To appear like she was functioning and taking care of a child and moving forward.

Through fall and winter, that was what Camille did. She followed the routine—the routine she'd developed and organized and recorded in a detailed spreadsheet. She color-coded her work appointments, Willa's childcare, the early-morning drop-offs, the army of babysitters on call for Camille's work emergencies, the food that Willa should be fed, the bills that needed to be paid. Camille listed everything that needed to be done, and then she did it. Because that made it appear that she could handle everything.

But she was just pretending. At night, after the emails from work stopped and Willa was tucked into bed, Camille would turn on the television, because silence was unbearable. She'd listen to the news and see that the world was moving on while she was immobile. She couldn't sleep; she couldn't bear to lie in a bed and relax without Ben beside her. There was no book or movie that could distract her from her loneliness. She'd spend the night awake and anxious, paralyzed with fear of living a whole life without Ben.

The only time she felt a break from the emptiness was when she was working. The demands of her job and its ability to consume her thoughts were a welcome reprieve. She poured herself into her clients, taking on new cases and volunteering for new projects, because she knew that while she was doing the work, she could force her brain to forget that Ben was gone. Some nights, if she read through files for long enough, she'd find her body collapsing on a heap of paper, sleeping for a few glorious hours, before her mind awoke and realized she was alone.

When springtime came, Camille was surprised. It was shocking that the seasons could change, that the weather could feel warm, that flowers could bloom, and Ben could still be dead. It was her job as an attorney to keep track of time, to record even the smallest fraction of an hour to bill her clients. Somehow, Camille had forced time forward, billing more and more hours, filling every minute of the day with tasks, so that days and weeks and months could pass. When Camille saw the cherry blossoms lining the streets of DC, she was genuinely surprised that she'd managed to live six whole months without Ben.

◆ 5 ◆

"I AM READY FOR school," Willa announced, walking into Camille's bathroom. Camille glanced at her daughter. Today's outfit was a combination of a Wonder Woman costume on top and pajama pants on the bottom. There were also snow boots in the mix. Snow was unlikely in late April, but Camille shrugged as she glanced at the clock. They had ten minutes before they had to be out the door. If the school had a problem with Willa's outfit, they could deal with it. Camille didn't have time for a battle with Willa over school uniforms. It wasn't even a worthy battle, because Willa was right: uniforms stifled creativity. Plus Camille didn't feel like she was in a position to judge anyone's appearance these days.

Camille glanced at her dress. It was a brown relic she had found shoved in the back of her closet, but it was clean. It hung on her frame. She kept forgetting to eat, which sounded like something girls with eating disorders said. Food seemed to be the last thing she thought about. She also forgot to pick up the dry cleaning, even though it was on the spreadsheet, bolded in red as a priority. She kept forgetting things, little things like grocery items, and big things like filing deadlines at work. It was the lack of sleep. Once she got through the meeting today, she was going to call her doctor and ask for a prescription. Plenty of people had insomnia; she'd take some pill and then she'd be fine. But first, she had to get Willa to school and then get to the office in time for her meeting. She closed her eyes briefly, trying to make herself focus on what needed to happen so she wouldn't forget.

She glanced at the clock again. Seven minutes before they had to leave. She'd already showered, a rarity these days, but she figured it was occasionally necessary. She pulled her hair into a wet ponytail. It would be a ball of frizz once it dried, but she wouldn't know that, because she never looked in the mirror anymore. She should have so much more time now that she wasn't getting weekly blowouts or spending her mornings on useless beauty routines, but that extra time seemed to evaporate. Grief sucked time like a vacuum.

She walked downstairs, Willa following, relaying details of the class caterpillar and her predictions for metamorphosis, a word Willa couldn't quite pronounce but stumbled through in an adorable way.

Camille gathered her purse and Willa's backpack and then glanced at the clock again. One minute ahead of schedule. "Okay, ready to go?"

Willa looked at her suspiciously and asked, "Can I eat breakfast?"

Camille had forgotten about breakfast. "Yes. Of course," she quickly said, even though they didn't have time to eat. She reached into her bag and pulled out an energy bar. "Here you go. I have one of the chocolate peanut butter flavors."

Willa grimaced. "They taste too chewy. Can't I have eggs? Or oatmeal?"

Camille shook her head. "No, we have to leave now." She opened the fridge and pulled out a container of leftovers. "Half of a bean burrito?"

"That's a weird breakfast, Mom."

"Yes, weird and wonderful." Camille tossed the burrito to Willa, who continued to eye it suspiciously. "You'll be fine. Eat the burrito. But walk and eat. We have to go."

Camille ushered Willa out the door. At the school drop-off line, she avoided eye contact with the principal. She was sure there would be a phone call later about the uniform guidelines, but it would be a polite phone call. No one wanted to scold the widow.

Camille hurried down the street, knowing it was faster to walk the few blocks than to try to find a cab. She glanced at her watch as she walked into the office lobby. She was three minutes late. It was fine; that was the meet-and-greet time, the chats about the weather, discussions about how everyone was doing. No one wanted to hear Camille's answer to that question, so they'd all be relieved she was three minutes late.

She walked into a conference room full of people and took the open seat next to the client. She smiled warmly as the meeting began. It was an important presentation, multiple partners reporting to the client about the full-scope risk assessment of the company's operations.

Paige sat across from Camille, ready to report on the civil litigation risks while Camille handled the regulatory risks. A senior partner at the firm was introducing the methodologies of the review when Paige looked at Camille and mouthed, *Are you okay?*

Camille quickly nodded her head and then smoothed her ponytail, guessing it was the state of her hair that gave Paige concern.

Camille made the motions of following along with the presentation, but she struggled to keep her eyes open. She hadn't slept at all the night before. She'd heard Willa cough and spent the night spiraling, wondering if her daughter had caught something from the playground, wondering if it would turn into the flu or pneumonia, wondering if Willa would stop breathing and Camille would be left alone.

If Ben had been there, he would have calmed her. He would have said, "It's probably allergies, but I'll peek in her room to make sure she's okay." But Ben wasn't there to share the worry, to be a part of the plan and the solution. Camille was left alone with her thoughts, and so she'd spent the night wondering and worrying until the sun came up and she showered and put on the awful brown dress and came in to work to sit in this meeting.

Camille flipped through the pages in the report as Paige began her presentation. Camille was next, so she started noting the three major risk categories she wanted to emphasize, but looking down at the paper made her eyes heavier. She heard Paige's soothing voice describe product liability litigation, and Camille's eyes closed momentarily.

Except it wasn't just a moment. It was several moments, or maybe it was several minutes. Camille wasn't sure. She opened her eyes when the associate on her right nudged her foot under the table. The client was staring directly at her, asking, "Camille, can you please describe the risks being assessed in phase two?"

Camille swallowed hard. She flipped quickly through the report and rattled off the list of foreign offices and operations that would be the focus of the regulatory risk review.

The client shook his head. "No. Paige went over all of that. I want to know about the testing protocols for the business lines that have already been designated high risk. It seems ridiculous to test them with the same phase-one standards."

"I agree. Let's review those protocols." Camille flipped through the report, but she couldn't find the chart summarizing the information she needed. Seconds passed in silence, an eternity when all the eyes in the room were focused on her. She looked up, searching the room, panic shooting through her body.

Paige spoke up. "If we all turn to page fifty-four of the report, I think we'll see the information you're asking about. This is my fault. I kept talking and took over a part of Camille's presentation, so I think she lost her place."

Camille quickly flipped to page fifty-four and mouthed *thank you* to Paige. She stumbled for a few more moments but eventually found her place and wrapped up her portion of the presentation. But the damage was done. The client barely made eye contact the rest of the morning.

At the end of the presentation, the client stood abruptly and said, "I'm going to check in with Duncan. Thank you for the report. I'll be in touch about next steps." A few other partners followed him out, nervously shaking their heads and shooting glances at Camille.

Camille slumped into her chair. She couldn't remember a worse presentation, and now the client was going to speak to Duncan Hatch, the managing partner of the firm.

Everyone seemed to leave the room as quickly as possible. Everyone except Paige.

Paige walked around the giant conference room table and sat next to Camille. Paige kicked off her heels and asked, "Want to talk about it?"

Camille sighed. "Not really. How bad was it?"

"It was . . . not great."

Camille nodded her head before asking, "How long was I asleep?"

"Five, ten minutes maybe? I saw you nodding off. When I finished up my section, I kept going. I thought if I kept talking, the client wouldn't notice you had fallen asleep and I could transition it over to you when you woke up."

"You shouldn't have done that. It made you look bad too. But thank you for trying." Camille put her head on the table. "I cannot believe I fell asleep."

"It's okay. It happens."

Camille shot her friend a sideways glance. "It happens to college freshmen after a bender. Not grown, professional women."

"What can I do to help?" Paige asked.

Camille shook her head. "Nothing. You already did too much in the meeting. I'll fix this. I'll go talk to Duncan, smooth things over. We'll write off my time for this meeting. Clients love it when they get things for free. I'll send them a revised phase-two report tonight. This will all blow over. I can probably get started on some of the testing protocols over-night and send it to them by the morning."

"Camille, stop."

"You don't think that will be enough? More of a discount on the bill? I'll make sure Duncan knows this was all my mistake. You were just covering for me."

"Camille, stop. I couldn't care less what this client thinks of me. You don't need to fix anything with Duncan. You fell asleep in the meeting because you're exhausted. Be honest—when was the last time you slept for a full night?"

Camille rolled her eyes. "College, probably. When was the last time you slept for a full night? Who sleeps anymore?"

"I get seven hours of sleep every night. That is how I look so amazing every day. I'm guessing you sleep maybe one hour, two if you're lucky." Paige leaned forward as she said, "I say this with love, but you look like absolute shit. There are rumors around the office that you have a drug habit."

"What?"

"You have that Kate Moss early-nineties look going—way too thin, pretty strung out. You need a cheeseburger and an Ambien immediately."

"Okay, Paige. I'll get right on that. I'll wrap up this letter to the client, finish the two dozen other things my clients need, pick up my daughter, grab a couple of burgers, sleep for eight hours, and then wake up from a dream life where I have the time and energy to do any of those things."

"Make the time. I'm serious, Camille. I'm worried about you."

"I'm fine. I *am* a little tired, maybe. I'm going to talk to my doctor about taking something to sleep. I'll take a nap this weekend."

"You need more than a prescription and a nap," Paige said, reaching for Camille's hand. "Let me help you. I'll take Willa this weekend, and you can have some time to yourself."

Camille yelled, "I don't need time to myself." She saw Paige's face freeze and immediately regretted her reaction. She knew Paige was trying to help, but the thought of a weekend alone made Camille nauseous. There was no way being apart from Willa would help. Camille wanted everyone to treat her like normal, because then she could pretend everything was normal.

Camille cleared her throat and said, "I'm sorry I yelled. I'm going to talk to Duncan. Everything will be fine."

Camille walked out of the conference room. She heard Paige calling her, but she kept on walking. It was hard enough to lie to Paige once. Camille couldn't tell Paige she was fine again, so she walked to her office, where she could bury herself in work.

A few hours passed before Camille's secretary knocked on her door and said, "Duncan Hatch would like you to come up to his office."

Camille had known this was coming. She nodded and made her way over to the elevator. She had been to Duncan's office a handful of times, most of them celebratory—when she'd won a case, the day she'd found out she'd made partner—but this was clearly a very different meeting.

When she arrived, Duncan opened the door and said, "Come on in, Camille. Want a coffee? Some water?"

He gestured toward his secretary, but Camille waved her hand. "I'm fine."

"Okay then," he said, closing the door behind him.

A meeting with Duncan was bad, but a closed-door meeting was even worse.

Duncan stood in front of the window with the expansive view of K Street and Farragut Square. He turned toward her and asked, "How are you, Camille?" and then immediately added, "I should have been asking you that more these last few months. I'm sorry."

"It's okay. It's not an easy question to ask someone . . . in these circumstances." Camille still had a hard time saying *Ben died*. The words didn't seem to want to form in her mouth.

"Tell me, then. How are you?"

"I have good days and bad days."

Duncan nodded. They were not close. He was not a friendly mentor. He was a looming figure, and their whole conversation felt forced. Camille decided to cut to the chase.

"This was obviously a bad day. I'm assuming you met with our client this morning."

Duncan nodded his head. "He's not happy."

"I know. I've spent the last few hours reviewing the report and outlining a response to get us back on track. Don't worry; I'll fix this, Duncan."

Duncan shook his head. "Camille, the damage is done. This isn't something you can fix."

Camille scoffed, "Of course I can. I had one bad meeting."

"That's not what I've heard."

"What do you mean?"

Duncan sighed. "After my meeting with the client, I made a few calls. I spoke to the associates on the team, a couple of your other clients, the partners in your group. This is not one bad meeting. Your work has been erratic—emails to associates at all hours of the night, assigning research projects, and changing your mind. Your work product has been sloppy." Duncan shook his head and handed Camille a piece of paper. "You sent this to your practice group at four AM last week. None of it makes sense. And I hear this isn't the only example—your colleagues have been covering for you, fixing work, editing in the background, but it can't keep going like this. It is becoming a liability for the firm." Duncan paused and then looked at Camille. "I met with the executive committee, and we've decided—"

Camille cut him off. "Are you firing me, Duncan?" She waited for his response, filled with equal amounts of fear and anger.

Duncan shook his head. "Of course not. You're one of the most talented young lawyers at this firm." In Duncan's mind, anyone under fifty was considered a young lawyer. He sat in his chair and then looked at Camille with regret in his eyes. "You're off your game, Camille. It's to be expected. Take a few weeks, a few months if that's what you need. Take some time, then get back in it."

Camille felt the tears threaten to burst forward, but she held them back. She nodded her head as Duncan continued.

"I can't put you in front of clients like this. You can't fall asleep in meetings. I have to fly out tomorrow to wine and dine the general counsel to keep this client across the firm. We can't afford to lose their litigation work because of your performance today."

"I know. I'm sorry. I can help you fix this; I have a whole outline ready to send," she said, handing Duncan her notes.

"No. You don't need to fix things with this client. I can handle that. This is not one problem that needs to be fixed. You can't yell at associates. You can't submit reports to regulators full of typos. You can't keep working this much, because your work is sloppy. You need to fix yourself. Go see a counselor. Take a trip to the spa. Do whatever you have to do."

This was as personal and as gentle a conversation as Duncan could have with another person, and they both wanted it to end as soon as possible. Camille nodded her head again and again. She kept repeating that she was sorry, but she stopped talking because her voice was starting to crack.

Duncan stood and walked Camille to the door. "You are officially on leave starting today. In a few weeks, I'll check in, and we can discuss if you're ready to return."

Camille quickly walked away, feeling her lip quiver. The entire trip back to her office, she held in her emotions as tightly as she could manage. When she was finally back at her desk, with the door closed, she burst. She choked in air to muffle her cries, but she couldn't seem to calm herself down.

Camille had worked so hard to get here: the years of studying, the drudgery of all-nighters and weekends spent in the office, nights and vacations and special occasions away from her family, because there were deadlines to meet, and she always met her deadlines. She always prepared for meetings. She always researched and planned and reviewed. She was always perfect. That was how she had gotten to this place—a partner in one of the best law firms in the country.

Now she was a mess. Ben's death had ruined her, and she had no idea how to get back. She was supposed to take some time off to fix herself, but she had no idea where to begin. It seemed laughable that there was any solution to fixing the hole Ben's death had left in her life. She grabbed a few items off her desk—a photo of Willa, a mug Ben had painted when they were first dating, the charger for her phone. She shoved them in her bag and walked out of her office. She had no plan, but at least the tears had been replaced with bubbling anger. She just wasn't sure if she was madder at the firm, herself, or Ben for leaving her all alone.

♦ 6 ♦

IT HAD BEEN A week since the meeting with Duncan, and Camille felt worse every day. She had no idea how to pass time without the distraction of work. The pain was increasing, growing and becoming more consuming instead of lessening. She didn't know what to do, what magic pill to take to make herself better and convince everyone around her that she was okay—that she could handle her job and her child and her life.

The only thing pulling her out of bed each day was Willa. Today Willa insisted on going for a bike ride. Sometime during the last month, Willa had learned to ride her bike without the training wheels. Someone had taught her—a babysitter, a neighbor, one of the army of grown-ups who swooped in and cared for Willa while Camille was working.

Camille sat on the couch, tying her sneakers as Willa's excited narration bounced around the room. "The key to not falling off is to keep your tummy tight, like this," Willa said, squinting her eyes and scrunching her nose. "Feel how tight my tummy is, Mommy."

Camille looked at her daughter, lightly touched her stomach, and said, "Very impressive, but you should probably keep your eyes open when you do it on your bike."

"Obviously," Willa said, as she snapped on her helmet and walked toward the door.

Camille smiled and shook her head at Willa, amazed at this confident bundle of child.

Camille threw a hat over her hair and accidentally glanced in the mirror hanging in the entryway. She didn't recognize herself. The circles under her eyes had moved beyond dark to soot. Her hair hadn't been brushed in so long it was basically one long matted strand hanging down her back. Her pale skin was translucent, blue veins peeking out of unnatural places. For the first time in her life, Camille felt like the world might knock her down rather than the other way around. She pulled her hat down lower and shut the door behind her.

Willa was off, careful to stop at the lights before crossing the streets. The spring weather was bringing the city back to life, but Camille barely noticed the blooming flowers and greening grass. She jogged behind Willa, letting her mind wander.

She should have realized where Willa was heading, but it was hard to think ahead about anything. Normally, Camille was careful not to take this route, Never to walk down P Street, past the pizza restaurant where Camille had bartended all through law school. It was where she had met Ben. Camille didn't go past these places, but Willa wasn't thinking about any of that. Willa was just thinking about a ride in the park.

Camille looked across the street, seeing the familiar place where her whole life had begun, and told Willa to wait.

She remembered every detail about the night she'd met Ben. It was a simple restaurant with perfect pizza and a large selection of imported beers. Camille had been bartending four nights a week, starting the semester she moved to DC. She needed the money and craved the energy after long days in the classroom and law library.

Those days, before corporate clients and K Street offices, Camille was glamorous, exotic, even. When Ben met Camille, she wore layers of gold jewelry, bracelets up her forearms and multiple necklaces hanging over a simple white tank top. Between her ruby hair and blue eyes, Camille had always thought her body was colorful enough to keep her clothes simple. But she'd never met a piece of gold jewelry she didn't love, and her hair was halfway down her back, exploding in wild tendrils.

She noticed Ben immediately. It was early in her shift, and he sat at the end of the bar. He had thick, shaggy hair that he'd tucked behind his ear and wore jeans with a button-down and a blazer. She watched as he pulled a book out of his messenger bag, probably some historical biography. Camille walked over and asked if she could get him anything to drink. He barely looked up at her and asked for a Bud Light.

She laughed, then popped the cap off the beer and set it in front of him. He finally made eye contact. Ben would later tell friends that Camille took his breath away from the first moment they met. He'd say that every room she walked into was immediately captivated by her. That her sky-blue eyes were so light, they had an unsettling effect if you stared at them for too long, but he was willing to take that risk.

All Camille remembered was the wide smile across Ben's face and the way his eyes crinkled.

Camille told him, "You know, we have sixty-four beers on our list, from all over the world."

"I like what I like," Ben said, smirking.

"That I can respect, but you're missing out on a lot of adventure."

Ben paused, seeming to contemplate his next move. "I guess I need someone to guide me."

Camille rolled her eyes. "That sounds an awful lot like a line."

"Is it working?"

Camille caught herself blushing and told him, "Maybe."

Ben stayed at the bar all night, nursing beers and commenting on other customers and Camille's coworkers. Camille got him to try two different beers, which he admitted were an improvement over his Bud Light. By the end of the night, he had nicknames for everyone, and Camille felt like they had developed their own secret society. She was smitten with the tall architect with kind eyes. Falling for Ben was as easy as breathing.

He waited for her shift to end and walked her out into the warm summer night. She was buzzy from the excitement of the bar and the butterflies of meeting someone new. He pulled her close, his body pressed against hers. She was certain he was going to kiss her, but he waited with a giant smile across his face and whispered, so close Camille could feel his breath tracing her lips, "Nice to meet you, Camille Graves."

He kept his arms around her waist, staring into her eyes, and Camille thought she might explode waiting to feel his lips, so she stopped waiting and leaned in.

She could still feel his hand on her back, the way he pressed her even closer so that there was no beginning or end to their space. She could still feel her heart race as his hand moved into her hair, his lips beginning firm and then softly melting into hers. It was a perfect first kiss. It took her breath away.

Ben loved telling everyone that he was seduced by a sexy bartender who made the first move, but they both knew that Camille would have followed Ben anywhere that night. Camille did follow Ben for most of their relationship, trusting him and his wise, practical approach to everything from retirement accounts to designing their dream house.

Camille was lost in the memory of that first night with Ben when Willa came up and grabbed her hand.

"Look, Momma, that lady has hair like yours," Willa said.

Camille looked up and saw a couple walking out of the restaurant, hand in hand. The woman had red, curly hair. The couple turned to each other and laughed as the man kissed the woman on the cheek.

Camille saw them and inhaled. She would never again hold Ben's hand. She'd never feel any more of his kisses. It made her so sad and so angry that tears filled her eyes until the whole scene was blurry, and then suddenly she couldn't see anything at all. The air stopped filling her lungs, and everything went black.

♦ 7 ♦

CAMILLE WOKE TO BRIGHT, buzzing, fluorescent lights. She didn't know where she was, and panic immediately set in. She sat up and saw the sterile setting of the hospital—paper gowns, monitors beeping, and a wire attached to her chest. She called out, and a nurse immediately walked in. "You're up. How are you feeling?"

Camille tried to stand but immediately felt dizzy. "My daughter. Where is my daughter? Willa." Her voice began to rise.

The nurse walked over to Camille's side and held her wrist, taking her pulse. In a low, calm voice, she looked at Camille and said, "She's right outside, honey. She's been helping us organize our tongue depressors. I'll bring her in and let the doctor know you're up."

The nurse left the room. Camille stared at the ceiling, her mind spiraling with all the varying horrific scenarios that could have played out, finally landing on how much she felt like a complete and utter failure. Only moments had passed when Willa walked in and leapt onto Camille's bed. Camille was immediately calmed by her seemingly unfazed daughter.

"Momma, you're awake," Willa exclaimed. "They told me you were taking a nap. Guess what? I saw blood. I didn't get scared, but it was really red. I also talked to Nana. She is very upset with you and so happy that I am such a good girl."

Camille's thoughts continued to spin. She was taking it all in—the hospital room, a bouncing Willa, the nurse moving about—when the doctor came in the room.

The doctor picked up Camille's chart, and between her explanation and Willa's colorful observations, Camille was able to piece together the last hour. She had collapsed on P Street. A couple had called an ambulance. Willa was by her side the whole time. They used Camille's cell phone to call her mother, Marion, and find an emergency contact to meet Willa at the hospital.

The doctor looked at Willa and said, "Do you know, we make some excellent orange Jell-O here. Would you like to try some while I talk to your mom?"

Willa placed her hand inside Camille's and squeezed tightly. She looked at the doctor and said, "You can tell me that you want to have grown-up conversations. I'm used to it. I'm not eating orange Jell-O. That stuff is gross."

Willa and the nurse walked out of the room as the doctor smirked and said, "Well, she's a pistol."

Camille looked at the doctor. "Yes, she is."

The doctor sat in the chair across the room and said, "You're lucky. She's charmed the whole fourth-floor nursing staff."

Camille put her hand on the monitor on her chest and asked, "Why did I collapse? Is it my heart?"

The doctor shook her head. "No. We ran some tests, and your heart is fine. It looks like you had a panic attack. A pretty severe one." The doctor took her time, looking down at her chart and then taking a deep breath. "Willa mentioned that her father recently died. Grief can have physical manifestations.

I'd like to keep you for another hour to monitor you. Then I'm going to refer you to a therapist specializing in grief counseling."

Camille stared out the window. She was a mess. This was the definition of a mess. She could barely make eye contact with the doctor.

The doctor cleared her throat and said, "You two have obviously been through a horrible time. Willa is a resilient child, but she was understandably very upset when we brought you in. You've got to take better care of yourself. These panic attacks are not going to go away. They're only going to get worse."

The doctor left the room, and Camille sighed deeply. She knew she didn't have a choice. She reached for her phone and called her mother.

Marion picked up on the first ring. "Camille, is that you?"

Camille tried to make her voice sound stronger than it was. "Yes, Mom. It's me. I'm fine."

"Oh, thank goodness. What the hell happened? That doctor wouldn't tell me anything—like there should be patient privilege with someone's mother. Just that you had been brought into the hospital."

Camille knew it was bad if Marion was cursing. She was careful to tell her mother what had happened as simply as possible. "I collapsed on the street. I'm fine, but the doctor thinks it was a panic attack. I wasn't paying attention to where we were, and suddenly I looked up and we were in front of the restaurant where I met Ben. I couldn't breathe."

Marion paused, then asked, "How long have these panic attacks been going on?"

Camille sensed the lecturing tone in Marion's voice and knew she had to tread carefully. She quickly replied, "This is the first one."

Marion huffed, "Camille, I know I'm a simple woman, but I am not an idiot. How long?"

Camille was quiet. "I guess since Ben died, I've had a few times where it was hard to breathe. A few dizzy spells. They've been happening more, but I thought I wasn't eating enough. I didn't realize what was happening."

"And who is with Willa?" Marion asked.

"She's at the nurses' station just outside my door. She's fine too."

"No, I mean, when you've been having these panic attacks, who has been taking care of your daughter?"

Camille started to get defensive. "They mostly happen when I'm by myself. Willa is doing great."

"Your child's father died. Her mother is having panic attacks and got taken to the hospital in an ambulance. There isn't a chance that Willa is doing great."

The reality of it all was too much to take, and Camille broke. She started crying and tried to form words, but she couldn't. She knew her mother was right, but the last thing Camille wanted to hear was that she was failing, especially from her own mother.

Finally, Marion interrupted Camille's sobs and tenderly said, "You need help, sweetie. You have acted like a responsible adult since you were toddling around the living room. It's my fault for assuming that you didn't need it before now. I got Ben's parents on the phone. They're on their way to the hospital, and then we will sort all of this out."

"No, I know what I need to do. I need to go home."

Camille could hear the exasperation in her mother's voice when Marion firmly said, "You collapsed on the street. You cannot take Willa back to your house like none of this happened."

Camille said, "No, Mom. I need to come home. To Alabama. I just . . ." Camille's voice hitched, and she struggled to get the words out. "I can't do it anymore. This whole life here feels like too much. Every day, it's all too much. Maybe a few weeks in Alabama will fix me."

Camille and Marion sat in silence. When Camille left for college, she had made it clear to any and every person she met that Alabama was a part of her past. There was no way she would ever live there again; it was too small for the big life Camille planned to live. Camille hadn't referred to Alabama as home in years. It was the place she was from. The fact that Camille was proposing a visit to Alabama as a solution betrayed her desperation.

Camille's statement hung in the air, and then Marion said, "Of course you will. I'll book your tickets." They discussed logistics briefly and agreed that Camille would call back once she left the hospital to finalize the details.

Camille hung up the phone as Willa came back into the hospital room.

Willa climbed into the bed and rested her head on Camille's shoulder. The room was quiet except for the beeping of monitors, and Camille relaxed into the bed with her daughter.

Willa's small voice cracked as she asked, "Momma, are you going to die too?"

At that moment, Camille thought her heart might break, that it might stop just like Ben's. She couldn't believe everything Willa had been through, and how she had been so wrapped up in herself.

Camille shook her head. "I'm very healthy, and I'll be tickling you for a very long time." Camille brought Willa closer. "I'm sorry I scared you. You were so brave. Let's go back to the house. We're going to pack a bag."

"For an adventure?"

Camille marveled at Willa's ability to switch from scared to excited, sad to hopeful, to feel the emotion of the moment. She took a deep breath, setting aside all her thoughts and worries, her hesitation about going back to a place she had been so happy to leave. She recognized that sometimes a step backward was necessary, especially for the sake of a person you loved. Camille looked at her daughter and said, "Yes, it will be an adventure."

✦ 8 ✦

I N THE SMALL BAY town of Fairhope, Alabama, the air was different—calmer, saltier, thicker. Camille took several deep breaths, inhaling the briny medicine of familiarity. She sat in a rocking chair as the soundtrack of early evening played: sea gulls fighting over dinner, fishermen packing up for the day, early-evening joggers slapping the pavement. It calmed her momentarily.

Coming home tangled Camille's emotions. There were a million reasons she had left Alabama, and those reminders always made it hard to relax in the place she had abandoned.

She was thirty-five now, a single parent, back in her parents' house. She knew there were circumstances outside her control that had brought her back, but at the same time, she couldn't help but feel a pang of failure. She'd thought she was better than her home, and returning humbled her.

Lying in the hospital bed, it had seemed like a reasonable decision—spend a couple of weeks in Alabama while she figured out a plan. But sitting on her parents' porch, back in the place she had left behind, felt like a mistake.

Camille had never fit in Alabama. The South was full of boxes—antique silver boxes passed down from generation to generation, simple wooden boxes that served a purpose but never tried to do anything more. These boxes seemed determined at birth, and it was hard to stay in the South if the box didn't fit.

Camille hadn't quite been able to make herself into the daughter her mother wanted, the daughter Marion still tried to make her into. So she had quit trying and left, a brazen eighteen-year-old asserting that she would never live in this place again, because the best way to beat rejection was to claim supremacy.

Camille's mother's family had lived in Fairhope for generations. Marion was a debutante and a member of the Junior League. Her best friends today were the women she had grown up with, a history Marion had hoped to pass along to Camille. Camille's childhood had been filled with girls who were just what their mothers wanted—blonde hair tied back with large white bows, monograms in the center of their crisp smocked dresses, always remembering their manners and saying *please* and *thank you* and *yes, ma'am.*

Camille, on the other hand, had spent mornings battling with her mother over how to control her wild, crimson hair, fighting about the rips and stains in her clothes, and constantly forgetting her manners because all those rules seemed so useless. The older Camille got, the worse it became—the divide between Camille and Marion grew as Camille became more interested in politics and challenging authority and less interested in attending football games, defiantly refusing to be a debutante and participate in such an "antiquated display of patriarchy."

They were just very different people. That's what her father would always say, attempting to defuse the constant tension between the two women he loved so much. Whenever Sam and Marion visited Camille in DC, Marion seemed to accept that Camille's life and her choices weren't up for debate.

But now, back in Alabama and in her parents' house, Camille could feel the day of judgment coming. Marion would likely cut her some slack for a few days—being a widow was a powerful shield—but Camille knew the comments would start up soon. Comments about her appearance, the focus on her career, and worst of all, the way she parented Willa. Camille knew she needed to figure out a plan, at least a concrete departure date, so she could make her escape before she suffocated under her mother's criticism.

Camille saw Willa wading into the bay. Marion was watching closely and instructed Willa to only go in up to her knees. Camille knew that was a futile request, and she watched as the water reached the hem of Willa's shorts and giggles bubbled from her daughter's mouth.

"Goodness me, Willa Taylor. You're not dressed for a swim." Marion's voice was firm and a touch frantic.

Marion waved Willa toward the shore. Willa started to slowly walk back but stopped to examine the tiny darter fish scurrying in the shallow waters. It was too much temptation for a six-year-old and Willa plopped down, scooping up handfuls of water and throwing them over her shoulder.

Marion's jaw dropped as she yelled, "Willa, you are soaked. What are we going to do with you?"

Unfazed, Willa continued searching for tiny fish and replied, "Oh, Nana, it feels wonderful to be naughty."

Watching the scene unfold, Camille couldn't help but laugh. For the first time since Ben's death, she didn't think about her grief but just experienced the joy of watching her free-spirited daughter pitted against the formidable Marion Graves. Usually, it seemed impossible to feel any emotion but sorrow. However, at this moment her heart was filled with the joy of Willa.

Camille joined her mother. Willa saw Camille and waved, as if she were greeting someone who had been away. Camille waved back.

Marion looked at Camille and gently squeezed her shoulder. "I'll go get a towel for that daughter of yours."

"Get two," Camille said. "I'm going to join her."

Marion shook her head. "Of course you are. Have fun."

Camille shrugged. "Fun? Can't remember the last time I thought about that."

"The bay is a good place to look for it. I knew a girl who had the time of her life in those waters. It'd be nice to see her again. I know her daughter would like that," Marion said, pointing at Willa, who was now squealing at all the tiny fish and begging Camille to come look.

Camille sighed, realizing the truth of her mother's statement and the difficult task ahead. She knew it had to become her singular goal: to find any bit of joy she could sift out of the grit.

Marion walked into the house as Camille joined Willa in the bay. They both stood in the water, fully dressed. Camille turned to Willa. "You know, there are mussels in these waters. You can hunt for them with your toes."

Willa cocked her head to the side and asked, "What's a mussel?"

"It's a type of seafood. It's something that grows in the bay," Camille answered.

"Show me," Willa said, reaching for her mother's hand.

Camille cradled Willa's hand, and they moved slowly together, dragging their feet on the bay floor. Camille felt the familiar bump in the sand and smiled at her daughter.

"Okay, Willa, reach down and grab the thing that feels like a rock under my foot."

"Will it bite me?"

"Nope."

Willa reached into the water and ran her fingers around her mother's foot. She pulled the mussel out of the water and showed it to her mother with amazement. "I did it! I captured a mussel."

"Yes, you did."

"What do you do with them?"

"Well, you can eat them, or at least we used to. When I was your age, I would carry a bucket around collecting mussels, and then Gramps would grill them." Camille held the mussel in her hand and pointed to the center line. "When you heat them up, they pop open and you can eat the meat inside." Camille handed the mussel back to Willa and said, "But tonight, we're going to throw it back."

Willa gave the mussel a gentle toss back into the water. They held hands as they walked back to the shore. Playing in the bay was one of Camille's best childhood memories. She would spend most of the day in the water, hunting for mussels, while Marion read on the dock, occasionally dipping her legs in the bay to cool off from her suntan training, then returning to her book. It was a wonderland for children, and Camille could already tell that Willa was falling under its spell.

Camille saw her father working on the edge of the property, pruning vines with large shears.

Willa pointed and asked, "What is Gramps doing?"

"Oh, he's weeding. You have to stay on top of those brambles, or they'll take over all of his garden beds."

"But he's cutting all of those pretty white flowers."

"That's honeysuckle," Camille said, walking toward the property edge with Willa following.

Camille plucked a few of the small flowers and held them in her hand. She carefully showed Willa how to pull the flower apart and suck the sweet nectar.

Honeysuckle was the perfume of Camille's childhood. It was everywhere in the town of Fairhope, tangling the playground fences, lining the bay bluffs, bordering the edges of the woods. Camille would come home from a day of exploring the bay, covered in sand and dirt, with the taste of honeysuckle lingering on her tongue.

She watched her daughter tasting the honeysuckle for the first time, the hidden treat in the weeds, and was transported back to her youth, to those carefree times before death had consumed her thoughts.

Willa reached for another bloom and pulled her hand back quickly. Camille looked down and saw the scratch on her daughter's hand.

Camille gave her a kiss and explained, "The brambles and the honeysuckle grow together. Most other plants couldn't stand up to them, but not the honeysuckle. It always pushes forward. It's strong, even though it doesn't look it."

Camille watched as Willa continued to hunt for blossoms, being more careful to pull the flowers out without scraping her hand on the brambles. Camille joined her until they had both sucked dozens of flowers. They held hands as they walked toward the house.

Camille leaned in and whispered, "We have to be careful not to track muddy feet on Nana's floor or she'll fuss."

Willa looked up at her mother. "Well, she's probably going to do lots of fussing while we're here." Camille couldn't help but laugh again, for the second time, thinking that maybe, with Willa on her team, this wasn't such a mistake after all.

◆ 9 ◆

THE NEXT MORNING, CAMILLE woke early and crept through the quiet house out to the dock. It was a simple home because the bay was the showstopper. A crushed-oyster-shell driveway led to the white house with a metal seam roof. When they first walked up to the house, Willa was mesmerized by the driveway, picking up bits of shell and stuffing them into her pocket. Camille couldn't wait for Willa to hear the music of heavy bay rains against the roof.

The house was on a bluff, which provided safety from the fall storms that plagued all coastal towns but also created the most amazing view of nature meeting humanity. The backside was Camille's favorite part, where the order of the house opened into the wildness of the bay.

Sam had designed it all. He was one of the most sought-after landscape designers in South Alabama, and his home was his showpiece. He'd lugged rocks from the local milling company and researched native plants. It was his pride, and Camille loved seeing her father in his element. Sam was happiest covered in dirt, a trait he had clearly passed down to his granddaughter.

As she sat on the dock, her feet dangling into the water, Camille yearned for Ben to be next to her. Being anywhere without him felt foreign. Being back in her childhood home without him felt particularly painful.

Camille remembered the first time she had brought Ben to Alabama. The minute they walked out of the airport, she saw sweat beading on his forehead. She wasn't sure if it was the humidity or nerves at meeting her parents for the first time. Camille couldn't wait to introduce Ben to true southern food, and she had listed every restaurant they would visit over the long weekend and exactly what Ben should order at each place. He'd joked that he wasn't sure his stomach was that big, and she'd told him to "man up."

Then he had pulled her into his chest and said, "I'm falling in love with you, Camille." Of course, that was the moment her father pulled up to the airport. She looked at Ben, smiling, watching him squirm as her father walked over and gave her a big hug.

They chatted on the drive home, Sam asking about Camille's law school classes and Ben's design projects. Camille kept sneaking glances at Ben, hearing a nervous shake to his voice, wondering whether it was due to her father's questions or his almost-proclamation at the airport. Their conversation veered to dinner plans, and after learning that Camille had never cooked for Ben, Sam declared that Camille was in charge of dinner. "You haven't shown this boy who you really are if you haven't cooked for him," Sam scoffed.

They made a detour to their favorite seafood shop, and Camille and her father walked into Billy's Seafood the way some women walk into Tiffany's. Camille squealed at the fresh oysters. That night Camille made a homemade mignonette for the freshly shucked Apalachicolas and pan-fried grouper with a chive sauce. They all cleaned their plates as Ben charmed Sam and Marion. Camille found herself falling deeper for a man who wove himself seamlessly into her family.

Later that night, Ben had snuck down the hall to Camille's room and nuzzled her neck, whispering, "I love Alabama-Camille. I love you."

Camille smiled and asked, "Not just falling anymore?"

Ben looked straight into her eyes. "Not just falling. Fully in love. With you."

Camille wrapped her arms around his neck. "Good. I'm very lovable. It's about time you came to your senses."

He tickled her until she couldn't breathe, and she finally said, "I love you too, Ben."

As Camille sat on the dock now, she could almost feel Ben next to her as she remembered how much fun it had been to show him her favorite parts of Alabama and how at ease she had been at home as long as he was with her. It would be easy to sit with the memories all day, but instead, Camille made herself stand up and get ready to make new ones with Willa. She had to stop pretending, going through the motions. She had to try to start living again, and showing her daughter where she had grown up seemed like a good start.

Willa padded into the kitchen as Camille made a pot of coffee. Camille loved seeing the wild perfection of her daughter in the morning. At six, Willa's copper hair had thick, spiraling curls that spilled down her back. It was lighter than Camille's, with enviable streaks of gold. Willa's green eyes were framed by a smattering of freckles across the bridge of her nose. Every mother saw beauty in their child, but Camille knew Willa was stunning. Ben would always say that his genes had gotten left behind because Willa was a carbon copy of Camille. Camille would disagree, pointing out Willa's lanky legs and broad smile, but mostly she disagreed because Willa was so beautiful that it made Camille uncomfortable to get that kind of compliment.

This morning, Willa had a disheveled halo of hair covering her eyes as she sat at the kitchen counter. Camille gently swept the hair out of Willa's eyes as she handed her a glass of milk.

"How did you sleep, sweet pea?" Camille asked.

Willa pulled at her nightgown. "Mostly good, but these pajamas are itchy."

Camille looked at the crisply pressed white nightgown, trimmed with lace and Willa's initials monogrammed in pale pink across the chest. Camille knew Marion had a whole wardrobe of monograms and ruffles that she couldn't wait to put on Willa, along with a drawer full of bows and headbands and tights that would never last ten minutes without being destroyed or covered in dirt.

Camille wasn't exactly sure how Marion had even convinced Willa to wear the nightgown. Willa had a T-shirt that said *I* ♥ *NY* that was two sizes too big that she slept in almost every night. Marion must have laid it on thick to get Willa out of the T-shirt.

Camille smiled at Willa. "They look itchy. You can wear whatever you want. Nana may have some clothes for you, but if you don't want to wear them, you don't have to."

"My body, my choice. Right, Momma?"

Of course Marion would choose that moment to come into the kitchen, raising her eyebrows at Camille. Camille shrugged her shoulders. In DC, everyone took their kids to political rallies, and she couldn't help it if Willa had the memory of an elephant.

Camille pulled out a bag of granola and poured some on top of yogurt and fruit for Willa. As Marion poured a cup of coffee, Camille asked, "Dad already gone for the day?"

"Yes, he's got a project in Montrose that has gone off the rails. The owner wants to put in a Japanese pagoda in the middle of a pecan grove, and your father's overalls are in a bunch over it."

Willa asked, "So are we having a girls' day?"

Marion smiled. "Yes, ma'am, we are. I thought you and I would go up to Page & Palette Bookstore for story time. All the girls bring their grandkids, and I can't wait to show you off." She wiped a streak of yogurt from Willa's cheek.

Camille winced. The last thing she wanted was her daughter paraded around like a trophy, but she knew her mother had good intentions. Marion's lifelong friends all had children and grandchildren living nearby. Camille knew that Marion had yearned for the day she could bring her grandchild along. Camille could easily go up to her room and wallow, leaving Marion and Willa to a day together, but she also knew that wallowing for the last eight months hadn't made anything better.

Camille took a deep breath and said, "I thought Willa and I would go exploring today."

Willa immediately screamed, "Yes!" then looked over at Marion and grabbed her hand and calmly said, "Nana, I don't want to hurt your feelings, and you know I love stories, but I really, really love exploring."

Marion's face fell momentarily, but she gathered herself quickly. "I think exploring sounds wonderful. Where are we going?"

"I want to take Willa to Magnolia Springs. I know you think the river is full of bugs. You don't have to come."

Camille could see her mother's head spinning, knowing how much she hated Magnolia River. With no breeze from the bay, the mosquitoes would eat Marion alive. Sam and Camille had always joked that having Marion around was better than bug spray because they would bite her, leaving the rest of them unscathed.

Marion briefly hesitated and then pasted on a smile. "Oh, I don't mind. A day on the river sounds great."

Camille chuckled, somewhat impressed with her mother's ability to tell a complete lie. "We won't be gone all day. I think it might be nice for us to have the morning to ourselves."

"Okay then," Marion said, beginning to clean kitchen counters that weren't dirty.

Camille rubbed Willa's back. "Finish breakfast and then put on your swimsuit. I'll go pack us an adventure bag."

Willa shoved two bites of yogurt into her mouth and then took off upstairs.

After a few moments, ensuring that Willa was out of earshot, Marion asked, "Are you sure you'll be okay? By yourself?"

"Will I be okay with my daughter? On a river that I spent more time in than this house? Yes. I'll be fine."

"Camille, I'm not trying to criticize. I'm here to help."

Camille sighed deeply. "I know. I'll be fine," she repeated.

"Okay," Marion replied, looking unsure of whether to push the issue or let it go. She stared at her daughter and then added, "There's bug spray in the laundry room, and I picked up one of those Puddle Jumpers with this adorable seersucker cover, and a new swimsuit for Willa is in her top drawer. Should I help her get dressed?"

"We'll be fine, Mom. We'll figure it out."

"Right. Of course. Well then, I guess I'll just catch up on your daddy's books. They're a mess." Marion turned and walked out of the kitchen. Sam was a brilliant landscape designer, but much of his success could be attributed to Marion. She ran the back end, from accounting to marketing to staffing. Apart from Camille, everyone did everything Marion Graves asked.

Camille knew Marion was disappointed, but she was never sure how to navigate the tension with her mother, feeling like she was always saying and doing the wrong thing. Camille set those worries aside, recognizing that Willa was the priority. Camille had to get her life back on track so she could get out of Alabama for another beginning.

✦ 10 ✦

C AMILLE ENJOYED THE DRIVE, winding through the check-erboard of rural county roads that took them away from the bay through the South Alabama farmland. The drive to Magnolia Springs took twenty minutes. Willa was mostly quiet, mesmerized by the new terrain—the coastline replaced by fields of farmland.

When they got to the river, they parked by the boat access. Camille led them down a short, wooded trail that eventually opened at the riverbank. It was a weekday, so it was relatively quiet, but there were a few boats humming downstream, likely heading to the estuary before making their way out to Mobile Bay. Camille loved the mix of homes that dotted the creek. There were original cabins that had been built up high enough to survive the inevitable rising water. There were also beautiful new homes, several "modern farmhouses" that Ben would have found disingenuous, but Camille still enjoyed them.

Camille spread out a blanket as Willa made her way to the water. Willa had already taken off her shorts, ready to dive in for a swim.

Camille dug into her bag and pulled out a shovel and a bucket. "Hey, Willa," Camille whispered. "Want to see what I brought?" She handed the bucket and shovel to Willa.

"What're those for, Momma? I can't build a sandcastle out of mud."

Camille smiled. "I thought you might want to be a marine biologist today. This is a very special river. There are all kinds of animals that live here. If you stay next to the edge, you may be able to find salamanders."

Willa's eyes got large as she grabbed for the bucket and shovel. Camille smiled and said, "The trick is to look in the shallow water where it's really muddy. If the water is up to your shins, you're too far away. Think you can handle it?"

"Yes. I love muddy water."

"I know you do, sweet pea."

Camille leaned back on the blanket and watched Willa explore. Willa moved carefully along the side of the river, grabbing handfuls of mud and sifting slowly for discoveries. Camille knew that the boat launch area provided a shallow area for Willa to explore, but she watched her daughter carefully, remembering the sudden drops and swift currents that made the river so exciting for a child.

The early May sun peeked through the trees and warmed Camille's skin. It had been years since she had spent time just sitting, enjoying being outside. She envied Willa's ability to focus, to let the noise of the world disappear and enjoy the experience of the moment. Their life in DC had been so busy—responding to emails from the playground benches, ordering a grocery delivery on her commute in to work. She had prided herself on her ability to multitask, but now it seemed like such a waste.

Camille felt guilt all the time. Guilt about not working when she had worked so hard to achieve her career. Guilt about working too much when Willa had been through so much. It was easier to keep going instead of dealing with any of the emotions that accompanied Ben's death. She hadn't talked about it with Willa. She'd assumed that would lessen the pain, but everything was bubbling up inside. She didn't let herself think about all the moments she had lost, time she could have spent enjoying the feel of Ben's arms when instead she had been thinking about picking up the dry cleaning.

Camille watched the postman motoring down the river, making deliveries to the mailboxes that lined the bank. This was a unique, quaint part of Magnolia Springs that had its mail delivered by boat. The ability to hold on to tradition, especially those aspects that lacked all practicality, was one of the most frustrating and endearing qualities of Alabama. As a teenager, all Camille had been able to see were the things that needed to change. Now Camille saw the value in preserving something that was beloved, even if it lacked efficiency.

Camille wondered about the postman's life—on the water every day, following the same route, seeing the same faces. Being a lawyer was all Camille knew, all she'd ever wanted, but there was no calm predictability in that life. It was full of crises and deadlines. There was an energy and excitement in DC that had always been her dream: parties with diplomats, a corporate expense account for first-class flights, elaborate client dinners. She was surrounded by important people handling important issues. But without Ben at her side, the dream had been replaced by exhaustion.

Now she was sitting beside a river with no other agenda. It would have been unthinkable in her old life; she'd always been too busy thinking about schedules and work deadlines and social commitments. She was in some type of purgatory, not sure what life she wanted to live but knowing that nothing felt right anymore.

Willa's excited voice drew Camille's eyes back to the riverbank. "Momma, I got one, I got one!"

Willa came over with the bucket, and squirming inside was a small salamander. Willa sat next to Camille on the blanket and watched the salamander moving back and forth. "Can I keep it forever, Momma?"

Camille looked at her daughter and wiped the smudge of mud off her cheek. "I don't know. Do you think we should?"

"Probably not. He's probably got lots of salamander friends, and he would miss them and this mud. This is the best mud." Willa sighed and then tipped the bucket and watched the salamander disappear into the river. "Momma, I love this place."

"I do too. It's one of my happy places."

"Why?"

"I spent a lot of time here one summer. You see that house over there, kinda hidden up the side of the high bank?" Willa looked across the river and nodded her head. Camille continued, "Well, Gramps designed that backyard one summer. I came with him every day and helped spread all those pine needles and plant the azalea bushes. I'd work in the morning, and then after lunch I'd swim." Camille paused, letting the memories sink in, then looked at her daughter and tickled Willa as she continued, "And hunt for salamanders just like you."

She hadn't really hunted for salamanders much that year, but she did have her first kiss, standing under the setting sun at the edge of the dock. Camille could remember so many details from that summer. How mad she was that her dad was making her come to his job site when her friends were going to be spending the summer working at the Grand Hotel pool. She was in such a foul mood the first day they rolled up to the house in her dad's truck that she spent the morning sulking and sweating and threatening to file a child labor complaint against her father. At lunchtime, she saw a sleepy-eyed teenager walk onto his back porch, chestnut hair swooping across his forehead as he drank a glass of water. Camille hid behind a bush by the river and watched him. She could hear his deep voice laughing as he scratched the ears of his dog. Although she could tell he was a few years older than her, he became her summer goal.

She'd made a pact with her friends that they would all have their first kiss the summer before they started high school, and now Jeremy Easton was her target. Camille spent the summer cutting her jeans off shorter and shorter, reapplying lip gloss, and waiting for hidden moments to flirt with the boy next door. Her crush on Jeremy was fast and furious in the way that teenage romances bloom and burn. It had all fizzled out by the end of the summer, when the prospect of a long-distance relationship—they lived twenty whole minutes away—seemed like an insurmountable obstacle. But she had gotten that perfect first kiss one early summer evening.

It had been exhilarating and awkward and innocently ideal. She could still feel the way he moved his hands into her back pockets and remember her giggly realization that she was being kissed and her butt was being touched at the same time. Years later, Camille had found Jeremy on Facebook, and he was living in Atlanta, happily married with two kids. The whole thing made her smile.

Willa brought her back to the present. "Momma, did Gramps let you swim all by yourself?"

"Well, yes, but I was a teenager."

Willa sighed. "I can't wait to be a teenager."

"Oh, really? What happens when you're a teenager?" Camille asked.

Willa looked at Camille. "I eat what I want, I sleep when I want, I swim when I want. Nana told me that the teenagers who hang out at the playground are hooligans, and I cannot wait to be a hooligan."

Camille laughed. "Do you know what a hooligan is?"

"Not exactly, but it makes Nana scrunch her face in a funny way, so I figure it's a good thing."

Camille kissed the top of Willa's head. "Well, I'm very excited for you to be a teenager too, but I think you're pretty amazing at six. I wish I could freeze you just like this."

"But Momma, I have to keep growing."

Camille was quiet, letting the truth of Willa's statement hang in the air. "You're very right. We all have to keep growing."

They sat, their hands intertwined, watching the water roll down the river.

Camille ran her hand over the golden streaks in her daughter's hair and said, "Your daddy would have loved to see you hunt for salamanders."

Willa looked up, her round eyes clearly focused on Camille. "Did Daddy love salamanders too?"

Camille nodded. "He was the one who showed me how to hunt for them. He took me on a hiking trip in Shenandoah, and we had a picnic by the river. We found a salamander, and I thought it was pretty gross, but he told me lots of interesting facts about them."

"Like what?" Willa asked excitedly.

"Like the fact that they live in water and on land and that their tails fall off if they're scared, which is how they escape from predators."

"Daddy has the best facts," Willa said. She looked at the ground and softly whispered, "I miss him. I miss hearing about him."

Camille closed her eyes. With the sun shining on her face, she said, "I miss him too. I think I missed him so much that I thought it would be easier not to talk about him, because I thought it would hurt too much." She opened her eyes and looked at Willa. She stared into her daughter's eyes and said, "I was wrong. I'm sorry, Willa-bean. I promise to talk about him as much as you want."

"Sounds good, Momma." Willa rested her head on Camille's shoulder, and they sat together, enjoying the sun and the safety of each other's touch.

"Want some lunch?" Camille finally asked. "I made pimento cheese sandwiches with big tomato slices."

"What's mint cheese? That doesn't sound good."

Camille smiled. "I agree. Mint cheese sounds gross. This is pi-men-to cheese," she said slowly, exaggerating the syllables. "It's cheddar cheese mixed with red peppers, but they aren't spicy."

Willa hesitantly asked, "Did Nana make it?"

Camille shook her head, understanding Willa's reluctance. Marion was a horrible cook, and over the last few months of Marion's visits, Willa had eaten enough of Marion's meals to proceed cautiously.

"There's a little cheese shop in town that makes this. If you like it, we can make some ourselves. It's not hard. My favorite way to eat it is on sourdough bread with a slice of tomato."

Camille pulled out two sandwiches wrapped in parchment paper and handed one to Willa. Willa held up her muddy hands, and Camille held up a package of wipes. "I came prepared. I know my best girl."

Willa beamed. "I never met a pile of mud I didn't love." Ben's words echoed between them. Camille pushed down the sadness and just enjoyed Ben's memory surfacing in her daughter's small voice.

Willa scrubbed her hands, removing about seventy percent of the dirt, which Camille figured was better than nothing. They both unwrapped their sandwiches and took giant bites.

Willa hummed, always a sign that she liked something, then said, "This has excellent flavor and texture."

Camille shook her head. She and Ben often joked that Willa was a tougher critic than the *Washington Post*. "Oh, good. That's a relief. If you didn't like it, we may have to leave Alabama. It's kind of a requirement of living here." Camille winked, letting Willa know she wasn't completely serious.

But Willa was serious when she asked, "Are there other foods I don't know about?"

"Oh, sure. The South is full of delicious, weird food. Po' boys, and beignets, and crayfish, and cowboy caviar, and fried okra. It's going to take a while, but we will map out a plan to introduce you to all of the southern requirements."

Willa scowled. "I can't believe you haven't given me any of this food." Exasperated, she asked, "Is this food you had when you were a kid and you didn't even tell me about? Are there other things I don't know about you?"

It was such a simple question, but its power overwhelmed Camille. She carefully responded the same way she had to so many difficult conversations with Willa over the last few months: with the simplest truth. "Yes. There are probably lots of things you don't know about me, but how about I work on showing you?"

Willa seemed satisfied almost immediately. "Can we start with the food things? That's what I'm most interested in."

Camille hugged her tight. "Yes. Tonight we will have a shrimp boil." She started packing up their bag and said, "Let's go. I'm taking you to Billy's."

◆ 11 ◆

THE PAVEMENT ENDED IN a large parking lot, mixing gravel and crushed oyster shells. A white sign with red lettering read *Billy's Seafood*. Camille parked the car and the shell dust settled, revealing the dock perched over the inlet extending from the simple one-room store. In the thirty years Camille had been shopping at Billy's, nothing had changed. The parking lot was full of dry-docked boats in various states of disrepair and pickup trucks. The shrimpers, with their large nets hanging in the air, moved in and out of the marina. Willa was mesmerized. Camille grabbed her hand, and they headed toward the store.

They walked inside and saw rows and rows of seafood on ice. The smell always amazed Camille. She'd brace herself for the fishy smell that plagued grocery store cases, but at Billy's nothing stayed on ice long enough for the store to smell like anything other than salt air. The floor was spotless, and the cases were lined with brightly colored seafood. Whole fish, fillets, crabs, oysters, and octopus were neatly arrayed behind a short glass shield.

Camille walked Willa toward the shrimp, which came in various sizes, and pointed out the reds, Camille's favorite. There was no one behind the counter, but it was the middle of the week and school was still in session. Camille called out just as the back door opened.

She looked up as an imposing figure walked into the store. He was dressed in waders and a plain gray T-shirt and was so tall his head barely cleared the doorway. He had on a baseball cap, but chestnut waves flipped outward, skirting above his shoulders. It was unnatural for a grown man to have hair that color. It belonged on Pantene ads and chocolate Labs.

He washed his hands and then walked toward the seafood case. "Sorry for the wait, folks; we're short-staffed this week. What can I get you?"

He bent over to lift a handful of the 12/15 shrimp. "These are beauties. Freshly caught this morning."

Willa cocked her head and pointed to the sign labeling the shrimp, asking, "How do you know how old the shrimp are? Do they have rings like trees?"

Camille shrugged her shoulders. She was used to strange questions from Willa, but the fisherman seemed to take questions about his product very seriously. He looked at Willa, looked at the sign, and burst out laughing. "Well, that is confusing. The numbers aren't their age. These shrimp are called 12/15s because it takes anywhere from twelve to fifteen of them to make up a pound. They're big shrimp. These over here are 25s; they're a little smaller because it takes about twenty-five of them to make a pound. Don't tell my other customers, but I think the 25s are tastier."

Willa smiled. "That's what my mom said. She said the 12s aren't as sweet. This is my mom." Willa gestured with her arms like on a game show. "Her name is Camille, and my name is Willa."

The man came out from behind the counter and shook Willa's hand. "Very nice to meet you, Willa. My name is

Mack." He smiled at Camille, and she nodded her head awkwardly, then looked at the floor. It felt strange to be in a room with a man her age who wasn't a relative. She couldn't remember the last time she'd had a conversation with a new person. Although she wasn't exactly conversing—her six-year-old was doing most of the talking.

Mack turned back to Willa. "Okay, so you want some 25s. How much?"

Willa started counting on her fingers. "There are four of us for dinner, and I'm a hearty eater. How much do you recommend?"

Mack examined the girl, seeming to question whether a child that skinny could ever be considered a self-proclaimed hearty eater. "A pound and a half should do it, even for a crew of fishermen. It might give you some leftovers too. Anything else?"

Willa started walking back and forth in front of the display case and stopped at the oysters. "Momma, can we get oysters too?"

Mack turned to Camille. "Your daughter eats oysters? Please tell me what you have done to raise such a remarkable young human."

Camille smiled, and Willa proudly stated, "I love oysters, especially Olympias."

Mack walked over to the oyster display. "Olympias are delicious, but those live on the West Coast. I only have local oysters here."

"What kinds do you have?"

"Well, there are wild Gulf oysters and some new farmed oysters. They're both tasty, but different."

"How are they different?" Willa asked.

"Want to try some and see if you can tell?"

"Definitely." Willa did a little hop and reached for Camille's hand.

Mack looked in the case and picked up an oyster. He shucked it with a simple flick and handed the shell to Willa. She slurped it down, handed it back to Mack, and said, "Next."

"Yes, ma'am," Mack said, beaming. He shucked the next oyster and handed it to Willa.

Willa tossed it back and closed her eyes. "Both good. I'm going to do some thinking."

Mack looked at Willa with complete surprise, but Camille grinned. Willa was the youngest oyster expert; she had been raised on them. There had been an oyster bar down the street from their house in DC. Ben and Camille used to meet after work for a cocktail and a dozen oysters. It was their Wednesday tradition—"Something to look forward to in the middle," Ben would say. When Willa came along, they kept up the tradition, bringing her in the stroller and, as she got older, plopping her in a high chair. She was two the first time she tried an oyster. They expected her to spit it out, but instead she said, "More, more!" It became a very expensive Wednesday when their toddler continued demanding more oysters.

Willa finally said, "I like them a lot, but the first ones are better. They taste more like the ocean."

Mack said, "Well, there is going to be a very happy oyster grower when he hears that you picked his."

Camille had been enjoying the dynamic between Willa and Mack, but she finally interjected. "Really?" she asked. "Willa picked the farmed oysters? I can't believe it. Can I try one too?" Camille asked.

Mack said, "Sure," and shucked two more oysters, handing one to Camille and sampling one himself. "They're good, right?"

THE RIVER RUNS SOUTH

Camille tilted her head back, enjoying the briny, plump oyster. It was cold and slick and bursting with flavor. "I'm shocked. These are delicious."

Mack chuckled. "I was too the first time I tried them. There's a professor at Auburn who started growing them a few years ago. He's a great guy, doing it completely natural, no chemicals or additives. His students study what works and what doesn't. It's pretty great, especially since the Gulf is still recovering."

Camille said, "Well, I'm impressed. We'll take a dozen along with the shrimp, please."

"But Momma, there's so much more I want to try," Willa protested.

Camille put her hands on Willa's shoulders. "I know. Me too. But we have to buy the seafood and stop sampling the product before we get Mack in trouble with his boss."

Mack started bagging the shrimp and packing the oysters on ice. "Oh, I think he's okay with a couple free samples, especially since I'm the boss. This is my shop."

Willa beamed and immediately asked, "How come this place is named Billy's but your name is Mack?"

"Good question. Think I should change the name?"

"Yes!" Willa exclaimed at the same time Camille said, "Definitely not."

Camille continued, "You can't change the name. Who would come to Mack's Seafood? Billy's is an institution. You're only a caretaker."

Mack smirked and looked into Camille's blue eyes. "Do you always have such a hard time sharing your opinions?" Camille felt herself flush and looked away.

Willa responded. "No, she doesn't. Momma is very opinionated. Daddy says no one should get between Momma and her visions for how things should be done."

"Well, in this case, I agree with your mom. The name stays. It sounds like your daddy is a wise man," Mack said, handing them the bag of seafood.

"He's dead," Willa stated simply.

Mack paused, then stepped toward Willa and gently patted her arm. "I'm sorry. My dad died too. He was Billy."

Camille was taken aback. "I didn't know Billy died. When?"

"About three years ago. I'm guessing you aren't one of our frequent shoppers. Pretty sure I'd remember two adventurous redheads." He winked at Willa, and she gave him her biggest smile.

Willa answered, "We are from Washington, DC, but my momma grew up here. We're visiting Alabama so that Momma can work on getting her life together."

"Thank you for that detailed answer, Willa." Camille crouched down. "Have you been listening to my conversations with Gramps and Nana?"

"Of course. You guys should find somewhere more private than the kitchen. Or at least whisper. That's what I do when it's a secret."

Willa walked down the display case, examining the day's catch while making fish faces in the window.

Mack leaned toward Camille and whispered, "She's pretty remarkable." They didn't touch, but Camille could feel his presence in the air, and she immediately stepped back.

"Yes, she is." Camille looked at Mack. "I'm sorry about your father. He was such a nice man. I can't count how many times I came in here as a child."

Mack cleared his throat. "Thanks. Yes. He was great."

Camille watched as Willa tried to touch an octopus. She gently called, "Willa, do not touch the merchandise." Willa giggled and pulled back her hand.

Mack looked at Camille and asked, "Okay if I take her to the back room?"

Camille tilted her head. "Depends on what you plan on doing back there."

Mack chuckled. "Fair point. Willa, I have a bucket of krill that's going to get tossed back. You can look at those. If your mom doesn't mind, you can even hold one."

Willa ran up to Mack. "She doesn't mind. I touch gross stuff all the time and she's fine with it, right, Mom?"

"Yes, that is unfortunately accurate."

Willa and Camille followed Mack into the back room, where he pulled out a bucket of tiny crustaceans. The world disappeared into Willa's love affair with the bucket of krill.

Mack turned to Camille. "So how long has it been?"

Camille said, "She's been like this since birth."

"No, I meant since your husband died."

"Oh." Camille took a deep breath. "Eight months."

Mack nodded his head. "Around that time, I was slowly coming out of the Miller Lite–for–breakfast stage and entering the yelling-at-strangers-for-no-reason stage."

"Well, those sound like fun times to look forward to. I think I'm still in the shock, disbelief, and wearing-the-same-pair-of-yoga-pants-for-a-week stage. I'm clearly making tremendous progress."

Mack looked at Willa as she closely examined the marine life and then over to Camille, who was smiling brightly at her daughter. He nodded as he said, "I think you're doing better than you think."

Camille was suddenly self-conscious, wondering if he could see her dark circles. She tugged at the shorts that hung too low on her hips and the straps of her bathing suit that crossed over her bony shoulder blades. She was too thin and too messy to look capable in anyone's eyes.

And yet Camille locked eyes with Mack for a moment, and a sense of calm overtook her. Mack's words were the exact compliment she needed, reassurance that she would survive this from a person who knew nothing about everything that had happened. He was probably just saying it to be nice, but he didn't strike her as someone who used words unnecessarily.

"Thank you," Camille said nervously. She turned to Willa. "We better get home. I bet Nana and Gramps are getting hungry."

Willa popped up and grabbed her mother's hand. "Can we come back?"

Camille kissed Willa's cheek and then smiled at Mack. "Yes, definitely."

Camille and Willa walked toward the car, their red hair swirling in the light breeze and Willa's laughter carrying over the water. Camille glanced over her shoulder and saw Mack standing in the door, smiling, before he waved and turned away. When Camille saw her reflection in the car window, she was surprised to find a grin on her face.

MARION MET WILLA ON the back porch as Camille unloaded the groceries. "Nana, Momma is cooking dinner tonight. Can you believe it?"

"Well, this certainly is a special occasion," Marion commented, surveying the bags in Camille's hands. "You seem to be making a real effort, Camille. That is certainly a start."

Camille sighed. Only her mother could so expertly hide her criticisms in compliments. Camille watched her mother surveying Willa's appearance, smoothing Willa's rumpled shorts and tucking her hair behind her ear.

Marion asked Willa if she wanted to help cut flowers for the dinner table and Willa quickly agreed, leaving Camille in the kitchen. Marion always had freshly cut flowers and always used her china and cloth napkins, and she kept a folder of clippings for "tablescape inspirations." All the effort that went into the setting out and washing and putting away of all the things that Marion used daily mystified Camille. It seemed so useless, but Marion always insisted that these traditions were essential.

Camille heard Willa's chatter float over the bay as she relayed in exacting detail every event of the salamander hunt at the river.

Camille started gathering ingredients, pulling a jar of Spanish green olives from the cupboard and grabbing the Conecuh sausage out of the fridge.

Sam walked into the kitchen and asked, "What's for dinner?"

For as long as she could remember, Camille's father had come home from work, walking up the back stairs that led to his bedroom and showering away all the dirt and sap and pollen that he'd brought home from the job site. He'd stroll downstairs smelling of Dove soap and aftershave and ask, "What's for dinner?" He was always starving.

Her father loved food, but Marion hated cooking. On the weekends, Sam did most of the cooking, but during the week he was too exhausted. They suffered through years of *Family Circle* casseroles and grocery store rotisserie chicken. By the time Camille was twelve, she took over dinner duty. She'd read recipes on the weekend and make grocery lists. It was a relief to the entire family, and there was no one Camille liked cooking for more than Sam. Her dad was her first and most favorite diner. Her mother always asked too many questions about calories and fat grams.

Camille smiled. "I'm doing a shrimp boil. I also picked up a dozen oysters. Can you shuck them, Dad?"

Sam leaned down and kissed Camille on the top of her head. "Of course. It's fun being in the kitchen with you again."

"I know."

Camille got out the large stock pot and made a sachet with Old Bay, peppercorns, garlic, and thyme. She poured a bottle of beer into the pot, then filled it with water. She threw in the sachet and brought it all to a boil as she shucked corn and chopped potatoes.

Camille had made dozens of shrimp boils, perfecting the recipe over the years. They ate it throughout the summer and for all major celebrations—graduation, the Fourth of July, birthdays. She had started with a basic recipe, tweaking and adding until it became her signature dish. By the time she was eighteen, all her parents' friends would beg to come over anytime Camille made her shrimp boil.

The olives were her secret ingredient. They softened in the boil, and their tangy brine was the perfect complement to the shrimp. The local Conecuh sausage added a fatty richness. A bite of potato, a crumble of sausage, a plump olive all stacked on the lightly boiled shrimp was just about perfection.

Once everything was in the pot, Camille worked on the garnishes and dips. She sliced blood oranges and lemons. She made a saffron aioli and placed it next to a dish of melted butter and another dish of grainy mustard.

She fixed a platter with cocktail sauce and saltines and opened a bottle of Sancerre and brought everything outside. Willa was sitting on the dock, her toes drawing circles on the surface of the water.

"Come on over for cocktails. Dinner's almost ready." Camille poured three glasses of wine as Sam came outside with the platter of shucked oysters.

"Willa, there's a pitcher of lemonade in the fridge. Think you can pour yourself a glass?" Camille asked.

"Yes, but don't eat all the oysters without me."

Willa came back outside a few minutes later with lemonade in a wineglass, and Marion asked, "Where did you find that?"

"In that tall cabinet in the dining room. Can't I have a fancy glass too?"

Sam chuckled, "You certainly can. Tonight is pretty special. Your momma's shrimp boil is famous."

Willa sipped the lemonade, and Camille sipped her wine as Sam and Marion traded stories about the different shrimp boils

Camille had made over the years and all the fun parties that had come along with them.

Camille smiled at Willa. "Since this is your first shrimp boil, you get to prep the table."

"Okay, Momma, I'll go get the tablecloth and the plates."

Sam and Marion exchanged knowing looks as Camille stopped her daughter. "Nope, no tablecloth and no plates. Go get Gramps' newspaper from this morning and spread it out all over the table. We'll need lots of napkins. You can get a couple of forks for the old folks, but you and I are going to eat with our fingers."

Willa's eyes grew large, and she immediately ran inside for the paper. Camille moved into the kitchen, pouring the pot's contents into the large metal colander in the sink. While the steam was swirling above the kitchen window, Camille brought out a small tray with the dips. Once Willa was seated at the table, Camille went back to the kitchen for the colander.

She walked outside, and Willa's mouth dropped. She could see the shrimp and corn and sausage and potatoes overflowing. Camille took a deep breath and said, "Ready?"

Willa quickly answered, "Yes," and Camille poured everything into the middle of the table. The food spread, and everyone was immediately hit with the lingering Old Bay steam.

"The best facial in the South," Marion proudly exclaimed. Camille laid the slices of blood orange and lemon on top of the shrimp and placed the small dishes of aioli and butter and mustard in the center.

"You have to peel this shrimp, Willa. Gramps can help you. He's the fastest shrimp peeler in this family. There are three different sauces you can try too."

"I can't wait," Willa said. "I love to dip."

"Well, don't we all," Sam replied.

Marion slapped his knee and said, "Just peel the child some shrimp. You never forget your first shrimp boil."

They all enjoyed the meal, making their way across the table and making sure to teach Willa all the best combinations. Willa proudly declared that she was going to ask for a shrimp boil every year for her birthday dinner. Afterward, she left the table to catch fireflies and Marion, Sam, and Camille caught up on the day's adventures.

When Camille told her dad about their trip to Magnolia Springs, Sam chuckled. "You were my worst worker that summer. You were too busy kissing that boy to spread any pine straw."

Camille blushed. "I don't know what you're talking about."

"Oh, you two thought you were so sneaky. The whole crew couldn't stop gossiping about what was happening. It was the most unproductive work site in the history of Sam Graves Landscaping," Sam said as Marion poured herself another glass of wine.

Marion quickly added, "It was such an exciting summer for us all. Your father would come home every night, updating me on the progress of your summer romance. It was better than the soaps."

"Not much gets past you two, huh?" Camille said.

"I'm a very observant man." Sam replied. "This was a delicious meal, Cammy. It's nice to see you like this." He gently laid his hand on top of his daughter's, giving it an extended squeeze.

Camille looked back and forth between her parents. "I know. I like seeing myself like this. I just, I don't know, shut off. I know I need to get back to normal. Or a new normal, at least."

"Normal is overrated," Sam replied.

Camille smiled at her father. "Thank you for letting Willa and me visit. I think the change of scenery has been good for us. Hopefully in a week or two I can convince the firm that I'm ready to come back."

Marion stood up, looking down at her daughter. "So the plan is a week or two here and then back to DC?"

"Yes, of course," Camille quickly replied.

"Well, if you think that's best," Marion said, gathering glasses and stalking inside.

Camille looked to her father. "What was that about?"

He waved his hand dismissively. "You know your mother has ideas about how things should be done."

Camille eyed her father suspiciously. "And what exactly does she think I should be doing?"

Sam shrugged.

Camille stared back. "You know you should tell me. I need to be prepared for whatever agenda is going to be thrown my way."

Sam sighed, seemingly resolved to the fact that he would forever be navigating the tightrope between his daughter and his wife. "Your mother thinks it might be good for you two to move down here. Move in with us, so she can take care of Willa while you . . ."

"What? Wallow in despair?"

Sam shook his head. "No. Grieve. Give yourself time."

"I'm pretty sure she just wants to dress Willa up and parade her around her friends. This is much more about her than me."

Sam looked straight into Camille's eyes. "Now that's not fair. You scared us all when you ended up in the hospital." He sighed. "Take your time, Camille. You don't have to rush back until you're ready. That's all."

"I know." Camille looked out over the bay, reluctantly agreeing with her father.

Marion walked back outside, bringing a bowl for the leftovers. Sam grabbed one last shrimp and said, "This was delicious, Camille. Where did you pick up the shrimp?"

"At Billy's, of course." Camille started clearing the table and looked up as the conversation stopped. Her parents' faces were pulled into matching grimaces. Sam threw his napkin on the table and pushed his chair back. Camille looked at her father, surprised by his reaction. "I'm sorry, did I say something wrong?"

"Nope. I'm going to catch fireflies with Willa." Sam stalked away, his shoulders pushed up toward his ears and his hands shoved into his pockets.

"Mom, what was that about?"

"That is a long story." Marion sighed deeply. "You should know, we don't shop at Billy's anymore."

"What are you talking about?" Camille asked. "We've bought seafood there my entire life. Dad would refuse to buy a piece of cod from the Piggly Wiggly because he insisted that nothing was as good as Billy's." Camille looked at her father across the yard. "Now Dad's in a huff and you're telling me, 'We don't shop there anymore.' I'm going to need some more details."

Marion tightened her face. "It's really nothing for you to worry about. I just wouldn't shop there or bring up Billy's if you're around your father. Or me. It isn't something we're going to discuss, so drop it." Marion gathered the dishes and walked inside, letting the screen door slam behind her.

Camille sat back, taking a longer sip of wine and murmuring to herself, "Well, I thought it was a nice day, at least."

◆ 13 ◆

CAMILLE TUCKED WILLA INTO bed, snuggling beside her with a copy of *The Boxcar Children*. It had been one of Camille's favorite books as a child, and she had read it to Willa at bedtime so many times they'd lost count. Especially since Ben died, the story of four orphaned children seemed to resonate with Willa.

As Camille finished the chapter, she watched Willa's body become heavy, her eyelids battling to stay open, the rhythm of her breath extending into longer stretches. Camille pulled the quilt up to Willa's chest and moved the stuffed animals into the crook of her daughter's arm. She kissed her forehead, gently sweeping the stray curls out of Willa's eyes, and watched her daughter fall asleep.

Willa was sleeping in Camille's childhood bedroom. When they first arrived, Willa had gravitated toward the room where her mother had grown up. Marion had never changed a thing about the room, so it remained a shrine to Camille, a fact that always amused Ben. "This room is a time capsule," he would say. Camille had tended to "hold on to things" as a child, so there was plenty for Willa to explore.

The quilt wrapped around Willa was one Marion's mother had made when Camille was born. It was a classic fan pattern, made with brightly colored scraps of fabric. It was incredibly soft after years of wash and wear. Camille traced her fingers around the pattern, remembering the look on Marion's face when Camille insisted that she wasn't taking the quilt to college. Marion had said, "But you've never slept without it your entire life. It's beautiful; why wouldn't you want to take it?"

Camille had been dismissive, but mostly embarrassed at the thought of bringing some raggedy quilt to her college dorm. She had insisted on a polyester comforter from Bed Bath & Beyond. Running her fingers across the quilt that had provided so much comfort for so many years, Camille couldn't imagine how she had ever left it behind. It was oddly calming to see Willa asleep beneath a blanket that held so many safe and happy memories for Camille.

Camille looked around her childhood bedroom, seeing the relics of middle school confusion and high school angst. Her eyes lingered on the picture from her senior prom. She immediately remembered tiny details, like how her charcoal eyeshadow had smudged by the end of the night after she had jumped into the bay with a group of friends. She had come home soaking wet, and her father had laughed, commenting that they must have had a "hell of a time." Marion hadn't said a word, continuing the silent treatment that she had instigated weeks prior, refusing to even acknowledge Camille's appearance. Prom had been an epic standoff between mother and daughter, each exerting last-ditch efforts at control. Camille looked at the prom picture, a mixture of pride and regret swirling.

It had all started with Camille's prom dress. Marion wanted to take her to Mobile, to the formal wear stores that catered to the big Mardi Gras parties, but Camille refused. She said she would rather go naked than wear the pastel Jessica McClintock gowns she knew her mother would force on her. Camille told her mother that she had already found a dress at the Salvation Army after spending hours driving all over South Alabama scouring thrift stores. Camille pulled the vintage gold lamé halter dress out of her closet, displaying it like a trophy, but Marion shook her head and said, "Absolutely not. That is a Halloween costume, not a prom dress."

Camille pretended to be unfazed, but she was crushed. Apathy was her shield against her mother's judgment. Marion's needling comments over the following weeks made it worse, insisting that Camille's dress was "an embarrassment," that she would "look so foolish" next to the other girls. When Marion asked about Camille's prom date and Camille defiantly announced she was going alone, Marion threw her arms in the air. She said she "wasn't surprised" that no one had asked Camille to prom. Camille pointed out that plenty of boys had asked her to prom; she just didn't want to go with them. Camille told her mother, "I'm happy by myself. I don't need someone else to make my life matter." It was a hurtful thing to say, especially since Camille meant it. They drew their battle lines and didn't seem to care how much they hurt each other in the process.

Weeks after prom, Camille brought home the framed picture of herself. She had posed for the photo like she was shooting the cover of a magazine, smiling broadly, her arm confidently posed on her hip. It was her favorite picture of herself, and she put it on the center of her dresser, proud that there wasn't some forgettable boy sharing the frame.

Camille wondered what Marion thought when she saw that photo—if she remembered all the tears and screams that preceded it, the fights that exhausted them both. They didn't scream anymore; they just delivered well-placed comments designed to slice at each other's hearts. ·

Camille looked over and saw Willa sound asleep. She tiptoed down the hall to the guest room, bringing the picture with her. Camille wondered how she had gone from the girl who had fought to take a picture alone to the woman whose life had completely fallen apart without her husband. It turned out another person did make Camille's life matter, and she'd learned that hard lesson in Ben's death.

As she crawled into bed, she remembered to text Paige, who had already sent four messages teasing her about the conditions in the trailer park and asking whether there was running water. Camille was used to jokes about Alabama. Living in a place as elitist as DC, Camille had quickly developed a thick skin about her hometown. Joining in on the joke was usually the easiest response, but it was deceitful because it ignored the beauty and character of her home. It was pointless to discuss complicated emotions over text, so Camille replied, *My parents renovated the outhouse. You should come visit!*

Paige quickly replied, *No thanks. I require indoor plumbing and a general population with an IQ above eighty. When are you coming back to civilization?*

Camille looked upward, frustrated that she didn't have an answer to such a simple question. She wanted to be back in civilization. She wanted to see a street lined with restaurants, hear people discussing the Ayatollah in line for coffee, and yell at cabs driving through crosswalks. But she wasn't ready. She knew, as much as she wanted her old life back, that life didn't exist anymore. She texted Paige. *A few more weeks and I'll be back with a tan. Going to sleep. Catch up more later.*

She hated lying to her friend. Camille shoved her phone under her pillow. She wasn't going to sleep; she still couldn't sleep. Instead, she pulled out her laptop, hoping to watch a movie that would distract her from the reality of a future with little certainty. She found herself thinking back to her afternoon on Magnolia River and the stop at the seafood shop, quickly falling down an internet rabbit hole.

Camille read all the articles written about Billy's Seafood over the last few years. She read Billy's obituary—how he had died suddenly of advanced-stage lung cancer, how he was survived by his loving wife of forty years and their son, Mack. She found a few articles on Mack and read about his career as an ecology professor at a small California university and how he had moved back to Alabama after his father's death and taken over the operations at Billy's.

Then she found all the articles about the protests. In an article from two years ago, Mack said,

"I spent my youth playing in these waters. Now I'm working with fishermen who have dealt with hurricanes, oil spills, and polluted runoff water. Most of the fish have left, and who could blame them? If we don't start holding people responsible, forcing people to care about these waters, we are going to lose our community's greatest resource."

He had organized rallies in Montgomery, picketing the state's capital and pressuring the legislature for stricter regulations. He had worked with a national environmental advocacy group to stage protests in front of the state's poultry plants and paper mills.

Camille could only imagine how many feathers he had ruffled. Those companies were big employers in the state. But there was a lot of support for Mack's work too. Some of the staunchest environmentalists she knew were hunters and fishers; they knew how important it was to preserve the land. The more she read, the more she loved the work Mack was doing, and she started brainstorming ways she could help.

Just as she was about to close her computer, she saw the link to one more story: *Local Advocate Sues Land Developer and Landscaper for Polluting Water.* The article was from three months ago. A real estate developer had been working to build a new community of twenty homes along the Fish River. It had been advertised as a "Nature Lover's Paradise," with a community dock for canoes and kayaks, fire pits, and a riverfront playground. The lawsuit claimed that the construction had polluted the river, which fed into the local water supply. A group of residents was suing the developer and landscaper.

Samuel Graves Landscape Design was a codefendant in the lawsuit. Mack was the lead plaintiff.

♦ 14 ♦

CAMILLE ROLLED OUT OF bed as the sun was rising. She had spent a restless night, thinking of the lawsuit and of Mack. The gentle, patient man she had met at the seafood shop seemed in conflict with the person who would sue her father. Sam Graves was a fixture in the South Alabama community and a fierce protector of its land and water. He'd had clients over the years who had insisted on obscure ornamental plantings, but he always advocated for native plants, gently encouraging clients to respect and enhance their surroundings. It was laughable that he was being sued for damaging the environment.

Camille did what she always did when she needed to think—she went for a run. She didn't have Ben's dedication and had never been a consistent runner, but it always seemed to clear her mind, and that was just what she needed.

The running trail in Fairhope was one of Camille's favorite places. There was a path that wound around the bay, under a canopy of Spanish oaks and past perfectly manicured cottages. She ran the length of Mobile Street, through the Fairhope park and out to the end of the town pier and back.

By the time she returned to her parents' house, the sun was already high enough and hot enough to leave her dripping in sweat. She found her father on the porch, sipping coffee, and sat on the bench next to him.

"Don't sit too close. I don't like to get that sweaty until the end of the day."

She wrapped her father in a playful hug, and he grimaced as she chuckled.

"Good run?" Sam asked.

"Yes. Exactly what I needed." Camille wiped her forehead on the bottom of her shirt and looked out over the water. "Anyone else up yet?"

"Nope, but coffee is hot. Want some?" Sam asked.

"No. I'm too sweaty to drink coffee. I can't believe how hot it is already."

"That northern weather made you weak. We'll have to toughen you up this summer. You look like you need to eat a little more too, but it is nice to see a little color on those cheeks."

"One thing at a time, Dad." Camille eased back and sat quietly for a few minutes. "So you're being sued, huh?"

Sam shook his head. He looked up at Camille, then back into his cup of coffee. "You weren't supposed to find out about that."

Camille smirked. "Well, there is this thing called the internet. And I am a lawyer. Not sure how you thought I wouldn't find out about it."

Sam spoke carefully. "You've had some other things on your mind. Your mother and I didn't think it was anything you needed to worry about."

Camille knew he was coming from a good place, but she couldn't help but feel annoyed. "You have a daughter who is a lawyer, and you didn't even mention that you were being sued. And for environmental damage. It's ridiculous. I could help. You know I can help."

Sam smiled at Camille and put his arm around her shoulders. "I know, but I managed to find a great lawyer who's handling this. We don't need your help. We just want you to help yourself. You've got enough on your plate. It's not a big deal and certainly nothing for you to worry about."

Camille stood up. "How could I not worry? This is your business and your reputation and your money. It is a very big deal."

Sam put down his coffee and walked toward his daughter. "This is exactly what I wanted to avoid. Camille, I'm serious. This is not something I want you to think about."

"Well, it's too late. I've got this big brain, and it can't help but think."

Sam smiled. Camille knew he was remembering the fight they'd had when Camille was in high school and went through a vegetarian phase. She cited all kinds of statistics about the health and environmental impact of eating meat. Sam told her that she needed to stop talking so he could enjoy his steak. He told Camille her brain was too big for her own good. Eventually, Camille won over the whole family, and they spent a year being vegetarians until Camille mistook a fried oyster for a falafel and declared that it was the most amazing thing she had eaten in a year.

Camille sat down, and Sam joined her on the bench. She took a deep breath and turned to her father. "I understand you're trying to protect me, but sometimes it's nice to think about something else. To do some worrying about something I care about that doesn't have anything to do with Ben's death. Please let me help you. You can start by telling me about this 'great lawyer' you hired."

Sam shook his head. "He's smart and I trust him, and that's all you need to know."

"Absolutely not." Camille began firing questions at her father. "Where did he go to school? How long has he been practicing? Does he have experience defending these types of suits? Please tell me you didn't hire that relic that did your will."

A small smile crept across Sam's face. "Mr. Jacobson was an institution in this town, and I would have hired him if he hadn't died six years ago." Sam rubbed his chin as he mumbled, "Your mother is not going to like this."

Camille suspected that Marion was the driving force behind their secrecy. "Probably not, but it's too late. I know about the lawsuit. Spill it. Who did you hire?"

Sam sighed before finally answering. "Fine. The lawyer's name is Griffin Wood. He seems to be in his forties, although I didn't ask his birthday, because that's impolite. He went to a very fancy school up north and worked at some big firm in Atlanta before he moved here a few years ago."

Camille kissed her father on the cheek. "Thank you. Now please call him and let him know that I want to discuss the case. I'm going to take a shower, and then I'm going over to his office."

Sam elbowed her side. "Good. You smell."

Camille laughed. "I know. The Alabama sun is going to force me into a daily shower routine."

Sam nodded his head, grinning broadly as he said, "Alabama is good for you."

Camille stood and walked inside. As the screen door shut, she thought, *Maybe he's right.*

CAMILLE SHOWERED QUICKLY, BUT it took longer than she liked to get dressed. All her suits and business clothes were in DC. Her instinct was to dress professionally whenever she came near a law office, but anything formal seemed ridiculous in Fairhope. The whole town was casual. A pile of clothes and a trip to her mother's closet later, she settled on a pair of white jeans and a soft blue blouse. She added a pair of espadrilles and a thin gold necklace.

She stared at her hair in the mirror. Without keratin treatments and weekly blowouts, it was impossible to straighten. There didn't seem to be a point anyway, so she let it go, freeing the curls to do what they wanted. It was a risk curly-haired women played each day, never knowing if their hair would rebel or behave. She took two minutes to apply the bare minimum of makeup and headed downstairs.

Sam was already gone for the day, but Marion and Willa were in the kitchen, hatching plans for a morning at the playground. Marion looked up at Camille and inhaled quickly, before recovering and saying, "Well, doesn't your momma look nice, Willa."

Willa looked up briefly from her coloring book as Camille walked over and kissed her on the top of the head. "She sure does. She has on real clothes and she doesn't smell stinky," Willa said, before returning to her crayons.

Camille mockingly glared at them both. "Well, thank you. Yes, it is amazing what some basic hygiene does for a person." She grabbed a muffin from the counter and walked over to Marion. "I need to run an errand this morning. It will only take a few hours. Is that okay, Mom?"

Marion waved her hand toward the door. "You go take your time. Do a little shopping. Willa and I are going to have a great time."

Camille made the strategic decision not to tell her mother where she was going. She smiled and said, "I won't be too long."

Camille made the short drive to downtown Fairhope, arriving just before nine AM, and found a parking spot close to the law office off Section Street. She walked into the two-story brick building that also housed offices for a Realtor and an accountant.

Griffin Wood's office was at the back of the building, and Camille walked down a narrow hallway into a brightly lit and sparsely decorated reception area. There was a couch and one upholstered chair, both in a shade of very plain beige, and next to the door was a dark wooden desk. Behind the desk, a woman with lightly graying hair and an exceedingly proper sweater set sat typing at a computer. Camille walked over to the receptionist, who looked up and said, "Good morning. May I help you?"

Camille smiled. The desk was simple and tidy from the front, but behind that facade, every inch of open space was covered. There were worn photographs of children, pictures of flowers, inspirational quotes, and a very large bag of pork rinds. Camille imagined she could spend about five minutes studying the scene and learn everything about this person. The more Camille looked, the more she wanted to know. She was especially interested in the picture of this proper woman dressed head to toe in leather on the back of a very large motorcycle.

Camille cleared her throat and said, "Good morning. I'm Camille Taylor. I'm here to see Mr. Wood."

The receptionist raised one eyebrow. "Do you have an appointment?"

"I don't, but I'm happy to wait until Mr. Wood has some availability."

The receptionist turned to her computer. "Well, his schedule is full this morning, but if you'd like to make an appointment, I'm happy to review his calendar for an available time."

Camille nodded and then smiled broadly. "I'm sure he'll free up for a few minutes, and I don't mind waiting. I'll just sit on the couch."

Camille walked over to the sitting area and bent to sit as the receptionist said, "Now, let me use this legal dictionary to look up the definition of loitering. Yes, see right here, it says, 'Sitting on someone's couch when they have told you to make an appointment.' Textbook definition. Now how about you come back over here and make an appointment."

Camille hesitated, not quite sure what her next move would be, but just then the door to the office opened. The man who walked in might have been in his forties but probably could have passed for a decade younger—the advantage of a round face and a bright smile. He was dressed in the standard southern uniform—a polo shirt and khaki pants—and had closely cropped sandy hair.

He walked over to the receptionist's desk and said, "Mornin', Ms. Cowles. Now I know I'm late, but I had a little car trouble this morning."

"Good morning, Mr. Wood. There was no car trouble. You had a lesson with the golf pro, and he already called to tell you that he can squeeze you in for a follow-up on that slice issue of yours. Don't try to lie in a town this small." Ms. Cowles paused, staring at him in a disapproving way that made even Camille feel like she was being scolded. "You have a visitor this morning," she continued, gesturing toward Camille, "but I have already explained to this visitor what a busy man you are. I'm sure as soon as you are settled in, she is going to come back over to my desk and make an appointment."

Camille waved timidly, but Ms. Cowles continued, "In the meantime, you have a message from Sam Graves that his daughter is coming into the office today and he apologizes for her brazen attitude, as she has been living in the North for a while and has lost all her manners, but you're free to discuss the case with her." Ms. Cowles went back to typing.

Griffin chuckled and walked toward Camille. She swallowed nervously, feeling like a neon sign against the plain office furniture.

Camille stood and reached out, shaking Griffin's hand. "Well, I will have to thank my father for that wonderful introduction."

"You're Sam's girl. You're famous around here. We can't get him to stop talking about his brilliant daughter."

Camille couldn't help but blush. Her father was prone to talking about her accomplishments, beginning with an embarrassing display of bumper stickers when she was accepted at Georgetown. She had already done a quick search into Griffin Wood's background and knew his résumé was even more impressive—Ivy League education and one of the top firms in Atlanta immediately after law school.

Ms. Cowles scoffed. "Seems like the 'brazen' description was more accurate."

Camille decided to let the comment pass and turned to Griffin. "I'm happy to make an appointment for another day, but I was hoping to touch base with you briefly about my father's case."

Ms. Cowles said, "His calendar is completely full this morning. He barely has time for this little exchange."

Griffin looked to Ms. Cowles and asked, "Am I really all booked this morning, or is that code talk?"

Unfazed, Ms. Cowles simply stated, "Mr. Wood, we have discussed this. You are never going to get out of here at a reasonable time unless you let me help you with your schedule."

Griffin walked behind the desk to the computer and looked at his schedule. "Okay, Ms. Taylor, I've got forty-five minutes. Let's start there, and then you can work with my warden here to find some more time later this week."

Ms. Cowles shook her head and pulled out a notebook, in which she scribbled furiously. Griffin started walking down the hallway and Camille followed him to his office.

"She may be the most intimidating secretary I've ever met," Camille whispered as she walked inside. "And what is she writing in that notebook?"

Griffin tossed his gym bag in the corner behind his desk and closed the door to his office. He gestured to a small round table and grabbed two bottles of water from a small fridge behind his desk. Camille sat as Griffin explained, "That is for my 'year-end report.' She keeps track of everything I need to improve upon from an office efficiency standpoint and delivers it as part of my performance review."

Camille's face was immobile. She pursed her lips, then said, "I'm sorry, you're going to need to explain that a little bit more. Your secretary gives you a performance review every year?"

"Oh yes, she's been doing it since I was a first-year lawyer. Used to drive me crazy, but about two years in, I realized she was my secret weapon to success. She had worked at my firm in Atlanta for twenty years, and for whatever lucky reason, when I started, she decided I'd be her pet project. When I told her I was moving here five years ago, it worked out. She has a daughter in Pensacola and wanted to retire closer. She works a few days a week and keeps me in line."

Camille and Griffin sat at the table and each took sips of their water. Camille smiled. "I am so intrigued. I think she hates me, and I might love her."

Now Griffin was smiling. "I think the same thing every day. I could talk about Ms. Cowles all morning, but I'm pretty sure you came here for another reason."

"Yes, sorry. And sorry for barging in this morning. I really will make an appointment next time. I just learned about the lawsuit last night, so I already feel behind, and I have a lot of questions."

"I figured as much. Sam told me about everything that has been going on, and I'm sorry for what you've been through."

"Oh. Thanks." Camille looked down. She knew there was no need to be embarrassed. Death wasn't something to be ashamed about, but the topic made her uneasy, and she was never sure how to handle these types of interactions.

Seeming to sense this, Griffin said, "I didn't mean to make you uncomfortable. But I figured you should know that I've eaten dinner with your parents a few times. I don't want to speak badly about your mother, but cooking is not her strength. I'm sorry about all the casseroles you must have suffered through."

Camille choked on a sip of water, resulting in a half cough, half snort. Then she started laughing. She genuinely laughed, and then she was mortified about the snorting.

Griffin smiled. "Took a risk there. Glad it was okay." He took a beat and then said, "I'm sorry about your husband too."

Camille felt oddly relaxed and said, "It's nice to laugh. I'm very disturbed by the amount of information you know about my family. And thank you for the other thing. I'm still not great with the response to that."

Griffin put a gentle hand on top of Camille's for a moment, then pulled back and opened a Redweld folder. "So, let's dig in. What are your questions?"

Camille sighed. "Well, it's hard to know where to begin. This has to be the most absurd case I've ever heard of, suing Sam Graves for environmental harm. I'm hoping you're going to tell me that a motion to dismiss is pending and this is a few weeks away from disappearing."

"I know, and I wish that were the case. I really do. Your dad has a strong reputation, but it's more complicated than you think. Unfortunately, your dad has a battle ahead of him."

Griffin walked Camille through the facts. He explained the partnership agreement that Sam had entered into with the developer, the reason Sam was being sued alongside the development company, and how difficult it was turning out to be to separate their actions and liability.

Camille was impressed with the way Griffin clearly laid out the issues, especially since this wasn't a scheduled meeting. But as reality set in, her concern for her father's case increased. She asked, "Are you saying there was real harm here?"

"Between you and me, yes. If we get to the point where we need to defend the conduct, then we'll do that. But I'm hoping we don't get there, because it will be a hard argument to win. The plaintiffs have provided some damaging water and soil samples. The bottom line is that your dad picked a bad partner, and then he didn't pay attention to what that partner was doing."

Camille sighed. "So this developer came in, wreaked havoc on the river and damaged the downstream community, and my dad is on the hook too because of their agreement."

"Yep, that's about right," Griffin said.

"Well, this is depressing." Camille slumped in the chair.

Griffin began gathering his notes and files. "I've seen worse, if that makes you feel any better."

"Not really. Any other news to cheer me up?"

Griffin paused for a moment, then said, "The muffins at Pop's Bakery across the street are delicious. They always boost my mood."

"I already ate a muffin this morning," Camille said, looking over her own notes.

Griffin tried again. "Well, I didn't, and I still have ten minutes left before Ms. Cowles comes hunting for me. Want to sneak out the back and grab a cup of coffee?"

Camille stared at Griffin blankly, not sure how to answer.

After too many uncomfortable seconds, Griffin said, "Sorry. It's probably too soon. And maybe a conflict of interest too? I guess I should check the bar rules on that."

Camille blurted, "I'm sorry, were you asking me out on a date?"

Griffin couldn't help but laugh. "I was trying to. Obviously not very successfully. I'm out of practice too. I've only been divorced a year."

"Oh. I'm just . . . I mean. No. I can't eat a muffin with you. I already ate a muffin, and I already told you that, and I can't eat a muffin on a date, or drink coffee on a date. I can't date."

Camille put her face in her hands, horrified at her inability to speak coherently in front of this very nice, very smart man.

She looked up, and Griffin said, "It's okay. I got it. I should have asked Sam's permission. I didn't know he didn't let you date."

Camille smiled, relieved that Griffin had made light of the situation and grateful that he was able to make her comfortable. She said, "That would be Dad's dream, especially since he wasn't very successful when he told me I couldn't date at fifteen."

Griffin said, "Oh, I know. He told me how you used to sneak out to the movies. Pretty scandalous behavior for such a virtuous woman."

Camille shook her head. "He has definitely told you way too much about me."

Griffin looked into Camille's eyes and said, "Oh, and I was just thinking he left out the best parts." The flirty smile he gave her made Camille's stomach flutter in a way it hadn't done in a while. "It was very nice to meet you, Camille Taylor. I hope you make an appointment to see me again soon."

Camille wasn't sure how she felt, but she walked out of his office and back into the lion's den to discuss schedules with Ms. Cowles.

♦ 16 ♦

CAMILLE LEFT GRIFFIN'S OFFICE, making the short walk downtown to meet her mother and Willa at the playground. When she called to check in, Marion said they were having "a little playdate with the girls." Camille silently groaned, dreading the thought of making small talk with her mother's friends, but it would be impossible to avoid them for much longer. Might as well rip off the Band-Aid.

Even though the playground was only a few blocks away, Camille instantly regretted her decision to walk. She'd forgotten about the suffocating Alabama humidity. After two blocks, Camille was sticky, and she could feel her hair inflating several inches. She knew there was a clown wig forming on her head and there was nothing she could do about it. Her shirt was clinging to her stomach, the silk beginning to darken from her sweat, and she briefly debated going home. She needed armor to meet these women, and instead she was walking in with an inviting checklist of faults.

As she walked to the playground, she was surprised to see a completely new park. The quaint wooden play set of her childhood was gone, likely having fallen victim to time and salt air. There were several new seaside-themed structures tucked into the aging oaks that shaded the park—an octopus climbing web, a whale slide, a seashell café for imaginary meals. In the center was a splash pad spraying arches of water for children to run under. As she walked through the entrance, she saw a sign that read *Made Possible by the Friends of Fairhope*, with a list of businesses and individual donors. *Samuel Graves Landscape Design* was the first name on the list.

Camille quickly spotted a circle of women next to the splash pad. Marion was holding court, surrounded by her friends, all dressed in their uniform of brightly colored Lilly Pulitzer dresses and coordinated lipstick.

Camille waved and Willa ran to greet her mother, wrapping her arms around Camille's waist and in the process streaking Camille's white jeans with an unidentifiable brown smudge. Hopefully mud, Camille thought to herself.

"Momma, have you ever seen a playground like this?" Willa was breathless with excitement.

"I haven't. It's pretty great," Camille said, looking around, her gaze landing back on Willa. Camille smirked, taking in the outfit Marion had selected for Willa. She was wearing cropped pants with ruffles at the hem and a matching top with a mermaid embroidered in the center and teal ribbons running through the sleeves. The entire outfit was pale pink, a beautiful color for bridesmaid dresses and baby blankets but unlikely to survive ten minutes on Willa without staining.

As soon as Willa turned around, Camille chuckled. Her entire bottom was covered in dirt. She'd have to talk to Marion about the practicality of all these outfits she had bought for Willa.

Camille walked toward her mother and leaned in to give Marion a kiss on the cheek, then waved to the group and said, "Hello, everyone."

Willa tugged on her arm and said, "I'm going to climb. Want to watch me?"

"I do. Let me chat with Nana's friends for a few minutes, and then I'll come watch."

Willa nodded and took off, a swirl of pastel pink and fiery red launching toward the climbing ropes.

Camille sat on the bench next to Marion and said, "Mother, this place is amazing. I had no idea you and Dad were involved in this."

"Involved? This place wouldn't be anything but a pile of dirt without your mother. They should have named the park after her." The way in which Marion's best friend, Muffy, described her mother's role in the playground made Camille shrink, embarrassed that she didn't know more about something that was obviously a big part of her mother's life.

Marion smiled broadly. "It took forever, but we finally finished it this winter. I love seeing all of these kids running around and smiling."

"Why didn't you ever mention this?" Camille asked.

Marion waved her hand dismissively. "Your dad talked to Ben about it all the time. They compared notes. Ben even helped send design plans. Surely you heard them discussing it?"

Camille shook her head. "I thought that was some hypothetical playground." She smiled, remembering how much Ben loved playgrounds. When Willa was two, Ben had taken her to dozens of playgrounds all over DC. He took notes as she climbed and slid and swung across DC. He came home that night and drew up plans for the ultimate backyard play space. Ben designed a slide that looked like a hollowed tree and a swing with fairy wings. It was a project that Ben and Willa revisited time and again, adding new components. Every trip they took, they would "research" the playgrounds in that area.

Willa would report on whether the slide was too slow or the monkey bars too far apart, and Ben would bring along a tape measure and take notes. Ben never got to build the dream playground for Willa, but it was oddly comforting knowing he had played some small role in a place Willa was enjoying now.

Camille looked to her mother. "I had no idea."

Marion beamed. "The whole town did it. We just helped organize everyone, and your dad supplied some manpower."

Muffy rolled her eyes. "Marion, modesty is one thing, but you are telling your daughter lies. Camille, your mother organized countless fund raisers, got donations from every town business, coordinated volunteers, and she even worked with the town attorney on permitting issues. None of this would be here without her. She is a remarkable force."

Camille sat silently for a moment and then said, "Well, it is very impressive, and it looks like Willa is loving it."

Marion nodded. "That was the whole point." She turned to Camille and narrowed her eyes. "Sweetie, you're melting over there. Why don't you go sit in the shade next to Muffy?"

Camille looked at her mother, not a hair out of place, the golden sun shining on her dry forehead. Camille never understood how her mother seemed to have an internal air conditioner that somehow had completely escaped Camille.

Camille stood and crossed to the shady side of the bench. "I walked over here. I should have known better; I'm not used to this heat." She wasn't sure why she felt the need to explain herself. Any normal person would be melting in ninety-degree weather, but not these women.

Camille sat between Muffy Stewart and Josie Meyers, two women who had been fixtures of Camille's childhood. Marion, Muffy, and Josie had known each other since high school. At times, Sam joked that he wasn't sure whether he'd married

Marion or the trio. The three women shared every major life event, from weddings to births to graduations. They all had homes within blocks of each other, and almost every morning they met to "exercise" by walking the loop through the Fairhope park. The fishermen joked that there was no point in trying to catch anything after they walked past the pier, because their laughter and voices scared all the fish away.

Camille looked around, realizing not for the first time that she was sitting in a den of three mothers who all wished she were just a little bit different than she was. For Marion's sake. It would be so much easier for Marion if Camille tried harder. If she were less sweaty. If she were less outspoken. If she were less herself and more like them.

Josie whispered to Camille, "You know, you can get Botox in your armpits. It helps with the perspiration. You might want to look into it."

"Thanks, Josie. I'll think about it," Camille said, knowing there was no way she was ever going to ask her dermatologist about that.

Camille turned to Muffy and asked, "How's Leslie?" Muffy's daughter Leslie was two years older than Camille. Growing up, Camille had always wanted to do everything exactly like Leslie, and Leslie had always been patient enough to let Camille try. Leslie was a southern mother's dream—polite, beautiful, respectful. A constant refrain of "Do you think Leslie would have done that?" had haunted Camille's childhood.

Muffy smiled. "She's wonderful. She took her oldest, Mary Beth, to her cheer competition in Birmingham this week. So I get the joy of having time with little Charlotte." Muffy gestured to her granddaughter sitting in the sandbox next to the bench.

Marion looked at Camille. "Leslie has four children now. Little Charlotte is her youngest." Camille knew Leslie had four kids. Camille and Leslie had lost touch after Camille moved away, but they still followed each other on social media. Leslie's posts were filled with pictures of four smiling children, usually dressed in coordinating outfits.

Charlotte was carefully filling a pitcher with sand and then pouring it into a larger bucket. When some spilled on her lap, she immediately stood up and walked over to Muffy.

"Grandma, I got sand on my lap," Charlotte said, her lip pouting.

Muffy quickly dusted Charlotte's clothes and then said, "All clean now!" with a cheerful clap of her hands. Charlotte turned back to the sandbox.

Camille watched Willa in the background, hanging upside down on the climbing ropes, her shirt almost falling off and her hair dragging the ground. She had to get Willa out of Alabama as soon as possible. There was no way she would fit in with the other girls here, and unlike her mother, Camille wasn't going to make Willa try.

Marion said, "Muffy and I were talking about how you and Leslie should get together, Camille. When she's back in town, you two should meet at the tearoom and catch up."

"I would love that," Camille said, wondering what it would be like to spend the afternoon with Leslie. For two people who had spent their childhood together, their lives had gone in such different directions. Camille wasn't sure if they had anything in common aside from the age of their daughters, although maybe that was enough. History and children were powerful bonds.

"How was your morning, honey? Did you do any shopping?" Marion asked.

"I didn't. I had a meeting in town. With Griffin Wood."

Marion inhaled sharply. Camille hadn't intended to say anything, but there was something about being in this group of women that put her on edge, and she wanted to surprise her mother. And maybe for a moment, to make her mother as uncomfortable as she always felt.

It didn't work, likely because Muffy and Josie were too polite to discuss the lawsuit.

Josie chirped in quickly. "What a great idea, meeting other lawyers in town. I'm sure Griffin had lots of tips about what it's like to practice law in Fairhope."

Muffy added, "If you decide to move back home, Camille, I'm sure someone like Griffin could help you learn how to open a practice and do all of that legal stuff."

"I'm pretty well versed in the 'legal stuff,'" Camille said defensively. "And no one is talking about me moving back home. I'm just here for a visit, right, Mom?"

"Yes. Of course, Camille. Although it is always a good idea to have an open mind, right?" Marion said as Josie and Muffy nodded.

Josie added, "Griffin is such a nice young man. My Bob says he's quite the golfer too. They play in the Saturday shootouts occasionally. It's a shame about his divorce. You know they never had any kids, and his wife moved back to Atlanta after she was the one that suggested they move here so that he wouldn't keep those long hours at the firm. Imagine, him making all those changes for her to save their marriage, and then she gives up and moves back to the big city. There are some people that can never be pleased. Anyway, Griffin is quite the golfer, and Margaret Winny told me that he's looking at a house on the bluffs, so he must be doing quite well for himself. Such a nice young man."

Camille bit her bottom lip, remembering the power of southern gossip. Only in Alabama could you mention someone's name and in the next breath know everything about their personal history, probably about half of which was true.

Willa walked back toward the group and announced, "I'm done climbing. Can I go explore over there?" She pointed toward the far side of the playground. Camille nodded her head.

As Willa walked away, she stopped at the sandbox and turned to Charlotte. "Do you want to go explore with me?"

Charlotte immediately whipped her head toward Muffy. Muffy smiled and said, "It's okay, hon. You can walk over there. Just make sure you can always see Grandma, and come get me if you need any help."

"Okay, Grandma," Charlotte said, and followed Willa across the playground.

Muffy turned to Camille. "Your Willa is such a beautiful little girl. To think of everything she's been through. You must be so proud."

Camille nodded her head. "I am proud of Willa. She's smart and creative."

No one seemed to pick up on the judgment in Camille's response. Josie commented, "We think it's wonderful that you're taking some time to focus on being a mother. I don't know how you've done it all those years, juggling a career and raising a daughter in that city. You must be loving this time to focus on the important things. To spend time with your daughter instead of getting reports from the babysitter. You know, one of the sweet ladies from the church nursery told me there was a working mom that dropped off her baby and didn't even know what size diaper she wore. Imagine that! Not being around your baby enough to know what size diaper the child needed. We are asking too much of these women to juggle a career and a child."

The entire comment rubbed Camille wrong. She knew that Josie had good intentions, but she felt she needed to stand up for working mothers everywhere. "It may be a juggle, but it's also a privilege to have a career and a child. I work very hard for both, and I'm grateful I get to do it."

"Oh yes, honey, we agree completely. But of course, things will have to change now. You can't keep working like you used to. Willa needs a mother who is present," Muffy plainly stated.

Camille felt her voice rise. "I am present. I have always been present for my daughter."

Josie and Muffy exchanged glances, and then everyone's eyes turned to Marion, who had been uncharacteristically quiet. Camille glared at her mother. "Is there something you want to add here, Mom?"

"We're trying to help, Camille. You don't have to get your feathers up."

Camille rolled her eyes, ready to get to the bottom of what exactly her mother had been telling her friends, when Muffy interjected.

"Oh goodness!" Muffy squealed. "Look at them. What happened? Camille, what did your daughter do to my sweet Charlotte?"

Camille looked up to see Willa and Charlotte walking toward the benches, covered head to toe in red Alabama clay. The dust coated their skin and clothes so that you could barely make out their faces.

Muffy ran toward Charlotte, everyone else quickly following. "What have you girls been doing?"

"Making snow angels," Willa explained.

"In what?" Marion asked.

Willa smiled. "In the dirt. See?" Suddenly, Willa and Charlotte lay down in the dirt to demonstrate. Their arms and legs moved back and forth, creating a cloud of dust as their giggles floated in the air.

"Charlotte Grace, you stand up this minute." Muffy grabbed Charlotte's hand and began dusting off her granddaughter.

Marion made similar motions toward Willa, but Camille interjected, "Mother, let her be. She's having fun."

Marion scoffed. "Oh Camille, don't be ridiculous. She's ruined her outfit. You have to set some limits for the child."

Camille rolled her eyes. "She has limits. She doesn't run out into the street or play with fire."

"Well, I should hope not. But I think some general hygiene might be useful to work on," Marion said, shaking her head.

Camille replied, "Mom, she's six. There are no limits on getting dirty. She's doing exactly what she's supposed to be doing. Caring more about her outfit than having fun is unnatural, especially on a playground."

Marion turned to Muffy. "I am so sorry about this. I don't know what got into Willa. What can I do to help?"

Muffy gathered her purse and waved her hand. "I'm going to take her straight home and get her cleaned up. Hopefully, a bath and a good soak for this outfit should do the trick."

Josie picked up her things. "I'm going to head out too. I need to get home and change for tennis this afternoon. I'll see you girls in the morning for our walk."

Marion waved to Muffy and Josie and then turned back to Camille. "We should probably head out too," Marion said.

"You can head home," Camille replied. "I'm going to stay with Willa. She's having fun."

"But she's filthy."

"She's fine." Camille turned to her daughter and said, "Willa, why don't you go rinse off in the splash pad?"

"Okay," Willa said enthusiastically, running over to the water feature.

Marion whipped her head toward Camille. "She needs a bathing suit!"

"Why? Her clothes are ruined anyway. Let her have fun."

Marion shook her head and sat back on the bench. "Well, this did not go the way I planned."

"It never does with me, does it?"

"What does that mean?"

"Well, what was all that talk with Muffy and Josie before the kids came over? Is there something you want to say about my parenting?"

"No. There is nothing I want to say."

They sat in silence, both knowing there was so much left unspoken, debating whether it was better to ignore the conflict or try to have a conversation.

"I know you would love it if I did this all day," Camille said, gesturing around the playground. "If I stayed home with Willa and met up for playdates, but I can't do that. It's not who I am."

"I know that," Marion replied. "You don't have to say it like it's a bad thing. Caring for your child is not a lesser life."

"I know."

"I don't want to fight with you, Camille. I just think you have some more learning to take from Ben's death. All your life is wrapped up in that career. Think of all the time you could have spent with Ben when you were at the office."

Camille recoiled from Marion's comment, both in its bluntness and its truth. "That was cruel."

Marion reached for Camille's hand. "I never want to be cruel. But I think your priority should be your daughter, not getting back to that job."

Since she had arrived in Fairhope, Camille had spent most days drafting a proposal to her firm about how she would more effectively manage her caseload and clients. She had been checking with the associates, getting updates on the status of cases, and drafting what she thought was a very compelling presentation. She knew Marion rolled her eyes every time she opened her computer, but wasn't that the point of this time at home? For Camille to have some support from her parents, help in caring for Willa, while she figured out how to better balance everything? The fact that Marion still didn't understand how important her job was infuriated Camille.

Camille shook her head. "They aren't separate. Getting my job back, taking care of my daughter, and taking care of myself. They're all wrapped together."

"Well, you seem a lot more focused on getting back to that career than on how your daughter is handling her father's death. Have you talked to her? Seen how she is struggling?"

"She's fine. We're all fine."

"Fine? Collapsing on the street is fine? Nightmares are fine? You don't sleep, but when you do, you scream. Every night. I asked Willa about it and she told me you scream every night, and she's used to it by now, so she just goes back to sleep. Does that seem okay to you?"

Camille shook her head. "I didn't know."

Marion continued, "Willa refuses to ride the bike we got her because she's afraid you're going to collapse again. She thought you collapsed on the street because she was riding her bike the wrong way. She also carries a Corona bottle cap in her pocket because she says she needs to remember Daddy and you don't like to talk about him. When she misses her father, she rubs the bottle cap. Did you know that?"

Camille shook her head. She felt her lip start to shake. "I'm not a bad mother."

"No, you aren't. But you have been gone, mentally, physically. And Willa needs you. That is the most important thing. You have to realize that."

"I know. Of course I know that." Camille turned toward her mother. "You have to realize that I may never do things the way you want. You have to accept who I am."

"Of course, Camille. I love you."

"I know. You've always loved me. But accepted me? No. I don't think you have ever accepted who I am. I think your life would have been a lot easier if I went to the University of Alabama like Leslie and dressed my daughter like Charlotte and settled down here with a boy from a good southern family. I think that's what you knew, what made you comfortable. I think you look at me and there's a whole lot you don't understand, and you don't want to try to understand, so you try to change it. I feel like you spend a lot of the day biting your tongue around me."

Marion shook her head. "I want what's best for you. That's all I've ever wanted."

"I spent the first half of my life trying to be what you wanted, but I was no good at it. So I left home. And I got lucky. I found someone who loved every inch of me. Who accepted every inch of me. And now he's gone. And my job is gone, or at least it feels like it's gone. So yes, I'm focused on getting my career back, and getting myself back, and figuring out how to do life when I seem to be messing everything up and the only person who made me feel like I was doing things right is dead. But I'm doing all of that for Willa. I want her to be exactly who she is, and I don't want her to have to fight for it. I want her to keep on waking up every morning with the blissful ignorance that she doesn't have to change an inch of herself to make other people happy."

Marion sat quietly, her lips opening and closing, seemingly unable to find the right words. She finally looked into her daughter's eyes and said, "I love you. I want to help, that's all."

Camille sighed. "I know." Camille stood up and called Willa. Willa ran toward her mother, and Camille scooped her into a hug, twirling her in the air. They held hands as they left, the muddy, messy, wet duo walking out of the playground and through the streets of downtown Fairhope, away from Marion.

CAMILLE WAS UP EARLY again, rising before the rest of the house. Her mind was filled with the tension from her conversation with her mother and her concern over her father's lawsuit. She made coffee and reviewed her notes. Griffin had sent over the case files yesterday, and she spent most of the evening reviewing the filings and Griffin's research. It felt so natural to spend an afternoon reviewing legal documents, but it also allowed her to avoid Marion. She started outlining a plan for potential legal defenses, but she needed more information. There was somewhere she needed to go, and she was prepared to battle with her parents over it.

Willa walked into the kitchen carrying a blanket, a cardboard box, and a doll missing its clothes.

"Morning, sweet pea. How did you sleep?"

Willa yawned, stretched, and then declared, "Good. Can I have oatmeal with bananas?"

"Yes. You sit at the counter and I'll get it started."

Willa walked over to the kitchen counter and set the cardboard box on the stool. She walked over to Marion's desk and pulled out scissors, colored pencils, and paper and returned to the counter.

"What are you working on there, Willa?"

"Nana gave me this doll. We were playing fisherman on the dock, but Nana said the doll wasn't dressed appropriately for fishing. So I'm fixing her up."

"What was she wearing?" Camille asked, pouring milk, cinnamon, and brown sugar into a pot. She slowly poured in the oats as Willa began her explanation.

"Some dress that matched one Nana gave me. They're both upstairs in my closet. I figured Nana wouldn't want her fishing naked, so I'm making her some clothes and a boat, and then she'll be ready to go fishing."

Camille stirred the banana slices into the oatmeal, thinking that Marion would probably prefer it if Willa didn't fish with the doll at all but instead had tea parties and sleepovers. Although Willa was right that Marion would probably be even more appalled at the idea of playing with a naked doll than she was about getting the doll's dress dirty. Camille set a small dish of raisins in front of Willa and said, "I'm sure Nana will be thrilled about that."

"Thrilled about what?" Marion asked as she and Sam walked into the kitchen.

"I'm making my doll a fishing outfit," Willa proudly declared.

Marion reached for the doll and turned it around in her hands. "Where is the outfit I gave you?"

"It's upstairs. Those clothes were just too constricting, Nana. She needs to move freely on the water."

Sam smirked. Marion raised her eyebrows as she said, "Oh, she does, does she?"

Willa didn't even look up from her coloring as she replied simply, "Yes."

THE RIVER RUNS SOUTH

Between bites of oatmeal, Willa continued constructing an outfit for her doll that was largely squares of paper secured in countless wraps of tape. Marion's eyes kept getting larger and larger as Willa decorated the doll in pencil drawings and oatmeal droppings. Camille could almost see the visions of tea parties dissipate above her mother's head as the reality of Willa settled in. Camille and Sam exchanged glances, and both stifled a laugh as Marion moved about loudly in the kitchen.

Camille nudged the bowl of oatmeal closer to Willa. "Eat up, sweet pea. You need your fuel; we've got another adventure day planned."

Willa set aside her doll and dug in. "Are we going to the river again?"

Camille nodded. "We are. But we're going to a different river this time."

Willa beamed, and her eyes widened. "There are two rivers here?"

Camille sat next to her daughter and began to explain the basic layout of Baldwin County. "There are two main rivers. We visited the Magnolia River, but there is another river to the north called the Fish River. Both rivers flow into Weeks Bay estuary. The estuary is a special place, because the fresh river water mixes with the salty bay water, and it's the home of some very special animals."

"Can we go to the estuary?" Willa asked in a voice that verged on squealing.

"Oh, definitely," Camille quickly replied. "When I was your age, going to the estuary was one of my favorite things to do. But today, I want to go to the Fish River."

Marion and Sam both looked at their daughter, mouths agape. Finally, Marion said, "You are not going to the Fish River site."

"Yes, I am. I need to see it," Camille replied definitively.

Marion looked over to Sam, wondering when he was going to chime in. She continued, "That is not a good idea. We didn't want you finding out about this lawsuit. But after your little meeting with Griffin yesterday, it appears that ship has sailed. So fine, have some conversations with your father's attorney, but visiting the site? Why?" Marion crossed her arms and stared straight at Camille. "Besides, you're leaving soon. What's the point of getting involved in this mess? You need to focus on your career, getting back to DC, right?"

Camille glared at Marion. "I'm pretty sure I can juggle it, like I've done with so many things, right, Mom?" Camille turned to her father. "Dad, I can help. You both know I can help. That's why I need to go see the site."

Sam took a long sip of coffee, then set it on the counter and looked at Camille. "I'll take you. I need to go too."

Marion threw up her hands.

Sam said, "I'll take you, Camille. But let's leave Willa here." He turned to Willa and asked, "Sweetie, do you think you and Nana can take your doll fishing off the dock today? We'll plan another day for a river trip."

"When?" Willa asked.

"Soon," Camille replied.

"Nope. I need to know the real day that we will go." Willa crossed her arms across her chest, then quickly added, "And the estuary too."

Sam looked at Camille. "She's even tougher than you were at this age."

"She's tougher than I am now," Camille replied. She looked at Willa. "Tomorrow. We will go to the river and the estuary tomorrow."

Willa quickly answered, "Deal." She turned to her grand-father. "I'm not sure how much fishing Nana is going to do today, but she can probably watch me. I need to build my doll a boat too."

Marion sat next to Willa and said, "Well, I'm actually an expert cardboard boat builder, and I can help you with that fishing outfit. I might not fish, but I can certainly dress for the occasion."

"Thank you, Mom," Camille said. She bit her lip, wanting to say more, but also afraid of what her mother would say back. Instead, she smiled and kissed Willa on the cheek and said, "Try to listen to Nana. And no swimming in the bay without your floatie."

Willa gave a nod and a thumbs-up.

"I have to pick my battles with this stubborn crew," Marion replied. "You two don't be gone too long," she said to Sam and Camille.

Sam grabbed Marion around the waist and kissed her on the cheek. "I'll have her back before lunch. I have to visit another site this afternoon."

★   ★   ★

Camille and Sam made the short drive over to the Fish River. The two rivers were similar, but Fish River was bigger, with a lower elevation. Downriver, near the bay, Fish River would expand and contract, creating expansive wetlands that were home to the state's treasure of birds and fish. An occasional restaurant would pop up along the river, drawing customers from Fairhope and Foley, but mostly it was a rural, fertile land-scape that divided the bay from the farming communities. The river narrowed out upstream and had homes similar to Mag-nolia River.

When they drove down the gravel road to the development site, Camille could hardly believe what she was seeing. The whole site had been cleared. The land bordering the river was usually covered with trees and wild grasses, the occasional cottage peeking through pines. This was an expanse of seventy acres with over a thousand feet of direct river frontage, and it was barren. There wasn't a tree or a bush in sight, just red Alabama clay pushed and moved into unnatural mounds in front of the open river.

They got out of Sam's truck and walked toward the river. Camille didn't think she could be more shocked until she looked into the water. The developers had attempted to build up the bank and, in the process, graded the land, resulting in a dump of sediment. It didn't create an elevated building site; instead, the cleared trees had resulted in an eroded riverbank that was seeping across the build site.

They walked along the riverbank together. Camille wasn't sure what to say. She was relieved when Sam spoke first. "Pretty bad, huh?"

"I've never seen anything like it." Camille took in the land. Her heart was breaking for so many reasons—from the damage to the river, the fact that her father was a part of it, and the reality that this lawsuit was a real problem. Finally, she asked, "Dad, how did this happen?"

Sam sighed long and hard. He looked up at the sky, then kicked the ground with his boots. "I don't know, Cammy. I just don't know."

"Well, try," Camille responded immediately. "Try to tell me how it got like this. Because I've been to hundreds of your job sites, and I have never seen anything like this."

Sam closed his eyes. He reluctantly began his explanation. "Camille, this piece of property is the crown jewel of Baldwin

County. All the sites along the bay are developed, and besides, if you're a serious fisher, you don't want to live on the bay. The water is too shallow to boat without a long pier. The river is calm, deep, and at this part, it's so wide you feel like you're on a lake inlet. Ten minutes down the river and you're in Weeks Bay, and a short drive east or west and you've got grocery stores, restaurants, shopping. There isn't a more attractive development site in the state."

Sam walked toward the river, and Camille followed. She listened. She had a million questions, but she knew Sam needed to tell the story in his own way and she needed to hear it.

Sam continued, "The only problem with living here is the floodwaters. It has scared off developers for years. But I still thought it could work. I tracked the flood levels, monitored the watershed studies for years. I thought the right developer could build this property at the right elevation, and of course I would landscape it so that it looked like that was how it was always meant to be. It costs a lot of money to move dirt around, but I thought it would be worth it."

It was hard watching Sam struggle through the story, laying out how his vision had washed away on the banks of this river. It was Sam's dreamer's heart that endeared him to everyone around him. Marion was practical, supporting the good dreams, reining in the frivolous ones. Sam always said Marion was good at reminding him of his happy place: back on the earth instead of floating in the clouds.

Camille prodded, "So tell me about this developer you found."

"I've known Trident Development for decades. They've worked throughout the Southeast. Family run with a solid reputation. Everyone in real estate knows about this property and knows how much I've studied it. When the Cornwall family announced they were ready to sell to the highest bidder, Trident called me and set up a meeting. The son was taking the lead on the project—he was young and ambitious. He told me this was going to be the future of Trident. We talked for months and months. When I pitched a community marina, shared open space with preserved wooded areas, and trails throughout the property, they were thrilled. There was only enthusiasm for my ideas. Maybe I should have realized it was too good to be true. We went over the numbers, got estimates. Everything was lining up—the sale price from the Cornwalls, the permitting from the town. This was not some shot-in-the-dark project. We worked on this for a long time, and it felt like it was really going to work. Like it was meant to be."

Sam started looking for rocks, picking them up and throwing them out to skip on the calm river water. "Your mother and I talked about it, and I approached them about taking an ownership interest in the project. I believed in it, and we wanted a good solid investment to retire on." He looked over to Camille. "Before your eyes fall out of your head, you should know I wasn't a complete idiot. I put some money in. Not all my money. But enough to give me an interest and apparently ownership in this mess they created."

Camille said, "Well, at least there's comfort that you're not totally destitute."

Sam laughed. "Not yet, anyway." Then he got serious. "But I know I could be. If I lose this lawsuit, I could be." Sam shook his head. "I can't believe how much harm was caused here. It makes me sick to think about."

"That's what I still don't understand," Camille said. "How do you go from your dream project to this?" She turned around in a circle in the open space that should have been filled with so much life.

"We'd agreed to wooded homesites with a small marina and a cleared pavilion at the river's edge for community gatherings. That's what we agreed to. It's my fault I trusted them to do what they said they would do. I take the blame, and now I need to figure out a way to fix it."

Sam started walking back to his truck. Camille stopped him.

"That's not the whole story. Tell me the whole story, Dad."

"There really isn't more to tell. I visited the site a few weeks after they started clearing, and everything was gone. They were supposed to mark off the homesites and start building the elevation on the riverbank, but they told me once they got started, they had to change plans. Their appraiser came back and said they couldn't recoup the construction costs if they preserved the trees; it was faster and cheaper to clear everything and then increase the planting budget. I lost my mind when I saw this and immediately went into crisis mode. I told them how much this would harm the river, especially the neighboring homesites, but they said they were permitted and the government approved the clearing."

"I still don't get it. You live at job sites. I've never known you to go a day without visiting an active site. They could maybe clear a couple trees, but not this whole place without you knowing. Where were you?"

As soon as she asked the question, Camille saw her father's face change. She saw the slight pull of pain across his eyes before he shook his head and said, "Couldn't be helped. I made a mistake in trusting someone I shouldn't. Now, we've talked about this enough."

Camille knew Sam meant to shut down the conversation then and there. Under different circumstances, Camille would have relented. But the nagging in her stomach, the waves of nausea coming over her, meant that she had to know. She needed him to say it.

"Dad, when did they clear the land?"

"Enough, Camille. I've said all I'm going to say."

"You know I can look it up. I'll have Griffin pull the documents. Tell me."

Sam swore under his breath. He never cursed, especially not in front of his daughter. But this was different. Finally, he said, "They cleared in October. They started the day after Ben died."

"They cleared in October," Camille repeated.

Sam was quiet.

"And you and Mom were with us in DC. You were with us for weeks."

Sam gently held his daughter's hands and said, "That is exactly where we were supposed to be."

"This is all my fault." Camille didn't cry. She wouldn't allow herself that luxury when she was clearly such an expert at messing up everyone's lives.

"No. Absolutely not. I picked a bad partner. If he didn't mess things up at the land-clearing stage, he would have messed up the build site. This is on me."

Sam blew out a steady stream of air and started mumbling to himself. Camille caught bits and pieces of rumbling about "tagging trees" and a "total waste of time."

"Dad, what are you babbling about?"

"I get so worked up every time I come out to this place. Especially considering all the time I spent with my crew, walking the property, tagging every tree, reviewing clearing plans with the surveyor and the architect. I accounted for every blade of grass. I left explicit instructions for where the dirt should go and where it shouldn't. They told me sometimes they have to make on-site adjustments, but never in my wildest dreams did

I think it would be this. I knew the clearing permit gave them a lot of leeway; I just didn't think they would take it. We didn't need to take it. It wasn't what we planned for. All that work and those guys flattened it."

"Did you tell Griffin about the tagging?"

"I don't think so. Tagging trees is something we do at every construction site. I'm sure he knows that."

Camille stared at her father. "When you look at Griffin, do you think, *That's a man who knows his way around a construction site?*"

Sam chuckled. "Fair point. Boy can golf, but not sure he's used to dirt on his boots. He probably doesn't know about my process. Honestly, most of my conversations with Griffin have been about the partnership agreement and the emails and conversations we had setting up the relationship. Why do you think he needs to know about the tree tagging system?"

"Just a hunch. I'm going to go back and take a fresh look at your agreement with the developer. It may be nothing, but it's worth thinking about. If you get a chance, make a list of the crew that worked with you on the tagging project. Also see if you have copies of those instructions you left with them for the dirt moving. I'm guessing you didn't email those?"

Sam looked at Camille sideways. "Have you ever seen a construction crew that reviews emails before getting to work?"

"That's what I thought. Check and see if you have a copy. Mom loves to make copies of your plans."

"I always hated homework," Sam said.

"I know. But this time it may be worth the effort." Camille jumped into her father's truck. "We better head back before Willa drives Mom crazy."

They drove off, a cloud of dust trailing the truck as Sam looked in the rearview mirror, shaking his head.

◆ 18 ◆

CAMILLE HAD TO STAY. There was no way she could go back to DC after seeing the site and understanding the seriousness of this lawsuit. She could help. The reason her father was involved in this lawsuit was because she had needed someone to take care of her after Ben's death, and her parents had done that, no questions asked.

As her father pulled into the driveway to drop her off, she knew she'd extend her time in Fairhope. She'd work with Griffin and file a motion for the court to reconsider the dismissal. It might take a few weeks, a few months more likely, of really digging in, but she might be able to make the lawsuit go away. At the very least, she could try.

Maybe she was also thinking about what her mother had said about her needing more time with Willa, about needing to connect with her daughter without the distraction and chaos of her job in DC. In the last few weeks, she'd already talked to Willa more about Ben than she had in the previous months since his death. One look at Willa and it was clear she was thriving in Alabama. Maybe extending their time here could help everyone.

If Camille was going to stay, she had to tell her office, and she wanted to call them now, before she changed her mind. Camille always had a hard time putting herself before her job. It was a job that made constant demands, loud demands, and sometimes it was easier to just do the work than think of the cost. But this time she needed to put the people she loved first.

Camille sat on the front porch and tentatively picked up her phone to call Duncan Hatch. She hoped for voice mail, but his secretary answered and said he was wrapping up a meeting. While Camille was on hold, she began rehearsing what she would say, ultimately deciding that it was best to cut straight to it.

"Hello, Camille. Great to hear from you."

"Hi, Duncan. I'm calling because I'd like to discuss my return."

"Well, that's what I was hoping to hear. We're ready to have you back."

"I hate to disappoint you, but I'm calling because I'm not quite ready. I need a few more weeks." Camille swallowed hard. "Actually, I need to take off the rest of the summer. I'm in Alabama with my parents, and I need to stay here until September."

Duncan exhaled. "Well, Camille, obviously we want you to take the time you need." He cleared his throat. "Here's the thing. We can manage for a few weeks, since that's what we were planning on. We've been keeping your seat warm. But September? That's a long time. There are active matters and active clients to think about. It's more than covering a few meetings."

"I know, Duncan. I hate to inconvenience anyone, and I wouldn't do it unless I felt it was necessary."

"I understand. But Camille, you know what this means. I'm going to need to reassign your clients. I'll have to bring in other partners for those relationships."

Camille had known this was a possibility, but her stomach sank. "I'll be available on email. I'll make phone calls to check in. These are relationships I've been building for years."

"Camille, our clients expect a certain level of involvement, and they can't get that while you're in Alabama. Do you really think you can manage these relationships, manage their cases?"

Camille knew he was right, but she also knew what it meant. "Duncan, if you reassign all my clients, I'll have nothing. My entire book of business will be sucked up by the other partners in the group."

"Camille, this is a firm. We support each other. No one would steal your clients."

It's what Duncan had to say, but Camille knew it was a lie. She pleaded, "Let me try to juggle it. I think I can do it. I need this time, but if you reassign my clients, you're going to make my return exponentially harder."

"Camille, I don't want to make anything harder for you. We're willing to give you all the time you need, but this is a business. A client service business. You haven't been giving your clients the level of service they expect, and that's an issue for the firm."

Camille sat in silence. She felt a growing knot in her stomach, not sure how to fight, or even what to fight for.

Duncan broke the silence. "Take the summer and we'll chat in September, figure out a plan then. You will always have a place at this firm, but we might think about another role for you. Coming back as a senior counsel instead of a partner, for instance. You can have some time to rebuild."

Duncan must have thought he was being generous, giving her the time and flexibility she requested, but Camille was angry. She choked down the tears she felt bubbling up as she said, "Let's make this clear, Duncan. If I come back now, I keep my clients; I keep my partner status. But if I take the summer off, take the time I need, the time you said I can have, I'm potentially coming back as a counsel. Giving up everything I've worked the last decade to build?"

"That's not what I'm saying. We're talking in hypotheticals here. You've surprised me with this news. We all thought you'd be back in the office by now. We're discussing options for all of us to consider."

"Got it," Camille huffed.

She thought about how miserable she had been those last few months in the office, trying to go through the motions of her life, to survive the daily hustle of her job and being alone with Willa. Then she thought about the last few weeks in Fairhope. Despite the tension with her mother, she had smiled more, felt more relaxed, more alive than she had since Ben's death. And she was needed here. She could help her father. Back in the office, it was clear there was a list of people who could fill her place.

She took a deep breath and said, "I need to be here. Until the end of the summer. I'll call you then, and we can discuss all the possible scenarios for my return. I appreciate the firm's willingness to give me this time."

"Of course. Take care, Camille."

"Thanks, Duncan."

Camille ended the call with her heart racing. It might be the right decision to extend her leave, but it still felt reckless. She was watching her career trajectory plummet so that she could spend a few more months in Alabama? It didn't seem like a responsible decision, especially for a single parent with a daughter to support. But then again, if the firm could replace her so easily, maybe none of it really mattered. Maybe none of her sacrifice, her time away from her family building this career that was the center of her world, mattered at all. Maybe it was time she started figuring out what did matter.

She needed to clear her head and do something to take her mind off the law firm. She walked inside to see Willa and Marion standing over the kitchen sink. Marion was showing Willa how to clean dirt from her fingernails.

Marion had a dish brush and was scrubbing the tips of Willa's hands. Willa said, "Nana, that kind of hurts."

"Oh goodness. I'm sorry, Willa. It's just that this stuff is really stuck," Marion said as she poured more water over Willa's hands.

Camille closed the door and said, "Mom, Willa has had dirt under her nails since she could walk. That is a pointless exercise."

"Oh, you're back," Marion said, looking up from the sink. "How did it go?" she asked.

"It was informative," Camille replied. "How were things here?"

Willa pulled her hands away and jumped down from the stool by the sink. She hugged Camille as she said, "Nana and I couldn't get the boat to float. The whole bottom sunk, so I dug it out, but Nana said I got bay gunk all over my hands."

Willa held up her hands, and Camille kissed them gently. Camille said, "Okay, how about this? Nana has a rest time and you I go to the estuary this afternoon?"

Willa jumped. "Yes! Tomorrow is way too long to wait."

Marion slumped into the couch and said, "That's a good plan. I may take a little rest. You two have a good time."

Camille figured getting outside and spending the afternoon at the estuary was just what she needed after the call with Duncan. Familiarity was the best antidote to anxiety, and Camille couldn't think of a more familiar place than the Weeks Bay estuary.

On the short drive over, Camille told Willa about Weeks Bay. In the 1990s, a foundation had been set up to preserve the wetlands and provide educational experiences for the community. A visitors' center was built, with boardwalks that traversed the marsh.

As they pulled into the parking lot, Camille was relieved to see the view was largely unchanged. They walked into the visitors' center, and Willa was mesmerized. There were display cases providing information about the animals and even specimens to touch. Camille and Willa grabbed a map, filled their water bottles, and headed out onto the boardwalks.

Willa cupped her hands and formed makeshift binoculars. She immediately started pretending she was a "world-renowned" explorer, about to discover a new species "any minute now."

Camille raised her eyebrows. "Well, if you're going to be an imaginary explorer, I suppose you should be world renowned."

They made their way to the end of the boardwalk and the open dock. There was a smattering of boats on the water. The gentle breeze barely disturbed the calm waters, and the salt air filled Camille's lungs. Camille pulled the baseball cap lower over Willa's face, and Willa immediately pushed it back. Camille knew it was going to be a constant battle this summer to protect her fair-skinned daughter from the Alabama sun. She had already noticed new freckles appearing on Willa's nose, matching Camille's. Thankfully, Camille tanned easily, and her daily runs had brought more color to her skin. She looked down at her cutoff jean shorts and the Pearl Jam T-shirt she had found buried in a dresser drawer. She smiled at how much she preferred this daily uniform to the suits she'd been wearing months ago.

They sat on a bench at the end of the dock, and Camille pointed out all the unique things about the estuary, how it created the perfect conditions for so many creatures to live with the mix of salt and fresh water.

A boat came close to the end of the dock, and Willa started to wave. Camille looked quizzically at her daughter. "Who are you waving at, Willa?"

"Mack's Seafood!" Willa shouted.

Camille looked up to see Mack's boat continuing its approach.

As he pulled up to the end of the pier, he kept the motor on idle and said, "Well, this a nice surprise. What are you two up to?"

"We are exploring the estuary," Willa replied. "I'm planning on putting on my scuba gear and finding a new species to put in the visitor center."

Camille quickly replied, "It's a shame that we left our scuba gear at home. Plus I think we should focus on the basic swim strokes before we attempt underwater exploration." Camille turned to Mack. "How did you know we were here?"

"I didn't. But I spotted you from the end of the pier and decided to motor over. You two stand out, especially with the sun shining down on all of that red hair."

Willa beamed. "Two firecrackers, right. That's what Daddy would say. I'm destined to stand out wherever I go."

"You are. You both are." Mack smiled.

Camille was becoming increasingly uncomfortable. She turned to Willa. "Okay. We have to go, Willa; it's time to head out." Camille abruptly walked away, then turned back to find Willa immobile, arms folded across her chest and feet firmly planted.

Willa said, "Momma, we just got here. I don't want to leave; besides, I've got some questions for Mack."

Mack killed the engine. "I can't wait to hear these questions."

Camille knew she should scoop Willa up, kicking and screaming if necessary. She couldn't make simple chitchat with the person suing her father.

Willa took Camille's hesitation to mean victory. She relaxed and turned to Mack, asking, "What do girl fishermen wear?"

Mack seemed to consider the question thoughtfully before answering, "Same thing as me. Waders, boots, hat to keep the sun out of their eyes." Mack did a twirl, displaying his fishing clothes to full effect, and neither Willa nor Camille could stifle a laugh.

Mack looked up at Camille. "Do you really have to head out? I'm done for the day, and I was going to head over to the blueberry farm. Want to join?"

"Where is there a blueberry farm?" Camille asked at the same time that Willa declared, "Absolutely."

Mack chuckled. "Weeks Bay Estate is an organic farm now. Their blueberries are famous around here. They're mostly picked out, but I happen to know about some hidden bushes."

Willa's entire body started vibrating with excitement. "I really want to go, Mother."

"Well, if you're calling me *Mother*, I know it's serious."
When a child had been through as much as Willa, you said
yes to every moment of joy you could bring, even if it meant
interacting with the person suing your parents. Camille said,
"Okay, we can do that." She looked at Mack. "We'll drive
over and meet you."

Mack said, "It's a quick boat ride. I can take you over and
back faster than you could get there by car."

"Plus," Willa added, "riding on a boat is so much more
fun."

Mack chimed in, "She's right. It is so much more fun.
Come on, you can see their dock around the bend. I know the
owner, and we can borrow their ATV and ride up to the fields.
Up for an adventure?"

"Momma is always up for an adventure!" Willa squealed.
It was true; Camille could never turn down an adventure.
Whenever Ben needed to convince Camille to do something,
especially mundane tasks like running errands, he would tell
her, "It'll be an adventure," and Camille would always go
along. Adventure was her Achilles' heel.

She knew she was outnumbered. Plus she did want to see
the farm at Weeks Bay Estate. Camille threw up her hands and
said, "Okay, you guys win, but we have to be back by four. I
told Nana and Gramps I would cook dinner tonight."

Mack and Willa both had giant grins on their faces. "Deal,"
they both said.

Willa loved the boat ride. She strapped on the life vest and
sat close to the front of the boat while Camille stood back with
Mack.

Camille refused to make eye contact and rebuked all of
Mack's efforts at small talk.

After a few silent moments, Mack said, "I seem to have pissed you off, and I'm not real sure what I did, since I haven't seen you since you were in the shop. Here I was pleasantly surprised to bump into you again, and you don't seem to feel the same way."

Camille blurted out, "I'm Camille Taylor. Sam Graves is my father."

Mack continued motoring the boat through the bay. "I'm a little out of touch on my South Alabama gossip. Am I supposed to know who that is?"

Camille scoffed. "Oh, I guess you sue so many people it's hard to keep track."

Mack drew his brows together. Confused, he said, "I only have one lawsuit going on, and it's against Trident Development."

"Yes, Trident Development and Samuel Graves Landscape."

"The landscaper." Mack paused, connecting the dots. "The landscaper is your father?"

"Yes," Camille stated.

Mack took off his hat and ran his fingers through his hair. "Okay, first, I didn't sue your father. Trident did something called a . . ." Mack searched for the word, and Camille filled it in for him.

"A joinder."

"Yes, Trident filed for a joinder and brought in your father. I had no idea about their partnership agreement. If I could leave Sam Graves out of this, I would, but that isn't up to me."

"Why? Why don't you settle or drop the lawsuit? Do you know anything about my father?"

"I'm learning more and more," Mack said. "I can't drop the lawsuit, because if I do, these developers will keep tearing this place up." Mack gestured around the bay. "These waters are my life, my livelihood. Used to be the same for a lot of people."

Mack gripped the boat's wheel as he continued. "All up and down this river, it's the same. The original houses are gone; these giant boxes are in their place. The trees have been cleared for better views, and when the water keeps rising, everyone wonders why. Without the tree roots, everything erodes away."

Camille listened to Mack, finding herself nodding along with his statements. She turned to him and said, "I know."

"You know?"

"Yes. I'm Sam Graves' daughter. He has spent his life saying the same things. He's the last person you need to inform about these issues. It's insanity that he's part of this lawsuit."

"I'm sorry. I wish there were something I could do."

"You could. You could drop the suit."

"Something other than dropping the suit. I'm not dropping the suit."

As the boat neared the dock at Weeks Bay Estate, Camille whispered, "Let's talk about this later."

"Of course," Mack agreed.

Unaware of the tension between her mother and Mack, Willa excitedly grabbed both of their hands and dragged them down the dock.

At the end of the dock, there was a utility vehicle, and Mack easily found the hidden key. Willa's squeals of delight almost eased the tension between Camille and Mack. "It's like the biggest golf cart I've ever seen," Willa exclaimed.

"Yes, and I'm sure Mack is going to drive it very responsibly, right?"

"Oh, of course, I'd never go fast or purposefully drive over big bumps."

"Well, that's a shame," Willa said. Camille and Mack laughed.

It was a short drive over to the blueberry fields. Mack pointed Camille and Willa toward the best bushes and handed them two buckets. He said he would join them in a few minutes, as he needed to find the owner to discuss a project.

It was a beautiful farm. You could see the bay in the distance and the old farmhouse and barn that had been turned into an event venue. Everything was surrounded by meticulously maintained grounds.

Willa was in her element, skipping through the rows of blueberry bushes, placing a few in her bucket but more straight into her mouth. After about thirty minutes of moving up and down the rows of blueberries, they had two full buckets.

Willa and Camille walked toward the farmhouse to join Mack and the owner. There was a farm stand set up by the parking lot, and Camille looked over the various bins brimming with brightly colored local produce. Camille found herself filling another basket with beautifully misshapen heirloom tomatoes, field peas, and ears of corn. She paid for her selections, along with the buckets of blueberries, while Willa chased butterflies among the lavender bushes.

Mack introduced Camille to Milly, the owner of Weeks Bay Estate.

"You here on vacation?" Milly asked.

"No, I'm from here. We're visiting my parents, Marion and Sam Graves."

Milly beamed. "Your dad is fantastic. I picked his brain for hours when I was setting up this place. Please tell him I said hi."

"I will. The whole property is stunning, and I love what you're doing with the farm and the events." Camille pointed toward the brochure of private events that she had picked up from the farm stand. "I'm pretty sure we could spend every day here."

Milly quickly replied, "Well, you should think about bringing your daughter to one of our summer camps. If she doesn't mind getting dirty, they're a lot of fun. Fishing, swimming, hikes through the marsh, and some gardening basics." Milly handed Camille a flyer.

"Well, that sounds like Willa's dream day. I'll definitely sign her up." Camille started filling out the paperwork for the next camp.

"Thanks again for all of your help, Milly." Mack lifted the stack of papers in his hands. "I'll confirm with these last vendors, and then we should be ready."

"Sounds good, Mack," Milly replied. "We're all looking forward to it."

Camille handed Milly the form for the camp and followed Mack. He walked back to the utility vehicle quietly. After their interaction on the boat, Camille understood his reluctance to talk.

Unable to contain her curiosity, Camille pointed toward the papers in Mack's hand and asked, "What was that about?" Then she immediately apologized. "Sorry, I'm being nosy. I shouldn't have asked."

Mack seemed grateful that the silence had been broken. "Oh no, its fine. No state secrets down here. Milly and I have been planning a summer festival. Weeks Bay Estate is going to host, and we've signed up lots of local vendors and a few live bands to play music. It should be a fun event. Just hammering out a few details."

"What kind of vendors?" Camille asked as they drove back to the dock.

"A little bit of everything. We're bringing oysters and a shrimp boil. Milly is going to have stands with produce, berries, wildflowers. We have a cheese maker, someone selling local honey, organic soaps and lotions. We're working on the permits for alcohol. There's a local beer brewer and bourbon maker that we have lined up if those come through."

"This sounds fantastic. I can't believe all of these businesses exist down here—this sounds better than the farmers' market at Dupont Circle in DC."

They climbed off the utility vehicle and walked onto Mack's boat. He effortlessly untied from the dock and started the motor, easing the boat back into the bay.

"Well, that's part of the problem," Mack said as he steered the boat upriver. "These businesses need help getting the word out so they can survive and grow."

The boat pulled up to the pier at the end of the nature preserve.

As the sound of the engine waned, Willa said, "My mom makes the best shrimp boil in the whole world. You should hire her."

Camille kissed Willa on the cheek. "Nothing gets past you," she said, marveling at her daughter's ability to take in Mack's passing reference to making a shrimp boil for the festival. "I make the only shrimp boil you've ever tasted. I'm sure Mack makes a good one too, sweetie."

Mack killed the engine and said, "Well, I'm not sure I'd go as far as calling it *good*, but I get the job done. I basically follow the directions on the back of the can of Old Bay. It is all about the shrimp anyway. I don't want to mess them up."

Camille stared. "I mean, I agree. It is all about the shrimp, but you can certainly do more than shake a little Old Bay in the water. Shrimp boils are sacred. You need to respect the craft."

Mack smiled. "A craft, huh? I didn't realize I was dealing with a shrimp boil expert. Sounds like I could use some help.

Maybe I should hire a chef. Know anybody that's interested?"
He cocked his eyebrow.

Camille shook her head. "Not me, for many reasons,
Mack." She raised her eyebrows at him. "Plus I'm not a chef. I
just dabble in the kitchen." She looked down at her watch.
"Okay, Willa, time to head back. We've got to get dinner
started."

Willa hopped off the boat, and Camille followed.

Willa asked, "What are we cooking tonight?"

Mack handed Camille her buckets of blueberries and her
bag of produce. Camille said, "Well, blueberry cobbler, for
sure. I also picked up some fresh corn at the farm stand. I was
thinking we could make a corn soup too."

"That sure sounds good. Like something a chef would
make," Mack said.

Willa whispered into Camille's ear, "Momma, you should
invite Mack for dinner. I can show him our dock and he can
give me fishing tips, and maybe he will hire you for the festival
and then you won't be unemployed."

Like most six-year-olds, Willa's attempt to be secretive
failed miserably and her whisper was closer to a muted scream.
Willa turned to Mack and asked, "Would you like to come to
my house for dinner?"

Mack smiled, replying, "I would love that," but Camille
immediately blurted, "Absolutely not."

"I'm sorry," Camille began again. "I didn't mean it to
come out like that, but you can't come over for dinner."

Willa began to pout and stomped up the boardwalk toward
the visitors' center. Camille shouted, "Wait for me inside,
please."

Willa shot back, "Yes, ma'am," in a tone entirely too sar-
castic for such a small person.

Mack tied up the boat. "You don't have to explain. I get it. It would be awkward, right?"

"What part? The eating dinner with the people you're suing part, or the bringing home a dinner guest without giving Marion Graves twenty-four hours' notice part?"

"Yep, it all sounds pretty bad," Mack replied. "In fact, I reject your charming daughter's invitation. Plus I find the texture of corn soup off-putting."

Camille was unnaturally defensive as she said, "My corn soup is delicious. There is no off-putting texture anywhere near my kitchen."

"Okay, okay. You convinced me, I'll come," Mack said, smirking.

"Mack, you have been surprisingly kind to Willa and me, and under different circumstances, very different circumstances, having you over for dinner might be nice. I'd consider it, at least. But you absolutely cannot come over to my parents' house tonight."

"Please, keep going. It's not every day a woman tells you that spending time together would be 'nice' or 'a thing they would consider.' My ego might sail this boat home."

"That is not a sailboat," Camille flatly replied.

"Are you always this tough?" Mack asked, with a glint in his eyes that felt exciting and dangerous to Camille.

"Yes." Camille sighed. "But I shouldn't be. Especially not to people who give me free oyster samples and show me amazing organic farms. I'm sorry. I've been rude. This situation feels complicated, and I'm working very hard to uncomplicate my life."

"You haven't been rude. You've been interesting. You are very interesting to me, Camille Taylor." Mack waited, his eyes meeting Camille's and holding her gaze until she looked away.

Mack turned on the boat and shouted, "By the way you're blushing, I think I'm interesting to you too. There are lots of shades of gray here. I'm not the bad guy. See you around, Camille," he said as he motored away, back up the river.

Camille stood on the dock for a beat before jogging up the boardwalk in search of her daughter and her sanity.

◆ 19 ◆

WILLA WAS STILL POUTING as they walked into the kitchen. Camille turned to her daughter. "I know you're disappointed, but we'll have friends over for dinner another night."

Willa quickly replied, "I don't want friends to come over. I want Mack to come over."

"You barely know him. Why do you want to invite him to dinner?"

Willa stuck out her chin and replied, "Because I like talking to him. He uses a regular voice. All the other grown-ups here use this squeaky voice. Except you. Plus I like his oysters."

Camille tried to defuse the situation with distraction. "Want to help me cook? I could use some help with these blueberries."

Willa's emotions turned on a dime, occasionally resulting in a tantrum or two, but this time her short-term memory played in Camille's favor and she relented. "Yes, I'll help, as long as we can snack while we cook."

"Of course," Camille said. "Let's get out a snacking dish and a cooking dish." Camille rinsed the blueberries in a colander and poured a handful into a small bowl and put it in front of Willa.

Camille grabbed ingredients to make the cobbler and tasked Willa with mixing the flour and butter. She showed her how to use a fork to cut the butter into the flour, but Willa shortly abandoned the fork for using her fingers. With Willa occupied, Camille set about putting together the rest of the dinner.

She took the Silver Queen corn and shucked it, then scraped the kernels from the cob. She poured most of the corn into a pot with chicken stock and sautéed onions and garlic. The remaining corn she would use to top the soup, along with some fresh crab.

Camille also decided to make a hot chili oil and a chive oil to swirl on the top. Once the corn had simmered, she pureed the contents and added a splash of cream and sherry vinegar. She put the soup in the fridge to cool and turned her attention back to Willa and the cobbler.

"Okay, Willa, let's make some biscuits."

"I thought we were making cobbler."

"Yep, blueberry biscuit cobbler. We're going to mix up these biscuits and put lots of sugar on top. The sugar melts as the biscuits are cooking. The blueberries get thick and syrupy, the biscuits are fluffy and soft, and the sugar turns golden and makes a crispy crust on the top. It's my favorite type of cobbler."

Willa's eyes got big. "It sounds like it's going to be my favorite type of cobbler too!"

They worked together. Camille loved cooking with Willa. That had always surprised Ben, because Camille could be so regimented about so many things. Camille knew he was right but justified her "intense organization" as something her legal job demanded. The kitchen, however, was a sacred calm in Camille's life. It was a place where she felt instantly relaxed, no matter what kind of chaos was swirling around in her life. She loved trying new recipes and testing different ingredients, but mostly she liked experimenting and taking the dreams in her head and putting them on a plate. There was no other part of her life where she had that much freedom. In a job where she felt pressure to be perfect, to never make a mistake, it was freeing knowing that, in the kitchen, any missteps were just exciting discoveries or lessons to take to the next meal. Cooking embraced and celebrated imperfections—the rustic apple tart, the misshapen pizza, the charred steak. When Camille cooked with Willa, she loved sharing the joy of food and embraced the process, oblivious to any little mistakes six-year-old hands might make.

Camille tossed the blueberries with sugar, a bit of cinnamon, lemon zest, and a little corn starch to absorb the liquid. She poured the blueberries into the buttered casserole dish and finished making the biscuits with Willa.

"Okay, sweet pea, this is the best part. We take the biscuit dough and drop it all over the top of these blueberries."

Willa nodded her head. "I can do that. Big drops or little drops?"

Camille pursed her lips. "I don't know. What do you think?"

Willa seriously considered the question before answering, "Let's go with medium drops."

"Sounds good," Camille agreed, squeezing Willa's shoulders.

Willa went to work. When there was dough sufficiently covering the blueberries, she asked, "Who gets to sprinkle the sugar?"

"You, of course," Camille said.

Willa's small hands carefully reached for the white sugar and slowly but very liberally spread it across the top of the biscuits. Camille smiled at her daughter, wondering how the chubby fingers of toddlerhood had so quickly disappeared.

Camille and Willa looked at each other and exchanged a brief high five. Camille said, "All right, into the oven, and then the hardest part."

"I know. Then we wait. I'm a horrible waiter. I have no patience," Willa said on a sigh.

Marion walked into the kitchen, enjoying the interaction between her daughter and granddaughter. She said, "You are just like your momma. She's never had any patience either." Marion gave Camille a quick peck on the cheek before walking over to the sink and commenting, "Smells delicious in here. You two are a good team."

"The Three Musketeers!" Willa exclaimed, then paused, catching herself. They weren't the Three Musketeers anymore, but the phrase Ben, Camille, and Willa had used so many times to describe their adventures, big and small, seemed impossible to erase from their language.

Camille's breath caught momentarily. She saw the sorrow in her daughter's eyes. There were no mistakes in the kitchen and no mistakes in grief. She didn't want Willa to feel bad for forgetting that her father was gone. His memory would always be wrapped around their shoulders.

Willa looked to her mother and asked, "What are we now?"

Marion quickly interjected, "What about the Terrific Twosome!"

Camille smiled, appreciative of her mother's efforts, but she realized this wasn't as simple as coming up with a new name.

She looked to Willa, whose face was slumped on crossed arms. "Not exactly the same, huh?"

"Nope," Willa quickly replied.

Camille laid her head next to Willa's. "I still feel Daddy with us. As long as you feel him and think about him, we can always be the Three Musketeers. We'll take Daddy with us on our adventures because he's in here." Camille put her hand over Willa's heart. Willa sat up and smiled. Camille continued, "Do you think he would like this cobbler? What do you think he would guess were the ingredients?"

Camille raised her eyebrows, knowing Willa couldn't resist the question. Ben had loved food, especially Camille's food, but he had a disturbingly inaccurate palate. Over the years, they would have a family competition to see who could guess the list of ingredients. Ben always lost, and his predictions were often so far off that they would all end up in fits of laughter.

Willa giggled as she said, "He would think there are grapes in the cobbler and potatoes in the biscuits."

"I think you are exactly right," Camille said.

Marion started wiping the counters and rinsing the dishes from the cobbler preparations. Camille sat next to her daughter and said, "You know, Willa. I was thinking we should come up with a list of adventures we want to have this summer. I've decided to extend my break from work. What do you think about spending the summer in Alabama?"

"We'd stay here? With Nana and Gramps? All summer?" Willa's voice escalated with each question.

"Yes. That is, if Nana is okay with it?" Camille looked at her mother.

Marion was twisting the kitchen towel in her hands. Her voice shook as she said, "I think that would be wonderful. I think that would be so wonderful for us all."

Camille quickly interjected, "Just the summer. This is not some permanent move, before you start scheming. I think I can help Dad with the situation with Trident."

Marion smiled slightly. "I wouldn't dream of scheming."

Camille turned toward Willa. "I'm going to help Gramps with a project, Willa, but I will have plenty of time to spend with you too. Lots of time for adventures, just the two of us."

"What kind of adventures?" Willa asked.

"Well, we have to come up with the plan together. We can make a list. Any ideas?"

Willa opened her mouth immediately, and Camille quickly added, "No international travel or life-threatening activities."

Willa closed her mouth and said, "Well, I'm going to need to do some thinking, then." A moment later, Willa sat up and declared, "I did my thinking."

"That was quick."

"I'm a good thinker."

"Okay, what do you want to put on the list, Willa-bean?"

"I want to go to all the places you went to when you were a kid, and I want to eat all the food you ate when you were a kid. You keep on giving me these foods that were your favorites, and I've never even heard of them. And you're taking me to your happy places, and I didn't even know about them. You never tell me anything, and I want to know everything."

The weight of Willa's statement sank into Camille. She purposefully avoided eye contact with Marion. There was nothing worse than being proven wrong in front of your mother. Camille scooped her daughter up and enveloped her in a giant hug. "I want you to know everything too. Let's fix this together."

Willa's curls brushed against Camille's cheek as they clung together. Camille looked up and met Marion's gaze. Marion joined the duo, grasping Camille's hand as she said, "I think you need to show your daughter all about where you came from. I think you need to see it too."

Camille took in a deep breath and said, "Okay, travel agent, pull out the family photo albums and let's start making our plans. It looks like we're doing a tour of South Alabama this summer."

IN THE DAYS THAT followed, Camille and Willa fell into a comfortable rhythm. They spent their mornings eating breakfast on the dock, their official planning zone to map the day's adventures. Willa would find a picture from the family album, and they would discuss the logistics. They took a day trip to Bellingrath Gardens in Mobile, and Sam tagged along. He was like a kid in a candy store, noting all the different varieties of crepe myrtle and zinnia and hibiscus. By the end of the morning, there was a group following them, asking Sam when he was going to start his next tour.

They hiked the path that connected Fairhope to the Grand Hotel, observing all the beautiful old homes that dotted the bay. Camille fell more and more in love with her daughter on every adventure. They were their own version of Thelma and Louise, except there was no crime spree and this Louise required multiple stops for snacks and bathroom breaks.

After Camille and Willa's morning adventures, Willa spent the afternoons with Marion at the playground or exploring the bay while Camille worked on the lawsuit.

After spending a few hours working, Camille and Willa would reunite and head straight to the kitchen. Willa would relay that day's playground antics while Camille prepared dinner. She was having more fun in the kitchen than she could remember, combing through the family cookbooks and putting her own spin on classic southern recipes. Willa loved to help and was full of questions about why okra had the same slimy feel as frogs and whether there was butter in butter beans.

Camille was spending real time with Willa. Sometimes being a parent was a box-checking exercise: *make sure child is fed, make sure child is bathed, make sure child is read to and put to bed*, repeat. For too long after Ben's death, and probably for too long before his death, Camille had been doing more box checking than truly connecting with Willa. She had been too exhausted to do more. It was an entirely different experience to parent out of joy and connection and awe at the shaping of a person you had made.

She went to bed with a sense of contentment that had seemed illusive for so long, and slowly she started to sleep. For hours at a time, she would sleep.

Camille eased into the routine for a week before making an appointment with Griffin. As Camille waited in Griffin's lobby on a Wednesday afternoon, Camille marveled at Ms. Cowles's efficiency. In the twenty minutes Camille waited, his phone never stopped ringing, and two other people tried to get in to have a "quick chat with Griff," but Ms. Cowles promptly dismissed them. When Griffin finally popped out of his office and apologized for keeping Camille waiting, she immediately said, "No, I'm sorry. I don't need much of your time. But I do have a favor to ask."

"Favor, huh?" Ms. Cowles scoffed.

Griffin ushered Camille back to his office. His desk was covered in papers, so he sat on the edge and said, "Good to see you, Camille. Now, what can I do for you?"

Camille looked over her shoulder. "She *is* your secret weapon. You weren't wrong about that. Imagine how efficient the world could be if Ms. Cowles were running it."

Griffin chuckled. "Please don't tell her that. I have a hard enough time reining in her authoritarian regime known as office management."

"I have a tremendous amount of respect for a woman I barely know."

"Me too," Griffin said, looking right at Camille. She quickly glanced down. Griffin was in a suit, but at some point in the morning he must have discarded the jacket and rolled up the sleeves of his button-down. Camille found herself staring at his forearms, unable to remember why she was in his office. Griffin cleared his throat. "Okay, so about that favor. I'm sorry, but I really do only have a few minutes today."

"Yes, right. Sorry. See, the thing is, I have a couple of ideas about my father's lawsuit, but I'm not set up to work at home. I need to do some case law research, and I'd like to spend some time reviewing the partnership agreements and the filings you've already made in the case. I know it's a lot to ask, but is there any way I could use some space in your office? I can come in early in the morning; you won't even know I've been here."

"Of course. Come in whenever it's convenient. I've got a spare office—we use it as a war room to prepare for trial, but it should have everything you need. I'll get Ms. Cowles to set up the case files for you and smooth over the logistics."

"Thank you, Griffin. I appreciate it."

"It'll be nice to see you around the office."

"You'll barely notice me. I'll stay out of the way."

"There is no way you could go unnoticed, Camille." He gave her a quick grin, slapped his knee, and walked toward the door. Their arms brushed as Camille walked out of his office, and Camille swallowed hard, thinking her new working arrangement was certainly going to be interesting.

Law offices could be intense places, and Camille expected a frenetic pace, conference calls arguing with opposing counsel, the urgency of crisis permeating the air. That's what Camille was used to. When Camille had first started practicing law, it was exciting, but over the last few years, the excitement had waned and been replaced by a pervasive sense of anxiety. She had been doing too much, at home, at work, and the constant sense that she was forgetting something, or didn't have time for something, made her worry all the time. But good lawyers couldn't worry all the time; it was an occupational hazard.

Over the next week, Camille spent her afternoons at Griffin's office, and she was surprised to find it different from anything she had ever experienced. She enjoyed hearing the friendly banter between Griffin and Ms. Cowles. Griffin seemed to juggle his busy schedule with ease. Being such a likable person helped. Camille heard calls that she knew should have been contentious, where he discussed extensions and scheduling motions, but Griffin had such a steady, reasonable nature. It was nice to be in his office. It was relaxing. Camille was practicing the parts of the law that she loved—using her brain, thinking creatively, and weighing strategies.

After a few weeks of work, Camille had a plan to help her father. She was wrapping up her research on Friday afternoon when she heard a familiar voice in the lobby of Griffin's office. Sam was chatting with Ms. Cowles when Camille popped her head out of the office.

"Dad, what are you doing here?"

"Well, I have an appointment with my legal team, so I thought I should show up."

Ms. Cowles looked over the edge of her glasses. "Your father is a very considerate person. He makes appointments and is very prompt."

Sam beamed. "Well, thank you, Ms. Cowles, I certainly try."

Ms. Cowles went back to her computer, and Sam walked over to Camille. He said, "I wanted to see what you've been up to."

"I'm almost ready to talk to you and Griffin about what I found. I need about an hour to pull everything together."

Sam put his arm around his daughter's shoulders. "You never did want to do anything without dotting all those *i*'s. Okay, let me chat with Griffin. Ms. Cowles, is it okay if I pop back to the big man's office?"

"Yes, sir, it is, and I appreciate you consulting with me first. You know, there are some people in your family who just walk in for a chat and interrupt his schedule. It's amazing he's able to get anything done."

Sam gave Camille a sideways look and whispered to his daughter, "You do not want to get on her bad side."

Camille shrugged. "Too late."

Camille went back to her office as Sam walked down the hallway. A few minutes later, he stopped by Camille's office and waved. "I'll see you back at the house. Griffin's going to come over for dinner tonight, and we can discuss the case then."

Camille looked up quickly. "What do you mean, he's coming over for dinner?"

Sam paused briefly. "You said you needed more time. The boy needs to eat. Seemed like the best solution. See you back at the house." Sam strolled out of the office.

A few hours later, Camille had gathered her work and made a quick stop at the grocery store for supplies on her way home. She found Marion and Willa on the dock and Sam deadheading the climbing roses that wound around the pergola columns.

"I'm home, with food and case files," Camille announced.

Willa ran up to her mother and wrapped her arms tightly around Camille's waist. Camille had only been gone for the afternoon, but the greeting was as enthusiastic as if she'd disappeared for a week. Sometimes Camille felt undeserving of such unconditional love. Other times, when Willa was covered with mud and full of spunk, she felt exactly that deserving. She brushed the hair out of Willa's eyes and asked, "Have a good time with Nana?"

"Oh yes. We met up with our group at the playground, and I organized a coup!"

Camille raised her eyebrows. "And what exactly does that mean?"

"I asked the same thing. Nana told me all about coups. It's when the little guys take over the big guys. All the mommas on the playground were very upset with me because I taught all of their kids how to paint with dirt."

By now, Marion had walked over. "All these precious children, smacking their muddy hands on the fences like they were cave dwellers. There was a pit of mud and they started making handprints on each other's backs. There is not enough stain stick in the county to clean up the mess your daughter made."

Willa sighed. "It was so fun."

Camille tried to suppress her laughter. "Well, it sounds like quite the adventure."

"Oh yes," Willa replied. "But next time I'm going to ask permission, right, Nana?" Marion nodded her head. Willa turned to Camille and whispered, "Otherwise I will be banned from playgroup."

Camille looked over to Marion, who took a long sip of her wine.

"Okay, looks like Nana has already given you a bath. How about you come into the kitchen with me to get ready for dinner. Did Gramps tell you we have a guest tonight?"

"Yes, he said another lawyer was coming over," Willa said with a sigh.

"What's wrong with that?"

"It's just . . . lawyers are so boring, Mom. Can't we have someone more interesting over for dinner?"

"You know, I'm a lawyer too. Are you saying I'm boring?"

"You are the exception," Willa said. "Why can't Mack come to dinner? You said we could have him over another night."

Sam stopped his pruning and walked over to his daughter. "What is she talking about? How does she know Mack?"

"I mentioned that we met him when we picked up shrimp at Billy's Seafood," Camille nervously replied.

Willa didn't grasp the mounting tension and continued on. "We also saw him at the estuary, and he took us to a blueberry farm. I got to ride on his boat, and he took us on a ride in a giant golf cart, but he didn't drive fast because Momma told him not to, but he did drive over one big bump and it made my stomach do a flip-flop."

Marion and Sam gaped. Their faces were covered with confusion, and Camille wished she could rewind the last two minutes. She knew it looked bad, like she had been hiding something from her parents. She hadn't intentionally omitted her run-in with Mack, but she hadn't volunteered the information.

She took a deep breath and started to explain. "We bumped into him, and he remembered Willa from the seafood shop."

Camille shrugged. "That's life in a small town, I guess. You can't escape anyone." She hoped the conversation would end there, but Willa interrupted.

"He is so great. He's a real fisherman. Like, for his job. That's what he does. And he's teaching me all kinds of things about different fish and how girl fishermen are just like boy fishermen. They wear the same clothes and everything. My doll can't wear a dress when she fishes. She needs waders, Nana."

Marion was the first to break the tension. "Why don't we go get that doll, sweetie. We'll let your momma and Gramps have a little talk before Mr. Griffin comes over for dinner." Marion gave Camille a look that could have burned a hole through the tablecloth that had been so carefully laid out.

Sam's face was tight. He was an even-tempered man, and Camille could remember only a handful of times she had seen him upset, mostly during her teenage years when her curfew was entirely too restrictive for her desires for independence. Looking at her father's face right now, Camille felt like she was sixteen again, about to have her car keys taken away.

"Dad, we just bumped into him, that's it."

"Oh, please. That's not it and you know it. Your face, Willa's face—you two are the easiest cards to read. Your girl's more excited about Mack than a mud pie."

"Willa gets excited about a new brand of cereal. That doesn't mean anything." Camille hesitated, then continued, "But Dad, you may have the wrong idea about him. He's not like you think."

"Oh, he's not? He's not the reason my entire business is at stake? He's not the reason my reputation in this community has been questioned because of his lawsuit? I know exactly what he's like, and I know what he's done to me and your mother. What are you thinking, Camille?"

"I think if you talked to him, this could get worked out."

"He could have talked to me. Don't you think I was bending over backwards trying to get plans in place to remedy the damage? He didn't have to sue anybody. We could have fixed this, but the minute he filed a lawsuit, everything changed. I knew that boy's father. Billy would be appalled at what his son has done."

"Dad, I think there's more to it. Some things you don't understand. Let's wait for Griffin and then talk through all of this."

Sam shook his head and stormed off, back to his roses.

Camille didn't follow him. Sam needed to cool off, and she hoped Griffin could help defuse the situation. She went into the kitchen and laid out her files on the table. Then she turned to dinner preparation, welcoming the distraction of cooking.

Camille had always been efficient in the kitchen, and in a few minutes she'd pulled together a platter of appetizers. When she heard Griffin's car pull into the driveway, the familiar rumble over the crushed shells, she exhaled with relief. She was hopeful that after she laid everything out, they could make a plan to fix this situation.

Griffin walked in the front door and gave a casual, "Hello."

"Back in the kitchen," Camille called.

"Am I too early for dinner?"

Camille walked out of the kitchen. "No, you're right on time. I thought we could chat before we eat, if that's okay with you? I've got some appetizers set out that we can nibble on while we work."

"Fine by me. This looks amazing." Griffin stared directly at Camille, and she wasn't sure if he was talking about her or the food.

Camille's tumble of wild curls was piled into a bun on top of her head, but rogue strands escaped, framing her face. Her black jeans and simple white tank top were covered in a beige linen apron tied snugly around her waist. She set out a platter of crostini with country ham, avocado, and fresh mint. Handing Griffin a cocktail plate, she said, "Let me go grab Dad."

Griffin sat on a kitchen stool, his eyes focused on Camille instead of the food as he said, "I'll wait here."

Moments later, Camille walked back into the kitchen, Sam and Marion following. Marion walked over graciously and gave Griffin a hug. "Good to see you."

"You too, Marion. Thank you for having me over for dinner."

"Well, I know you all have some business to discuss, but the real reason you came is for my home-cooked meals. Unfortunately, Camille is taking over the kitchen tonight, so I'll have to fix that Ritz cracker chicken casserole you like so much another night."

Griffin looked at Camille, and they shared a knowing smile. Griffin replied to Marion, "Sounds great. I'll take a rain check."

Camille looked at Marion. "Mom, do you think you can keep Willa occupied outside for a bit? I don't want her worrying about anything else, and that girl has ears like bats."

"Not wanting your daughter to worry—well, that sounds an awful lot like something another mother was criticized for a few weeks ago."

"She's six. I'm thirtyish. There's a difference."

"I know how old you are. I was there for both of those days. Of course I will take her outside, but I'm going to need another glass of sauvignon blanc first. That girl's will is stronger than steel."

Camille pulled a bottle of wine out of the fridge and poured a glass. She handed it to her mother, then put her hands on either side of her mother's face and said, "Stay strong and say no to predinner swims." Marion closed her eyes briefly, as if to prepare herself for the task ahead, and then made her way out to the porch to find Willa.

Camille turned to her father and Griffin. "Anyone else want a glass?"

"I'm gonna grab a beer," Sam replied.

Griffin quickly replied, "Make that two, Sam."

Camille poured herself a glass of wine and said, "Okay, now that we have our cocktails, let's discuss strategy." She sat at the kitchen table and pulled out her notes. "Here's my idea. The only way Dad is involved in this lawsuit is because of the partnership agreement with Trident. Right, Griffin?"

"Yes, that's right."

"Okay, Griffin, I'm sure you've explained this to Dad before, but I want to make sure he understands the joinder issue."

Griffin pulled a notepad out of his briefcase. "Okay, let's go over it again. Sam, you weren't an original defendant. In fact, the plaintiffs didn't sue you directly. Trident made you a party to the lawsuit because it involved the conduct of your partnership. If the plaintiffs wanted the lawsuit against Trident to continue, they had to sue you as well."

Camille waited a beat and then interjected, "Dad, I want to make sure you understand that. Mack didn't sue you, and he never made claims against you. He can't choose to only sue Trident—either he sues you both or he has to drop the lawsuit altogether."

Sam took a long swig of beer. "So this all falls back on Trident. And my stupid decision to enter into a partnership agreement with them."

"Yes," Camille said. Then she waited a few minutes, because it didn't seem like any of them wanted to talk.

Camille continued. "If the partnership was void at the time of the conduct at issue—the clearing of the land—then Trident wouldn't have grounds to join Dad in the lawsuit."

"The court already ruled on the joinder—we didn't have any arguments that the partnership was void."

"I think you do."

Griffin's eyes narrowed as he turned toward Camille. He bit on his lip nervously and said, "Okay, go on."

Camille took a deep breath and began explaining her idea— the weeks of work that she hoped would give them the solution they needed. "If there was a material breach of the partnership agreement, the partnership would be void and the joinder would be improper. Mack and the other Fish River property owners could continue their lawsuit with Trident and Dad would be out of it. I've spent the week researching case law in Alabama on improper joinder and what constitutes a material breach of an agreement. I think we have a strong argument."

"But how do we prove that the partnership is void? On what grounds?" Griffin asked, somewhat dismissively.

"Dad, tell Griffin about the tree tagging."

Sam had a puzzled look on his face. "*Tree tagging* are the only words I understood. You guys want to translate all of that legal stuff?"

Griffin interjected, "I think what Camille is getting at is if Trident did something they weren't allowed to do under your agreement, then we could go to the court and say there was no valid partnership, so there would be no reason to add you to the lawsuit."

"Exactly," Camille said as she took a bite of the crostini. "Dad, tell Griffin about the trees."

Sam explained the tagging process, how his crew had designated the trees that should be cleared and those that should be preserved. He explained the way they'd tagged the trees with different colors depending on their location and whether they could be removed. He also described the detailed plans that were provided to the Trident crew.

"Did you find copies, Dad?"

Sam nodded. He turned to Griffin. "We don't do any of this stuff over email. These crews move from site to site. I did what I always do. I made sure every single tree on the site was tagged and then I gave them a written plan, diagraming the key areas of preservation." Sam turned to Camille. "You were right; your mom made a copy. That woman makes copies of everything. I have it in the office."

Camille pulled out a copy of the partnership agreement and showed Griffin the key provisions. The agreement gave Sam the authority to make all decisions relating to the landscape design. Any changes had to be approved in writing.

Camille gave Griffin a memorandum she had drafted summarizing the key cases in Alabama that established a partnership agreement breach. She described her research and the argument she thought they could make before the court. As Camille spoke, a spark returned to her eyes that had long been missing anytime she was discussing work.

"So what do you think, Griffin? With the tree tagging and the plans Dad drafted, I think we could argue those were clear instructions that Trident intentionally failed to follow. Right?"

Griffin read through Camille's memo and flipped through the cases. "This is good. I think you're right, except, Sam, didn't you say Trident had the flexibility to take down more trees if needed?"

"Well, yes, sometimes when you get the machines in there to clear, things happen. That's why we have our tagging system. We color-code the trees so that they know what definitely has to stay, and what can go if they can't get around it."

"And who gets to make those calls?" Griffin asked.

"Well, me, usually," Sam said.

Camille looked away, but Sam reached for her hand, squeezing it reassuringly.

Griffin continued, "But you weren't there the day of the clearing, right?"

"No, I was with Camille, but my foreman was there. All that time we had spent, planning so carefully for every homesite so that it would have this tree house feel. They were only supposed to clear for the homesites, and the rest was supposed to remain wooded."

Camille looked to Griffin. "So, what's next? What do we do?"

"We need to talk to your foreman, get an affidavit from him confirming the tagging and what happened the day of the clearing. It will be important to establish that he didn't make any special authorizations."

Sam nodded. "Okay. I'll set up a meeting next week."

Camille looked to her dad. "I also think you should talk to Mack. With Griffin. I'm not suggesting that you start negotiations without your lawyer, but I also think there is a chance the two of you could work this out."

"I'll think about it," Sam said, sighing. "But I got to tell you, Camille, I'm just mad. I can't believe that boy would file this lawsuit without talking to me. Everyone downriver knows me or knows my reputation. I'd never do something to hurt them. The fact that Mack would run to a courthouse before talking something over—that's not the way we do things down here."

"That's why I think you should talk," Camille said. "I think you would both surprise each other."

Griffin broke the tension. "Let's talk to your foreman first, and then figure out what's next."

"I'm going to tell Marion about this," Sam said, standing. "We can all use a dose of hope whenever we can get it. Think you two can handle the dinner prep?"

"Yes, dinner is under control. Go join Mom and Willa."

Sam walked out the back door and down to the dock.

Griffin continued reading over the papers and then looked up. "Okay, put me to work. What can I do?"

"You can relax. Or read the cases I pulled. I can handle the cooking."

"I don't mind. I like feeling useful. I'm an excellent chopper."

"How are your stirring skills?"

Griffin rolled up the cuffs of his shirt. "See this forearm? It is primed for stirring."

Camille looked down. She had seen the forearm. She wasn't sure why she kept looking at it, but she found herself feeling warm, and she hadn't even turned on the stove. She quickly handed Griffin a spoon and said, "Okay, you oversee the cheese grits. Think you can handle that?"

"That seems doable."

Camille had a pot of water mixed with chicken stock on the stove coming up to a simmer. She poured in the stone-ground corn grits and turned to Griffin. "Stir. Don't let them burn, and make sure to turn that heat down to low once they start bubbling."

Griffin gave her a little salute. Camille pulled out a giant cast-iron skillet and turned the stove eye to high. "What are we having with the grits?" Griffin asked.

"Steaks, some sautéed spinach. Dad sprung this dinner on me; otherwise I would have planned something more. I figure the bar is pretty low if you're used to the Ritz cracker casserole."

"Steak dinner sounds pretty perfect to me."

"Good."

They stood next to each other at the stove, moving back and forth with the dinner preparations and making easy conversation about mundane topics like Griffin's golf game and the weather for the weekend. It felt easy, being in a room with Griffin, standing next to him and cooking dinner for her family.

After searing the steaks, Camille popped them in the oven to finish. She started grating a mixture of cheddar and Parmesan for the grits and leaned over the pot. "They're looking good. Arm tired yet?"

"I'll survive," Griffin said. Their bodies were so close, the heat from the stove rising in a cloud between them. Griffin smiled as Camille walked back to the fridge to pull out the spinach. "The breach argument was a good idea, Camille. You're a good lawyer. Ever think about setting up shop down here? Or would you miss the big DC office?"

"I've never thought about practicing here. Not once. I was out of here as soon as I graduated high school. I never fit in."

"You look like you fit to me," he said, enjoying the opportunity to give Camille a thorough look.

Camille raised her eyebrows. "I was the angsty teen telling everyone she was off to greener pastures. Being back for the summer, I'm not sure how I feel about it."

"The hometown girl having an identity crisis?"

Camille shrugged. "I'm living with my parents, supposedly on leave from my firm, but who knows what my practice will be like when I go back. Let's just say none of this was part of my life plan." Camille shook her head, refusing to let herself dwell too long on all the ways her life was upside down. "What about you? A law practice in Fairhope must be different from Atlanta."

"It is. It took a bit of getting used to, but I like people. I like representing people, and I didn't get to do much of that at my old firm. I also like setting my own hours, being my own boss."

"You are not the boss. Ms. Cowles is the boss."

"That is an accurate statement. I can't believe you never thought about coming back to Fairhope to practice law."

"I guess the law was my escape from here. I left for school and didn't think I would ever come back."

"And now that you are back, at least temporarily? The small-town law practice isn't the least bit tempting?"

Camille rolled her eyes. "No."

"I sense some judgment. I guess I should expect that from a DC lawyer."

"Oh, please. Not too long ago, you were an Atlanta lawyer."

"Yes, but I saw the error of my ways."

"Don't you get bored? Representing a local landscaping company when you used to work for the Fortune 500?"

"No. I don't. Mostly because I like the local landscaping company and most of the Fortune 500 were assholes. Practicing law in a town like this is a good life. But please, don't do it. I don't want the competition. You'd end up stealing all my clients."

Camille laughed and then eyed him suspiciously. "Did my mother put you up to this? This reeks of Marion Graves and her master plan to get me back to Alabama."

Griffin smirked. "Your mother sent me your résumé the week you came back. I think she was hoping I would hire you. I told her you were overqualified."

"That is mortifying. That woman has no boundaries." Camille shook her head but couldn't keep herself from smiling. "It has been fun working in your office. It's so different than my firm in DC. In a good way."

"I like having you in my office. Although I'm not as productive as usual. It's very distracting when I walk by your office, especially when you're scribbling in those notebooks with your hair piled up like that."

Griffin reached out, tucking one of Camille's curls behind her ear. She stared into his eyes, then reached for the wooden spoon, saying, "You need to keep stirring, or you're going to ruin my cheese grits." They stood there together, their bodies inches apart, Camille clinging to the spoon. He reached up to grab it and then set it back on the counter, taking one hand and wrapping it around Camille's waist and reaching the other hand up to her cheek. Camille leaned into him for a moment, feeling the warmth of an unfamiliar body pressed against hers. His hand felt strong as he wound his fingers into her hair. She knew she should step back. She knew she should open her eyes, but she didn't. For a moment, she wanted to melt into Griffin's body and forget about everything and everyone else.

Then Willa walked into the kitchen, Marion and Sam trailing closely behind. The screen door slammed, and Camille and Griffin jumped apart.

Nervous laughter filled the room and Camille quickly said, "Okay, we're almost ready to eat. Everybody wash up."

Willa looked at Griffin, then looked at her mother, and then walked away. For Camille, that was more unsettling than any question Willa could have asked.

Camille quickly finished the dinner preparations as Marion poured water and Sam opened a bottle of Cabernet.

Camille finished the grits, folding in the grated Parmesan and cheddar, but her hands were shaking. It wasn't like her to be so thoughtless. She wasn't even sure what had happened with Griffin, or almost happened. She focused on the food, avoiding eye contact with her family members, whose gazes were currently burning holes in her back. She placed pats of herb butter on top of the steaks and quickly sautéed some spinach in the iron skillet she had used to sear the steaks. She finished the spinach with some lemon zest and brought all the food to the table.

They sat down to eat. Sam and Marion's enthusiastic chatter with Griffin compensated for the silence steaming in from the other half of the table. Camille and Willa were quiet, pushing their food around their plates. Griffin kept trying to catch Camille's eye, but she avoided his face. A few bites in, Griffin said, "Camille, this is delicious."

"Oh, thanks," she replied dismissively.

"Our Camille has always had a talent in the kitchen," Marion proudly added.

Willa, who had been uncharacteristically quiet, eyed Griffin carefully. She put her fork down, carefully folded her hands, and said, "I'd like to be introduced to this lawyer friend of my mother's."

Sam raised his eyebrows, and Marion exchanged glances with Camille. Camille quickly turned to Willa. "I'm sorry, sweetie. This is Griffin Wood. Mr. Wood is helping Gramps with some of his business."

"It's nice to meet you, Willa. Your grandparents have told me so much about you," Griffin said, with a gentle smile.

"My mom used to be a lawyer," Willa replied tersely.

"Willa, I'm still a lawyer. I'm just taking a little break from work for now."

Willa turned back to her mother. "You don't have to go back to being a lawyer. You could work for Mack. He said he would hire you."

Sam's fork dropped, and silence overtook the room. "What's she talking about now, Camille?"

Camille reached for her glass of red wine and took a long sip.

Marion looked at Willa. "What are you talking about, sweetheart?"

"I got Momma a job. Mack's going to hire her to cook a shrimp boil for his festival. You're doing it, right?" Willa asked as the entire family turned and stared at Camille.

Camille continued staring into her wineglass.

"Momma, you don't have to keep being a lawyer. You love cooking, and you could be a professional chef now." Willa's naïve enthusiasm was oblivious to the larger issues circling in everyone's mind.

"Camille, are you working with Mack?" Sam asked.

Camille rubbed at her temples, hoping to smooth the tension away. "No, I'm not. He's planning a summer festival, and he asked if I would help him with the shrimp boil. I told him no. Obviously."

"Another thing that slipped your mind, I guess." Sam started cutting his steak with force, pushing the meat back and forth across his plate. He took a bite, swallowed hard, and continued, "Were you planning on letting me know, or were you going to set up some partnership with this guy? Seems bad judgment in partners runs in this family."

"Dad, there's nothing to tell. This is being blown out of proportion."

"That's not true, Mom," Willa couldn't help interjecting. "You can start with cooking for the festival, but then Mack might hire you for more things."

Camille sighed deeply, then turned to Willa. "Sweetie, I love to cook, and I love to cook with you, but it's what I do for fun. My job is being a lawyer."

Willa huffed and muttered that she was leaving to go play upstairs.

Marion looked across at Camille and stood. "I'll go upstairs with her. You three work this out." Marion left, looking back over her shoulder at her daughter.

"What do you think, Griffin?" Sam asked, pointing his fork at Camille.

Griffin hesitated, then said, "In these types of multiparty litigations, you have to be very careful about all your interactions. Any communication, with Trident or with Mack Phillips, should be in writing. I certainly wouldn't recommend you consider employment with Mr. Phillips."

Camille sighed. "Willa's exaggerating. There is no employment. We just had a brief conversation."

"That's not the whole story and you know it, Camille," Sam said tersely. He looked to Griffin. "Camille's been seeing him—doing things with him."

Griffin raised his eyebrows, but Camille immediately interjected. "Dad, that's enough. Willa and I ran into Mack once. I went to buy shrimp at Billy's once. Before I even knew about the lawsuit. The lawsuit you hid from me for months."

Griffin shifted in his seat. Sam pushed his dinner aside. Camille stared at the ceiling. Uncomfortable silence filled the room.

Finally, Griffin turned to Camille. "I'm not going to tell you what to do. You know the issues as well as I do. Having any type of relationship at this stage of the lawsuit creates unnecessary complications."

"It also pisses off her father," Sam added.

"Yes, you made that perfectly clear, Dad."

Griffin stood. "I'm going to head out. Dinner was delicious. We can chat at the beginning of next week about meeting with your foreman."

"Thanks for coming over, Griffin." Sam shook his hand. "I'm going to get some fresh air out back. Camille can walk you out."

Camille watched her father walk out onto the back lawn and then turned to Griffin. "I'm sorry about all of this."

Griffin waved his hand. "Nothing to apologize for. I have a family. There's no love without passion. Most of our family dinners end with screams—laughter or anger, hard to tell them apart sometimes."

Griffin grabbed his bag and papers and followed Camille to the front door. She reached for the door handle and then turned back to Griffin. "About earlier." She paused, not quite sure what to say next.

"I like having my arms around you, Camille. It's as simple as that for me. I know there's more for you to think about."

"Griffin, this is all so much."

"I know. I never did like half-assing anything. See you in the office next week?"

"Yes."

He reached his hand to her cheek and moved closer. "I can wait. It might kill me, but I can wait." Griffin walked out to his car, a silver BMW, and drove off, windows down.

★　★　★

After Griffin was gone and Sam had joined Willa upstairs, Marion and Camille were left to clean up.

Marion forcefully washed the dishes, letting the pans loudly hit the bottom of the sink.

"Something you want to say to me, Momma?"

"No," Marion said, spitting the reply.

"Well, your dishwashing technique certainly suggests that you have something on your mind."

"Maybe I do, but I'm going to bite my tongue." Marion looked to Camille. "There isn't anything I could say to you right now that you aren't thinking yourself."

"I know."

"Willa is resilient, but the last thing that child needs right now is a revolving door of confusing men."

"Mother, there is no revolving door."

"Mack Phillips has caused your father an unbelievable amount of pain. To think that you have been going around behind our backs and seeing that man. I have no words, Camille. I raised you better than that. He has no morals, to file this lawsuit against us. He has made a lot of enemies in this town. You should hear what people say about him."

"I'm not interested in hearing the town gossip about Mack. He has been nothing but nice to Willa and me. But you're right. I know the lawsuit has hurt Dad, and I don't want to add to that pain."

Marion softened, smirking at her daughter. "Now, Griffin. Nothing but good gossip about him. He did look very nice tonight, standing at the stove helping you with dinner."

Camille rolled her eyes. "I'm going to tuck Willa into bed."

"See you in the morning," Marion said, humming to herself.

◆ 21 ◆

SATURDAY MORNING, CAMILLE MAPPED out plans for a day away from the house. Her father needed space. Willa had been studying the family photo albums. After Willa found a picture of Camille milking a goat, Willa insisted on visiting the goat cheese farm. Camille figured a day trip to the farm was the perfect way to escape the tension at home. Camille was also curious to see how the local goat farm had grown from a small oddity of her youth to a nationally renowned purveyor.

When Camille visited the farm in the 1990s, goat cheese was an ingredient used by fancy New York restaurants, not something you would find in a grocery store in Alabama or on anyone's table at Sunday supper. When a husband and wife announced they were going to turn an old pecan farm into a goat-milking operation, there were rumblings and smirks across town. Camille's father, however, was fascinated. He loved visiting the Elberta Goat Farm, and Camille had been eager to tag along. The couple had stumbled into a booming business, and they were eager to share their love of cheese making. It was one of the businesses Camille checked up on occasionally, scanning restaurant menus in DC looking for their product and asking for updates from her parents.

On the drive to the farm, Willa was bubbling with excitement, peppering Camille with questions about how goats were milked and how long it took to make cheese. Camille was grateful that she had signed up for a tour in advance, hoping that many of the questions would be answered by the experts. By the time they pulled into the gravel lot of the farm, their stomachs were growling in anticipation.

Camille hardly recognized the Elberta Goat Farm. It used to be a simple hunting cabin that had been converted into a farm shop, with goats milling around the parking lot. But this place was a professional operation now, with a full manufacturing facility in the back and hundreds of goats in multiple fields. The only thing that was the same was the hunting cabin, but of course it had been expanded and renovated, with a two-story addition and multiple tasting rooms out the back. There was a sign for a bed-and-breakfast on the property. Taking it all in, Camille was both excited and reluctant. In all respects, the change and expansion of the farm had been positive for the business and community, and yet it was hard to move beyond the memory of the past—a simple farm, a couple with a dream, and a few good cheeses.

Willa pulled Camille inside, eager to explore. The tour was exactly what Camille had hoped for. They learned so much about how the business had grown and all the scientific intricacies of making cheese. Willa was a nonstop stream of questions, and the patient tour guide was unflappable, even when Willa asked if the goats' milk turned pink if the goats were fed beets.

After the tour, they made their way into the farm store for a tasting of the cheeses. Willa's favorite was the Blue Beard, the cave-aged goat cheese with blue veining. Camille preferred the Good Goat, a hard-rind cheese made in the style of a Gouda.

As they finished the tasting, Camille crouched next to Willa and whispered, "We will have to make this a regular trip for the Three Musketeers. Which cheese do you think would have been Daddy's favorite?"

Willa thought for a second and then said, "He would have liked the honey one, because it's sweet just like me, right, Momma?"

"I think you are exactly right."

Camille and Willa held hands as they paid for their purchases. They decided to buy one of each cheese, so that they could do a tasting at home with Sam and Marion. Camille figured she could bribe her father with food to help him forget he was mad.

Camille was packing everything into a small cooler when she heard a familiar deep laugh. She looked up and saw a tall figure emerge from the back room, gently lowering his head so that his frame could clear the low doorway.

For a moment, Camille caught herself smiling at the sight of Mack. He was dressed casually in shorts and a navy T-shirt that somehow made his green eyes disarming even across the store. He saw Camille, and the surprise on his face quickly turned to amusement. Camille immediately looked away as panic set in. She could not run into Mack Phillips again, especially not after the way her father had reacted. She quickly gathered her bag and tried to turn Willa toward the door.

But it was too late. Willa was running across the shop, straight toward Mack. By the time Camille caught up, Willa was breathless as she told Mack about cheese making and her favorite cheeses from the tasting.

Camille joined Willa, Mack, and the store manager, apologizing for interrupting their meeting. The manager shook her head and said, "Oh, nonsense. There is nothing better than hearing from a satisfied customer."

Mack agreed and said, "I like bumping into you two. We seem to have a lot of mutual interests." He winked at Camille, and she could not believe that her palms got clammy from a simple wink.

Willa seemed oblivious to the interactions between Camille and Mack. Willa explained their plans for the summer and how they had gone through all the family albums and made a list of adventures from Camille's childhood that they planned to re-create together.

Willa added, "And this was my most important stop. My momma came here as a little girl. I saw a picture of her milking a goat, and she told me that she used to come here all the time with Gramps and Nana, but she said it wasn't anything like this. She said it was just two people in a little building with a couple of goats wandering around the parking lot, and now look at it." She gestured around the farm store like Vanna White.

The manager had been nodding along with Willa and finally said, "Well, those two people in the little building are my parents. They will be so excited to hear that a customer from all those years ago came back to visit."

"Oh wow," Willa said. "You mean you own this place?"

"Well, my family does, yes. I was talking to my friend Mack about selling our goat cheese at his festival. Has he told you about his festival?"

Willa quickly replied, "Yes. He told us about it at the blueberry farm. My mom is going to make a shrimp boil for the festival."

"Oh, that's great," the farm manager said, turning toward Camille. "Mack mentioned he may hire someone to help with the cooking. You know, we could use help with recipe development. I'd love to discuss some ideas with you. Maybe some cooking demonstrations in the store and recipe cards to give to customers? Have you ever done anything like that?"

"I'm sorry, my daughter is getting ahead of herself," Camille said. "It sounds like Mack is too. I'm not a chef. I'm a lawyer. I just like making shrimp boils."

Willa quickly added, "She used to be a lawyer, but she's out of work and needs a new job, and she is the best cook in the whole world and she has a million ideas for recipes for your goat cheeses. She was just saying that to me. Isn't that right, Momma?"

Camille looked upward, briefly closing her eyes and wondering how she was constantly finding herself in these situations with her daughter. She knelt and whispered to Willa, "We have been over this. I'm not looking for a new job, Willa. I'm taking a little break from work to spend time with you and Nana and Gramps this summer."

Camille stood and apologized to Mack and the farm manager. She added, "My daughter is right about one thing. We tasted your cheeses, and they're delicious. My mind is spinning with all of the meals I want to make with them, but I'm not a chef. I just enjoy cooking."

The manager shrugged her shoulders. "Well, think about it. If Mack vouches for you, that's good enough for me. I'll give you my card." She walked back into the office and came back with a business card and a small tin. She handed the card to Camille and then bent down in front of Willa. "Would you like to try our newest product? It's a little different." She opened the tin and explained, "This is a caramel made from goat milk. We have two flavors—salted caramel and lavender caramel. Can you be one of my taste testers?"

Willa looked up at her mother, who nodded her permission. Willa popped one of each candy into her mouth. The manager asked, "So what do you think?"

"I think they're both amazing."

The manager smiled. "Do you think the lavender taste is too strong? Too weird?"

"No. I think it's just right," Willa declared. She put her small finger to her lip, savoring the bite of caramel, and then said, "I also think chocolate would be delicious."

The manager chuckled. "I like the way you think. Maybe you want to be my recipe consultant."

"Yes. I can do that," Willa solemnly replied.

"All right, how much do you charge?"

Willa thought carefully and then said, "I won't charge you any money if you let me milk a goat. My mom got to when she was little, and I'd really like to milk a goat."

"Well, most of our goats are milked by a machine. I think I've got an even better trade for you. We still have a few baby goats that are on bottles. Would you like to feed one?"

Willa's body started vibrating with excitement. "I could give a baby goat a bottle?"

"Yep."

"Definitely. Yes. This is turning out to be the best Three Musketeer adventure ever."

Camille watched the whole interaction and shared Willa's excitement. She bent down and hugged her daughter. "Oh, I agree, Willa."

Mack turned to the manager. "I've been coming to this place for years, and you've never let me feed a baby goat with a bottle. When's my turn?"

"Okay, okay, bottles all around. You guys head out to the back barn. I'll get everything ready."

"Momma, did you hear that? We all get to feed a baby goat, you and Mack. Isn't that exciting?" Willa grabbed each of their hands and pulled them toward the back barn. Willa turned to Mack and said, "I know you're used to fish. Don't worry; I'll help you. I'm really good with goats."

"Oh, are you now?" Camille asked.

Willa gave a subtle nod of her head and crossed her arms. "I am. I dreamed about it. The goats loved me."

Camille and Mack exchanged glances, and Mack whispered, "Do you think she's right?"

Camille shrugged her shoulders. "It wouldn't surprise me."

It turned out Willa was right. The baby goats swarmed her as soon as she was handed a bottle. The whole barn was mesmerized by how Willa seemed to instinctively know how to handle the baby goats as they nuzzled toward her, pushing each other out of the way. Willa made sure they each got a turn until the last goat fell asleep in Willa's lap.

It took some convincing, but Willa finally handed over the baby goat. Camille and Willa thanked everyone at the Elberta Goat Farm and headed for their car, loaded with a cooler full of cheeses. Willa held Camille's hand. "I liked this adventure, Momma."

"Me too," Camille replied easily.

"Daddy too?" Willa gently asked.

Camille took a brief inhale and squeezed her eyes for a moment, allowing the emotion she could feel bubbling up to temper down. She looked at her daughter and quietly replied, "Yes, Daddy too. Daddy would have loved this adventure."

Camille loaded the trunk and Willa asked, "Where are we going now, Momma?"

"Well, are you hungry?"

"Yes. I'm starving," Willa said, with the exaggerated drama only a small child could exhibit about hunger pangs after eating an entire cheese tasting only an hour earlier.

"Well, I thought you might be. We're going to stop for lunch. There's a restaurant called Lambert's Café that I used to love going to when I was your age. How about we add one more adventure to the list for today?"

"Yes!" Willa exclaimed.

Mack walked over to Camille's car and said, "It was fun running into you two again." He turned to Willa. "Well, your dream was right. You were excellent with goats."

"Thanks, Mack," Willa said confidently. Then she asked, "Hey, are you hungry?"

"I'm pretty much always hungry," Mack replied.

"Me too. We're going to lunch at Lambert's Café. My momma used to go there when she was a kid. Do you want to come?"

Willa immediately looked up at her mother. Camille narrowed her eyes and looked down at Willa.

Willa quickly responded, "Momma, you said we could eat with Mack another time. This is another time. And he's hungry. And we are going to lunch right now." Willa's arms were crossed emphatically across her chest.

Mack shrugged his shoulders, glanced at his watch, and said, "Sure. I never turn down a throwed roll. I'll meet you guys there." Mack strode toward his truck before Camille could find her voice to stop the looming disaster.

Camille winced. She should have hauled Willa away as soon as they saw Mack. Her father was going to be furious when he found out they had run into Mack again. But she hadn't planned any of this, and bumping into people was inevitable in

South Alabama. Still, her mind spun, wondering how to control the damage. Willa was incapable of keeping a secret. Her
parents would find out, so Camille decided to make the best
of the situation. She'd explain to Mack that they couldn't have
any more contact. Then she'd cross her fingers that she wasn't
around when Willa told her parents about lunch.

As soon as she was buckled in her seat, Willa asked,
"Momma, what did Mack mean by a throwed roll? Is that
another southern food?"

Camille chuckled. "No. It's a roll that has been thrown
at you. That's what they do at this restaurant. The waitresses
throw rolls at you, and then you catch them and eat them."

Willa's eyes were wide. "That sounds weird. And awesome."

"I think that is a perfect description. This place is weird
and awesome. That description kind of applies to a lot of things
in Alabama."

It was a short drive between the towns of Elberta and
Foley. The changes between the communities should have
been drastic—a sleepy southern town to the bustling center
of beach traffic. Pulling onto Highway 59 in Foley used to be
like crossing through customs into a foreign country. Foley
had always been the center of development—the road that led
to the white-sand beaches, cluttered with chain stores, outlet
malls, and mini golf. It used to be surrounded by farmland and
maybe the occasional country store.

Camille was surprised to find a series of strip malls and
new neighborhood developments. The beautiful old pecan
farms and horse properties that used to spread across the
county had been sold off and subdivided. Elberta was hanging on for dear life among growth and progress. Camille was
happy to see signs of stability in a community that could have
fallen victim to the poverty that plagued so many Alabama

communities, but she also longed for the character of the town that was being quickly obliterated. It was strange seeing the bait-and-tackle shops replaced with dry cleaners, nail salons instead of barbecue stands.

Camille sighed as she pulled into the restaurant parking lot, a place she'd been so many times as a child. It was tradition whenever they were in Foley. Her life was upside down, and she craved the familiarity of the tradition.

Camille glanced in her rearview mirror and saw Mack's truck parked in the row behind. She saw him pull off his worn baseball cap and run his hand through his wavy chestnut hair, smiling as he hopped out of his car. It was an enviable smile, especially to Camille, who felt so many complicated emotions about going to lunch with a man who was suing her father and made her stomach flutter.

The trio walked inside the restaurant and were quickly seated. The restaurant was decorated like an old-fashioned saloon, wood covering almost every surface from the walls to the floors to the booths. There were black-and-white photographs on the walls, and the smells of bacon and yeast perfumed the air. As soon as they were seated, Mack turned to Willa and said, "Okay, the key is to hold your arm in the air and be ready."

"I'm ready, I'm ready," Willa squealed.

Mack gave a slight nod to the young boy in suspenders wheeling around the cart of warm rolls. The boy gently tossed a roll toward their table, and Willa stood up on the bench, catching it easily. "More, more," she shouted. The bread cart boy nodded his head and tossed a roll high in the air, straight at Willa. She caught a second roll. Then Mack held up his hand, and the bread cart boy wound up, like he was pitching the opening game ball. Mack reached across the table but fumbled the roll, and it bounced to the floor.

Camille laughed, and Mack shook his head. "I'm off my game."

"That's okay, Mack. I'll give you one of mine," Willa said, already slathering butter on her roll and snacking happily.

A few moments later, a waitress came by and dropped off menus, waters, and sweet tea. Willa quickly pushed aside the children's menu. "All right, Momma. You order for me. Just what you would have ordered when you were a kid."

"You got it." Camille scanned the menu, not surprised to find that little had changed in the last thirty years. She handed the menu back to the waitress and said, "We'll have the fried catfish, hush puppies, turnip greens, and sliced peaches."

Mack nodded his head. "Sounds good to me. Make that three. Plus some banana cream pie."

"All right, that'll be right out. You folks seem to know the drill, but if you want any more rolls, just raise your hand."

"What do you think, Willa? Should we get some more rolls?" Camille asked.

Willa shook her head. She became uncharacteristically quiet. Camille looked over at her daughter fidgeting with her napkin and staring down at the table.

"Willa, what's wrong?" Camille asked.

Willa's voice was small as she replied, "I don't want to eat cat or puppy. I thought I wanted to try the foods that you ate as a girl, but I can't eat that."

Camille's mind quickly reeled as she remembered their order. "Oh, sweetie. Catfish is a type of fish. It doesn't have any cat in it at all. Mack, tell her."

Mack was laughing. "She's right. It's called catfish because they have these long whiskers. No cats will be harmed in the making of this meal."

"And the puppies?" Willa asked.

"Hush puppies. They're little balls of fried corn bread. No puppy in them at all."

"So no one is eating cat or dog here?"

"No. Absolutely not."

"Okay." Willa returned to nibbling her roll. "People in the South have really weird names for their food."

"They do," Camille and Mack said at the same time.

Mack enticed Willa into playing a game of checkers by the empty fireplace, which proved to be the perfect distraction.

As soon as Mack and Willa returned to their seats, the waitress brought out the plates of food. Willa looked at them suspiciously and then looked up at the waitress. "I want to make sure there is no cat or dog in any of this food."

Camille put her head in her hands, but the waitress seemed unfazed. "Nope," she plainly stated. "Need anything else? Want me to throw some more rolls at you?"

"No. We're all set," Camille quickly replied.

Mack chuckled as he started eating the fried fish. After a few cautious bites, Willa dug in. "This is really good, Momma. But do you think we could call these things something other than hush puppies? It's a horrible name."

"Sure thing. What would you call them?" Camille said, relieved that Willa had moved on.

"I don't know. But I wouldn't come up with a name that makes kids think they're eating dog."

Mack chuckled and said, "That is an excellent point."

Camille was surprised at how easily the conversation flowed, but it was mostly driven by Willa and her never-ending curiosity about fishing. Mack was patient, answering all of Willa's questions, even the one about fish poop, with a surprising amount of detail.

Camille remembered that he had taught at a college in California before moving back to Alabama. She almost said something about how he must have been a great teacher, but she caught herself. She'd forgotten that she was supposed to hate him because of the lawsuit. And she'd forgotten that she had internet stalked him, and people were uncomfortable when you knew things about them that they didn't tell you. Camille was quiet while Willa and Mack kept talking. She sat there enjoying the food—a little bit of crunchy fish, the tangy richness from the turnip greens, and the sweet juices of the fresh peach slices.

Willa and Mack looked at her. Mack asked, "You eat them all together?"

"Yeah. It's weird, right? I like the combination. I always have. I've always gotten the exact same thing here."

"Okay, I'll give it a go." Mack fixed himself a similar bite, combining all the flavors. "Well, it's strange. But for some reason, I want another bite just like that."

Willa finished her food and asked if she could play with the wooden train set at the front of the restaurant. Camille watched her daughter skip happily over and instantly make friends with a young boy about the same age.

As soon as Willa was out of earshot, Camille turned to Mack. "We can never do this again."

Mack sat back, raising his eyebrows. "Usually my dates wait until after I've finished eating to tell me that."

Camille shook her head. "This is not a date. This is absolutely not a date. This is a happenstance run-in with compounded awkwardness due to my adorable, persuasive daughter's invitation to lunch, which you should have declined, by the way."

Mack nodded his head slowly. "Please, continue. I'd like to hear more about the happenstances and the awkwardness."

"Mack. Please be serious. You are suing my parents. I cannot speak to you. I cannot meet you, ever again, at least not without a lawyer present."

"But aren't you a lawyer?"

"Yes. And I'm advising myself that this is a very bad idea."

Mack shrugged. "Not my fault. You said it yourself. It's that adorable, persuasive daughter of yours. I wasn't going to tell her no. Neither were you."

"Fine. But we cannot ever do this again. Agreed?"

Mack leaned back in his chair. "I'd like to agree. I'm generally an agreeable guy. But I feel a responsibility to educate the youth of America about sustainable fishing. I can't disappoint Willa. Plus, when you give me these lectures, you have these little creases between your eyebrows." He reached across the table and rubbed his thumb gently across Camille's forehead. "It's pretty cute."

She tensed for a moment, her heart thumping, filling her face with heat.

Mack smiled. "You're blushing again."

"I don't know why. You just told me I have wrinkles."

"Most adorable stress wrinkles I've ever seen."

Camille swallowed hard. "I can't see you again. You shouldn't want to see me again. My life is one giant messy complication."

Mack shrugged. "Messy is where the best things in life come from." He said it with such ease, as if it were the simplest, truest statement. Then he asked, "What if we kept bumping into each other? What if we even saw each other on purpose? There isn't a part of you that's interested?"

Camille closed her eyes, trying to force logic forward. He was suing her parents. Her husband had died nine months ago. The logic told her she wasn't interested. The problem was, her heart hadn't stopped racing from his brief touch of her face and she couldn't stop wishing that Willa would play trains for hours so that she could keep talking to the frustrating, confident, kind man sitting across the table.

The logic won. The logic always won with Camille. She opened her eyes and said, "I'm interested in getting my father out of this lawsuit. He's a good man, Mack. A good man that got caught up . . ."

Mack cut her off. "He got caught up with some really bad guys. Do you know what happened here?"

Camille nodded slowly. "I've seen the site."

"Then you know, almost a year later, it's still full of mud and silt. None of the fish or crabs can see to hunt, so they're leaving or dying. People have to treat this place better."

"My father has spent his life taking care of this place. This isn't his fault."

"It may not be directly, but he's wrapped up in it." Mack leaned forward. "Mobile Bay is this country's most diverse ecosystem. Not the California coast or the Florida wetlands. This place is home to more species than anywhere else, and our state is killing our most prized resource."

"How is suing my father going to fix this problem?"

"It's a start. A way to make people take care of the things that matter."

"My father cares. Suing him isn't going to make a difference."

"This is much bigger than your father." Mack sighed. "Do you have any idea what's going on in the bay? I want to swim in these waters, eat the fish out of these waters, without worrying. Don't you?"

Camille stammered. "Willa and I swim every day."

Mack ran his hand through his hair. "You should be more careful." He pushed his plate aside. "Are you done eating?"

Camille grabbed a hush puppy and said, "I am now. Why?"

Mack narrowed his eyes. "Because I'm about to talk about sewage."

"Okay," Camille said, as she put the hush puppy down.

Mack explained. "An hour north of here, in the Black Belt, the communities are so poor that there is no sewer system. People are supposed to put in septic tanks, but nobody can afford it, so they pump the sewage into their yards. Raw sewage, flowing from backyards into our rivers. Those rivers flow south to us. This county is a rainy place. When the rains come, the sewers overflow, spilling more into the rivers. Then you've got the muddy waters from the construction. There is so much development everywhere. It's great for jobs, but what about the water? Every new housing development, every new strip mall, they're dumping sediment and debris into our waterways."

Mack exhaled. "The sewage flows from the north, systems overflow, construction erodes the natural barriers, and all of this muddy, dirty water flows right into the bay, killing everything."

Camille sat quietly, Mack's words filling her head. In DC, it was easy to ignore the problems of home. But she was here now, even if it was temporary. The rivers and bay that surrounded her home were a part of her, and her heart ached thinking about what would happen if this problem was ignored.

Mack shook his head slowly. "I don't care who I piss off anymore. I'm going to do whatever I can to save this place. I have a plan, and some friends that have been helping me with that plan, to start holding people responsible. Making changes in this state. The first step is holding Trident responsible for the mess they created on the Fish River. I'm sorry your dad is caught up in this, but there is no way in hell I'm letting this go."

Camille nodded her head slowly.

"I ruined our lunch, didn't I? At least I waited until we were finished eating to bring up the sewage talk," Mack said, the sides of his mouth creeping into a smile.

Camille looked directly into his eyes. "You didn't ruin anything. I needed to hear that."

Mack raised his eyebrows. "Most people walk off when I start that lecture. It's not a popular topic around here."

"I can imagine." Camille sighed deeply. "I really do care about this place, but I care about my father more. I wish we weren't on opposite sides of this."

Mack reached over and grabbed her hand. "We aren't on opposite sides of this. This is about Trident."

Camille looked down, feeling Mack's rough palm on top of her hand. She slowly, reluctantly pulled away. "I can't hurt my father. I understand what you're doing, but this lawsuit hurts him."

Mack shrugged. "So fix it. Do that lawyer thing. Get him out of it. Make him understand why I'm doing all of this."

Camille rolled her eyes. "Okay. Sounds great. I'll just run off, fix the lawsuit problem for my father, and then—"

Mack cut her off. "And then run into me on purpose. Maybe sometime next week? We can meet for a drink?"

Camille laughed. "Sure. I'll get my father dismissed in a week, and then we'll grab a drink to celebrate."

"Okay, maybe not a week. But when you do get your father dismissed, meet me for a drink?"

"It's not that easy."

"What isn't?"

"All of it. The getting him dismissed. The seeing you. Being with you is not easy for me."

"I get that. I'm not looking for easy. You are a giant, messy complication."

"Yes, I am."

"I like those complications, Camille. I like your weird food combinations. I like the way you pretend to be a serious lawyer but are absolutely powerless with your daughter. I like it when your eyes come alive trying one of my oysters, watching Willa with those goats, fighting with me about this lawsuit. I also really like your legs in those shorts."

Camille gulped. Her hands were clammy, a wave of nausea rising at all the conflicting emotions churning in her stomach from Mack's words.

Mack winked. "I think you'll find a way to get your dad out of this lawsuit. When you do, I'll be waiting."

He slowly stood up and grabbed the check off the table. "I've got this. Best meal I've ever had at Lambert's." He smiled broadly. "Hope to see you soon."

Mack walked over to Willa and helped her connect the wooden train track before giving her a high five and waving good-bye. Camille watched him pay the cashier and walk out of the restaurant to his truck. He had an easy smile and nodded at other patrons as he left. An easy stride, confident and smooth. She couldn't take her eyes off him, even when Willa returned to the table to continue nibbling on the hush puppies and asking, "Momma, why do you have a funny look on your face?"

◆ 22 ◆

THE NEXT MORNING, WILLA trotted downstairs in her over-sized T-shirt and halo of red curls. Camille put her finger to her lip and whispered, "Nana and Gramps are still sleeping. Want to go on a breakfast adventure with me?"

Willa nodded her head vigorously and turned back to her room to put on shorts. A few minutes later they were outside.

"Where are we going, Momma?"

"To get muffins." Camille needed a peace offering to defuse the tension with her parents.

Willa must have mentioned Mack's name a dozen times, describing the farm and lunch in excruciating detail. Sam stormed off, muttering about a "complete lack of loyalty." Marion put on a better face, but once Willa was in bed, the lectures commenced. Camille figured muffins were a start, but what she really needed to do was get her father out of this law-suit as soon as possible.

Willa started walking toward the car, but Camille shook her head.

"I thought we would bike into town. What do you think?"

Willa hesitated. Camille bent down and said, "You love to ride your bike. Nothing is going to happen to me. Let's go for a little ride, together."

Willa nodded her head and tentatively hopped onto her bike.

It was still early, and the town was quiet. They rode the path under the Spanish oaks to downtown Fairhope and up Main Street to Pop's Bakery. Willa kept looking sideways, pedaling carefully, but after a few moments she found her rhythm, and she was smiling broadly as they rode into town. When they walked inside the bakery, Willa's jaw dropped. There were dozens of flavors of muffins, all lined up in the case, the scents of vanilla and cinnamon still clinging to the air.

"Oh wow, I want one of each."

"I know. Don't they all look amazing?"

Camille loved Pop's Bakery. It was an institution in Fairhope; the oversized muffins were famous across the bay. Camille could look into the case and use the muffins as markers of her childhood. There were the elementary years, when she would only eat the strawberries-and-cream muffin; the middle school years, when she would go down the line, picking something new each Saturday morning; the high school years, when she finally settled on her favorite, the morning glory, with its carrot cake batter and craggy, caramelized edges.

"We will definitely be back, but what do you want to try this morning?"

Willa walked back and forth in front of the case before settling on a snickerdoodle muffin, topped with a cinnamon-sugar crumble.

Camille walked over to put in their order. "One snickerdoodle, one morning glory, a blueberry, and a double chocolate chip."

She took their muffins outside and put them in the basket of her bike.

Willa said, "Let's bike home superfast. I can't wait to try my muffin."

Camille was thankful that a six-year-old's version of fast biking was a moderate pace, and she enjoyed the leisurely ride back to her parents' house. The bay was starting to perk up, a few boats on the water and fishermen lined up at the town pier.

When they pulled in front of the house, Camille suggested they eat their muffins on the dock.

"I'll drop these off in the kitchen for Nana and Gramps and get us some milk to drink. Sound good?"

"Yes. I'll wait for you out back."

"But not on the dock, right?"

"Not on the dock. I don't go on the dock without a grown-up. I know!" Willa refrained the rules as if she were a train conductor reminding passengers about exiting the platform.

Camille left the muffins on the counter for her parents with a note that said, *I love you. I'm sorry.* She grabbed a cup of milk for Willa and a cup of coffee from the pot she had made that morning. She met Willa in the back. Willa was waiting at the edge of the dock, her toes lined up with the first board.

"Okay, let's go sit on the end and let our feet dangle down."

Willa skipped to the end of the dock, removed her socks and sneakers, and dipped her toes in the water.

Camille handed Willa a muffin. Willa nibbled on the muffin and looked out over the water. She didn't speak, but Camille could see the ping-pong balls bouncing thoughts around her daughter's brain.

"What are you thinking about, Willa?"

"I really like it here."

Camille nodded. "I do too."

Willa smiled broadly. "Can we stay? Forever?"

Camille turned toward her daughter, seeing so much inno-cent hope on her face. "We live in DC. Our house is there. My job is there. Your school is there. That's our home."

"But you're so sad there. And you're happy here. Why can't we stay here?"

Camille reached out, grabbing her daughter's hand. "I'm sorry I was so sad in DC. I missed your daddy very much. It will be better when we go back, I promise."

"No. You were sad before Daddy died. You'd come home from work all grumpy. And we never did fun stuff like explore rivers or pick blueberries. I don't want to go back there."

Camille paused. "Willa, this is temporary. I have to go back to work. We'll make time for adventures. There are blue-berries to pick in DC too."

"Why can't it be better here? You're happy and you cook all these yummy foods and we go on all these adventures and we see Nana and Gramps all the time. We love it here."

Camille grabbed her daughter and pulled her onto her lap, wrapping her arms around her tightly. "Oh, sweetie, I wish it were that easy."

Camille sat and thought about what her daughter had said. It was amazing how children could be these mirrors, reflect-ing and magnifying all the good and bad in their parents. For the last nine months, Camille had been so consumed with her grief that it had left little time to reflect on anything else. It was easy to idealize every aspect of their lives together before Ben died. But if she was being honest, things hadn't been per-fect. And she certainly hadn't felt satisfied at work for some time. Camille had been on the cusp of burnout for years; Ben's death was simply an accelerant.

They had been in Fairhope for over a month and had found a rhythm to life here. She missed things about Washington, DC—the restaurants, the museums, the energy of the city—but it was nothing more than a passing pang of longing. There had been moments in the past week where she had felt energized while working out of Griffin's office, using a part of her brain that had been dormant the last few weeks. But it didn't make her long to go back to her old practice, to the constant stress and deadlines.

Camille asked Willa, "What makes you happy every day? What do you want to be?"

"Gramps."

"What do you mean?"

"I want to be just like Gramps. His whole job is digging in the dirt every day. And he knows so much about plants and flowers. I want to dig in the ground my whole life."

"I could see you doing that, Willa."

"I know. Gramps too. We talked about it. He's going to rename his company when I join. *Sam and Willa's Landscaping.*"

"Well, I would hire them."

"But you don't need to, Momma. I'll dig in the dirt for you for free!"

"I love you, Willa."

"To the moon and back, right?"

"Right. Should we go see if Nana and Gramps are up yet? Nana is going to be so excited for her chocolate muffin."

"The chocolate one is for Nana? But she never eats things like that."

"I know. These muffins are her special treat. She can never turn them down."

The muffins were a temporary fix, along with Willa. It was impossible for Camille's parents to act mad when Willa

was around to keep everyone laughing. They suppressed whatever anger and disappointment they felt toward Camille when
Willa was present and stuck to icy silences when she wasn't.

★ ★ ★

In the weeks that followed, Willa and Camille plugged away
at their adventure list. They took a day trip up to Clanton to
pick peaches. Willa declared the homemade peach ice cream
the most delicious thing she had ever tasted. They stopped
by Preisters Pecans, and Willa exclaimed, "It's like a carni-
val, but instead of rides, its pecan things everywhere!" They
sampled the praline pecans, the cinnamon sugar pecans, the
chocolate-covered pecans, and brought home a bag of each.
They had high tea at the Grand Hotel, and Camille had never
seen her mother happier.

After every adventure, Marion added photographs to the
scrapbook she was making. Willa loved flipping through it,
comparing it to the family albums from Camille's childhood.

Camille enjoyed the comparisons too. It was almost as if
she were getting a do-over. All the things she enjoyed, she
was experiencing again, appreciating new aspects, finding new
love for the place that had raised her.

Camille poured herself into the lawsuit, spending afternoons at Griffin's office and nights researching in her bed. She
couldn't shake the things Mack had told her, and the more she
dug, the more she realized that everything he'd said was true.
She'd sit on the dock, looking across the bay, wondering what
was happening below the calm surface.

But she focused on her father's case, on finding the best arguments to get him out of this mess. Working with Griffin was
easy. He was smart and thoughtful, and Camille was constantly
surprised at how much she enjoyed working in his office.

Marion gave Griffin a folder full of documents: the plans for the sites, the landscape designs, and the instructions that had been left for Trident. Griffin met with the foreman of Sam's landscaping crew and got an affidavit describing the tree tagging process and what had happened the day of the clearing.

After two weeks, Camille and Griffin agreed that they had a good argument and were ready to file the motion. The affidavit from the foreman was critical. It would be hard for Trident to argue against that evidence. Everyone's mood seemed to lift at the thought.

The day they made the submission to the court, Camille spent most of the afternoon at Griffin's office. It had been a long time since she'd done a filing, and she'd never done one that she cared about as much as this one. She wanted to do everything she could to make this lawsuit go away for her parents. She read over their motion again and again. She double-checked the filing procedures. They sat next to each other, staring at the computer, as Griffin clicked submit.

"Four hours before the midnight deadline. I'd call that a victory," Griffin said.

"It's already eight? I didn't realize it was so late."

"Me either. But I'm starving. Want to grab some dinner?" Griffin asked, casually raising an eyebrow.

Camille shook her head. "I should probably get back home. I'm sure they're wondering where I am."

"Call and check in. Then let's get something to eat. I'm guessing Willa's probably in bed by now."

Camille knew Griffin was right. Willa was high energy all day, but she was a blessedly good sleeper. She was out cold most nights by seven. Camille realized she was hungry, and she did want to celebrate. It had been a tedious day of work, but she was proud of the argument they had submitted to the court. Camille also knew that the idea of going out to dinner with Griffin was full of complications.

Griffin could see the wheels in Camille's head spinning. "Let's grab a pizza down the street. There is certainly nothing romantic or date-like about takeout pizza. It's a nice night. We could sit in the park. We'll use paper napkins and eat off our laps. It's the most un-date-like scenario I can imagine."

Camille smiled. "Could you see the fear on my face?"

"Yes. Did I convince you with my non-date pizza argument?"

"You did. You're very persuasive. Okay, let's go. Maybe even some ice cream after pizza. Go big or go home, right?"

Griffin laughed and held the door for Camille as they walked out of his office.

It was a warm night, typical for late July in the South, but Camille enjoyed the fresh air and the walk through downtown to the pizza restaurant.

Griffin said, "You know, if this was a date, I might try to hold your hand. But I'm not going to do that. I'm going to stand over here, at least two feet of space between us, and casually stroll alongside you, like a friend would do."

"I don't have any friends that say *casually stroll*. That only happens in movies where there's a British narrator."

"You've clearly been hanging out with a bad crowd. All those big-city people."

"I've been corrupted."

"It's a good thing you moved back home."

Camille paused, thinking about Griffin's statement. He saw her squirming and asked, "Did I say something wrong?"

"No, it's just . . . I haven't moved back. I'm leaving as soon as this lawsuit is worked out. September at the latest. This is temporary."

"Are you sure about that? You seem to like it here, even if you don't want to admit that out loud."

Camille searched for a way to describe her feelings. "Willa and I are relaxed here. It's easy. But living here? I don't know about that."

"Why is *easy* a bad thing?"

"Sometimes I think *easy* is failure. It's giving up on a chance for a bigger life."

"What do you want in that bigger life?"

Camille thought about his question. "When I was eighteen and leaving home, I wanted bigger. I wanted to see what was out there."

"And when you did it—moved to the city and got the big job? Was it what you wanted?"

"I thought so, but . . ." Camille trailed off. "I don't know. Willa said something to me, about how unhappy I was coming home from work. I never thought about it before, but maybe I was. Working at a firm in DC is one giant complaining competition about how long you work and how hard you work. That started to feel normal. Then I come down here, and I meet people that are passionate about what they do. I didn't realize that existed anymore, and that makes me sad. I want passion in my life again. I was wishing away time in DC— make it until the weekend, make it until the next vacation. I don't want to wish away my life."

"I understand. It was the same for me in Atlanta."

"And is it better here? A better life for you?"

Griffin winced. "Well, I'm divorced. Everyone seems to know my business, all the time. There are zero decent sushi restaurants. But I guess it is better. It wasn't at the beginning. It was a rough transition for me. But this place has a way of winning you over. Slowly. Plus there have been some developments this summer that make it much more attractive." Griffin winked at Camille as he opened the door to the pizza restaurant.

As soon as they walked inside, Camille's stomach grumbled. There was a giant wood-burning stove in the back of the restaurant. It was a casual place, with tables inside and out, an equal number of people staying to eat as taking their pizza to go. Camille looked at the menu and was impressed. Even after a few months in Fairhope, she loved discovering changes to her hometown, seeing how much sophistication was packed into a few modest downtown blocks. Sometimes Camille thought of Fairhope as being frozen in time when she'd left; its evolution was surprising and humbling.

"So, what's your order?" Griffin asked.

"The prosciutto and arugula sounds great, but I think I have to try Fisherman's Revenge."

Griffin grimaced. "I don't know if I can do that one—clams and pickled jalapeños? I'm more of a sausage man. Maybe some olives if I'm feeling adventurous."

"Then we should get two pizzas," Camille stated. "I'm starving, and I can't pass up trying this combination."

"Sounds like a plan." Griffin walked up to the counter and placed their order.

Camille wandered around the restaurant, admiring the old black-and-white photos framed on the wall. There was so much history in the town. There had been change, of course, but Fairhope Avenue still looked the same. Even some of the businesses had been fixtures for seventy years—the hardware store, the pharmacy, the toy store; the only difference was the cars parked out front. Camille loved it. She was wrapped up in the pictures when Griffin brought over two beers.

They sipped their drinks while they waited for the pizzas, comparing war stories about being associates in big law firms.

When the pizzas were ready, they took them to the town park, finding an empty bench under one of the town's grand Spanish oak trees.

As they ate, Camille asked, "How long until we hear from the court?"

"Couple weeks, probably."

Camille nodded and asked, "If we win, what happens next?"

"We celebrate while Trident and the Fish River residents battle it out. That lawsuit will take years. Trident will fight every step of the way. Every developer in the Southeast is watching to see what will happen. Deep pockets, long lawsuits."

"How is Mack going to do this?"

"Well, Mack"—Griffin hesitated, eyeing Camille suspiciously—"and the other Fish River residents have their own deep pockets."

"What do you mean?"

"They have local counsel, but their real lawyers are Preston Crane."

"The Seattle firm?" Camille was shocked. Preston Crane represented every major tech company on the West Coast. "How did they get involved?"

Griffin shrugged. "The gossip is—"

Camille cut him off. "Please. Alabama gossip is the worst. Let's not add to it."

Griffin raised his eyebrows. "Yes, but it is also surprisingly accurate."

"Okay, fine, what's the gossip?"

Griffin said, "Mack Phillips is very well connected. He brought them in. I don't know how he's paying the bills. I don't believe the gossip there."

Camille hesitated, took a bite of pizza, and asked, "What does that gossip say?"

"Lots of ideas. Drug ring is the most popular. Cocaine smuggled in salmon," Griffin said, smirking.

Camille laughed. She could imagine Mack doing a lot of things, but smuggling cocaine was certainly not one of them. He cared too much about the fish.

"What do you think? How is he so well connected?" Camille asked.

"You'd have to ask him about that. People aren't always what they seem, Camille."

"I know." Camille nervously bit her lip and then asked, "What if I kept working on the case? Digging into Trident and the damage a little more? There isn't any harm in being pre-pared while we're waiting for the judge to rule, right?"

Griffin shrugged his shoulders. "Sure. If you have the time. Anything in particular you want to look into?"

Camille smiled. "Pretty much all of it. The environmental regulations and the construction site standards and the water testing. I'm realizing that there's a lot I don't know about how the waters are protected."

"I can pull some of that for you."

"Would it be okay if I kept working out of your office?"

"Of course. I never mind having you around, Camille. In fact, I really like it. Still want ice cream?" Griffin asked.

Camille glanced at her watch and winced. "Can I get a rain check?"

"No problem. Maybe I could pick you up this weekend and we could bring Willa along. Kids love ice cream, right?"

"Everyone loves ice cream, my daughter included." Camille nervously bit her lip before she continued. "It is a thoughtful offer, Griffin. But I'm not ready."

"Okay. Are you telling me to back off?"

Camille sighed. "I like spending time with you. I like talking to you. I'm just not sure if . . ."

"If you want to do more than talk?"

Camille nodded.

"I've got no timeline, Camille. I like spending time with you too."

"Thank you, Griffin. You are a good friend."

"A friend you may or may not want to kiss at some undefined time in the future."

Camille couldn't help but laugh. She gave Griffin a short hug and said, "Thank you for dinner. I'm going home now."

Camille walked to her car, thinking about Griffin's offer. She wasn't sure why she had turned him down. It had been less than a year since Ben died. It seemed too soon to date, and yet it also seemed silly to follow some grief timeline. When she was ready, Griffin was the type of person she should date. He was smart, kind, and easy to be around. Part of the problem was that he wasn't Ben. The other part, the part that scared Camille more, was that he wasn't Mack.

◆ 23 ◆

CAMILLE PULLED INTO HER parents' driveway, a dull ache creeping across her forehead. It hadn't been an easy week. The judge hadn't ruled on the motion to dismiss Sam from the lawsuit, and the stress of waiting was wearing on everyone. Camille kept working out of Griffin's office, but neither of them brought up dating. The absence of that discussion seemed to suck out all communication. There was a lot of polite awkwardness.

The more Camille continued researching the standards of harm for citizen suits, the more worried she became. Griffin shared the water samples and damage report Mack had filed. It was heartbreaking to see the experts cite the harm that the land clearing had caused, to read the report about dead fish and animals choked by the murky water flowing into the bay.

The only factor weighing in her father's favor was that this had happened in Alabama. Any other state would have taken swift action—government mandates to fix the damage. But Alabama's enforcement of environmental violations was the lowest in the country. It was ironic that the state with the most rivers, the most species to protect, had so few rules and even fewer people willing to police the damage. As Camille saw it, there was no winner. If the judge didn't dismiss her father, then they'd have to fight Mack, a fight that would result in either financial ruin for her father or lasting harm to the river and everything downstream. Getting her father dismissed from the lawsuit was their only hope.

As she got out of her car, she heard laughter, women's voices craning over one another, and the squeals of children. She walked around back to find her mother and Muffy huddled together, holding each other's hands as they gasped for air between laughing fits. Leslie was sitting next to her mother as Charlotte and Willa played in the sandbox Sam had built.

"What's so funny?" Camille asked.

"Oh, you're home. Good. We were waiting for you," Marion said, smoothing her hair and trying to compose herself.

"I didn't realize you guys were coming over," Camille said, reaching out to give Leslie a hug.

"Muffy, Leslie, and Charlotte stopped by for a little playdate. Leslie was telling us about William's latest adventure," Marion said, stifling a laugh.

Leslie's blonde hair was cut into a chic bob that swung just above her shoulders. She had on a blue eyelet dress with ruffled shoulder straps. Her nails were perfectly manicured and painted a pale pink that coordinated with her Jack Rogers sandals. Leslie waved her hand dismissively. "Camille does not want to hear about ten-year-old boys."

Camille sat down next to Leslie and said, "Oh yes I do. Especially your ten-year-old."

Leslie tilted her head toward Camille. "Against my better judgment, we got him a phone, but he gave it back to us the next day. He said he couldn't handle the responsibility."

Muffy chuckled. "Tell Camille why."

Leslie continued, "He told us he had been sexting."

Camille's eyes widened. "At ten?"

Marion started laughing. "It's the best scandal of the summer."

Camille stared at her mother. "Mom, this is serious. Why are you laughing?"

Leslie patted Camille's shoulder. "It turns out William's definition of 'sexting' was texting the word *sex* to his friend, who then replied with *butt*, and then there were a lot of emojis. Honestly, I'm just glad they spelled the words correctly."

Muffy added, "And now you have an excuse to keep him away from phones. I honestly have no idea why you agreed to it in the first place."

Leslie rolled her eyes. "I know, but all his friends have phones. Parenting is much harder for us than it was for you two." Leslie pointed at Marion and Muffy as she put her arm around Camille.

Camille sighed. "I'm relieved that I have a few more years before all of that stuff. I don't know how you do it, Leslie."

Leslie shrugged. "Blind faith." She turned toward Camille, eyeing her faded black tank top and shorts, and said, "Go change. We have plans."

"What do you mean?" Camille asked.

"The grandmas are babysitting tonight," Marion said, beaming. "You girls are going out. You've been surrounded by children or old people for too long. It's time."

Leslie nodded. "She's right. Besides, there's only so much gossiping we can do with the little ones around."

Camille and Leslie had met up a handful of times since Camille had been back, mostly at the playground so that Charlotte and Willa could play. It had been nice to see her friend, but Leslie was right: there was only so much talking they could do when they were interrupted every three minutes to "watch this" or distribute yet another snack.

Leslie whispered, "I need real updates, especially about all this time you've been spending with a certain town lawyer. Go change, and then we'll head out for drinks."

Camille looked over at Willa, who was huddled with Charlotte, designing plans for their sandcastle. Marion and Muffy were happily chatting. Camille figured there was no harm in leaving Willa for a night.

"Are you sure, Mom? You can handle bedtime with Willa?" Camille asked.

"Yes. I will be fine. You two go have some fun." Marion waved her away dismissively.

Camille went upstairs to change. She grabbed her favorite coral silk slip dress. She added a gold cuff bracelet and slipped on a pair of emerald-green snakeskin heels. She glanced in the mirror, pleased she was having a miraculously good hair day. The Alabama sun had added golden streaks to the red, bringing her color closer and closer to Willa's. The humidity was a perfect diffuser, and the corkscrew curls trailed down her back. Some days she woke up and looked in the mirror ready to shave her head, but today, her hair was behaving perfectly. Camille said a silent prayer of thanks to the gods of curly hair.

She walked downstairs and said, "All right, I'm ready. Should we head out before they change their minds?"

Leslie nodded. Willa blew Camille a kiss, then immediately returned to sandcastle building with Charlotte.

Leslie said, "I'll drive and then drop you off on our way home. You are due for a night of fun."

"Where are we headed?" Camille asked, as Leslie pulled out of the driveway.

"The Wash House. It's still the best bar around."

Camille relaxed on the short drive to Point Clear. The Wash House restaurant didn't look like much from the parking lot, just a simple wood-clad building, but inside it was a hidden treasure. There were rough-hewn wood floors and white tablecloths with candles. It was an old house, so there were rooms and hidden nooks with tables tucked inside. Camille remembered it as the place they had always gone for special occasions: prom, her mother's birthday, the day she was accepted to law school.

The bar was off to the side, and the small crowd was an eclectic mix—the regulars that came in for their nightly cocktail on the way home; the couples grabbing a drink before dinner, shoulders brushing against each other as the anticipation for the evening built; a few stragglers having a business meeting or a solitary moment on their way somewhere else.

Camille and Leslie found two open spots at the bar. Camille could feel the energy of the room buzzing on her skin, exciting and uncomfortable. It felt strange to be in a bar without Ben.

When the bartender walked over to take their order, Camille quickly said, "I'll have a shot of tequila." The bartender raised an eyebrow, and Camille realized exactly how ridiculous she looked, a middle-aged mother ordering a shot of tequila. She nodded her head, confirming that yes, she would like to make this poor choice. The bartender asked, "Want me to chill it?"

"Sure. That would be great."

"You want one too?" he asked Leslie.

Leslie gave a small shake of her head and said, "I'll stick with pinot grigio tonight."

The bartender poured Leslie's glass of wine and handed Camille the shot, along with a wedge of lime.

Camille quickly downed the shot, and Leslie asked, "Feel better now?"

"A little bit," Camille answered.

"Good. Now look at the cocktail list and order a grown-up drink. And maybe some food too. I don't want you getting sick in my car."

Camille looked over the menu of cocktails and saw herbal infusions, handcrafted drinks, and even dry ice. Camille ordered the rhubarb gin shrub with basil. She was thankful the shot of tequila was already working, and she felt her shoulders easing as she watched the bartender mix her cocktail. The bar had a beautiful back patio; planters overflowed with sweet potato vines and impatiens. There was a light breeze this evening, and the dining room quickly filled up. Camille clung to the security of the bar and sipped her drink slowly, people-watching and scanning the room.

Camille and Leslie slipped into easy conversation, catching up on Leslie's kids and Camille's work in DC. When you'd known someone since birth, there was a familiarity no amount of time could erase.

Leslie raised her eyebrows as she said, "Your name has been a hot topic on our mothers' morning walks."

"I can only imagine. What have they been saying?"

Leslie smiled gently. "Mostly expressing strong opinions about things that aren't their business."

Camille looked up at the ceiling. "My mother thinks I'm doing everything wrong. My career, my relationships, how I parent Willa. My mother wants to fix me, and I know she has good intentions, but it just makes me feel like I'm broken."

Leslie narrowed her eyes. "You're not broken, Camille. You're the strongest person I know. My whole life I have envied you—moving to DC, going to law school, making partner."

Camille rolled her eyes. "That's a joke. You are perfection embodied, Leslie. You've never wanted to be like me for a minute."

Leslie took a sip of wine. "Nothing is perfect. My mother laid out a path, and I strolled right down it. I never even thought to dream of something different." She shook her head. "We make our choices. I made easy choices. You were so brave. You *are* so brave."

Camille shook her head. "I don't feel brave. I regret so much." Her voice was so quiet it was almost a whisper. "Sometimes I think if I had been a better wife, Ben wouldn't have died. If I were with him more, maybe I would have known he was going to have a heart attack. I have a lot of regrets, Leslie. Even if I couldn't have stopped his death, I should have loved him better. I should have worn the sweater."

"Worn the sweater?"

"Ben's office had this ugly Christmas sweater party. Every year, he begged me to dress up, but none of the other wives did. It was almost like this thing the guys did to see who could embarrass each other more. Last year he bought us matching sweaters, but I refused to wear mine. It's stupid, but I think about that sweater all the time. It would have made Ben smile. I should have done more things to make Ben smile instead of worrying about myself."

Leslie nodded. "I'm sure there were other sweaters, metaphorically speaking. Ben knew you loved him."

"I know, but I don't want to have those same regrets with Willa. I want to be everything she needs, and maybe that means I should listen to my mother."

"Maybe. Or maybe you figure it out yourself and let Marion keep her opinions to herself." Leslie raised her glass of wine and said, "How about we toast to that?"

Camille smiled as she clanked her empty glass against Leslie's.

"You need another round," Leslie said.

"No. I need food. Are the crab claws still good?"

"Yes, they are so good." Leslie looked across the bar. "Almost as good as that delicious man that just walked in."

Camille laughed. "You're a married woman. You shouldn't be calling men delicious."

"I'm married, but I still have excellent taste. And that," Leslie said, pointing across the room, "is someone you should think about tasting."

Camille turned around, and the blood drained from her face. Mack Phillips was standing at the door. He'd replaced his usual T-shirt and hat with a light-blue button-down and navy shorts. His usually unruly hair was brushed back, showing off his tanned face and bright smile. Camille looked away immediately, lowering her face into her hands.

Leslie saw the concern on Camille's face. "I'm sorry. I get it, you aren't ready yet. But if you were ready, that would be an excellent place to start."

Camille was silent.

Leslie continued, searching for the right thing to say. "Or maybe you've already found someone? We haven't talked about Griffin yet, and that was my number-one agenda item for this evening."

Camille shook her head, trying to make herself small so she could disappear into the crowd at the bar before Mack saw her. She whispered, "I don't know if I'm ready. I also have no idea what to think about Griffin. But none of that matters because we have to leave, immediately, before that man sees me."

Leslie eyed Camille suspiciously. "You are acting really strange. What's wrong?"

"That is Mack Phillips."

Leslie looked at Mack and then back to Camille. "That's the person suing your father?" Leslie laughed, her blonde hair falling back as she said, "Well, this is an interesting development."

Camille reached into her purse and left several bills on the bar. "Let's sneak out the side."

Leslie gave a little wave. "Too late. He's walking over."

"Stop waving at him," Camille demanded.

"I have manners," Leslie retorted.

Mack was grinning as he walked over and sat on the open barstool next to Camille, immediately holding up his hands. "I did not plan this. I come here every Friday night. Ask this guy," he said, gesturing to the bartender.

"Want your usual, Mack?" the bartender asked.

"Yep, thanks," Mack said as the bartender placed a beer in front of him.

"Can I get you ladies another round?" the bartender asked.

Leslie answered quickly, "Yes, please. And some crab claws and the fried green tomatoes." She turned to Camille and said, "You need something to soak up that shot."

"Shot, huh? Sounds like I'm joining a party," Mack said, smirking.

Camille shook her head. "No party, no you joining anything. We've been over this."

"Camille Taylor, there is no need to be so rude," Leslie said, extending her hand to Mack and introducing herself. "I'm Leslie, one of Cam's oldest friends. I've heard so much about you, Mack."

Mack chuckled. "I'm sure you have. Nice to meet you, Leslie."

"Cam and I were just discussing our dinner plans."

"No, we weren't," Camille quickly replied.

Ignoring Camille, Leslie continued, "Mack, since you come here so often, do you have any recommendations?"

"Well, I hear there's a good fried oyster special, and they have some beautiful Gulf grouper on the menu. Best of my catch."

Camille asked, "You supply the fish?"

Mack nodded. "Yeah, for this place and a few other restaurants around the bay. I still want to keep the business small, but we started branching out into commercial operations a few years ago."

Leslie motioned for the bartender. "We'd like to order some dinner too."

"No, we wouldn't," Camille quickly said.

"Ignore her. We'll have the oyster special and the grouper, blackened, please. Anything for you, Mack?"

"Your usual?" the bartender asked.

Mack smiled. "Yep."

The bartender walked away. Camille turned to Leslie and whispered, "What are you doing?"

"Getting some food in you. I promised your mother I'd show you a good time tonight."

"Please stop."

Mack cleared his throat. "I didn't mean to interrupt your evening."

"Oh, don't be silly. You aren't interrupting anything." Leslie looked down at her phone and exclaimed, "Oh no. I just got a text message from my mother. You'll never guess what she said."

Camille narrowed her eyes at Leslie, her voice as tense as her body, and said, "Leslie, whatever you're doing, stop."

Leslie continued, "My mother says she can't get Charlotte settled. I guess I'm going to have to leave and pick her up. I'm so sorry. But you two stay and eat. It's a shame to let all that food go to waste."

Leslie stood, gathering her purse with a large smile on her face. She put her palm to her forehead and said, "I forgot. I drove you here, Camille. Mack, do you think you could be a gentleman and give Camille a ride home?"

Mack nodded and said, "Sure. No problem."

Leslie leaned in to give Camille a hug. Camille whispered in her ear, "Leslie, I may never forgive you."

Leslie whispered back, "Oh, I think you will. It's time you had some fun, and that"—she gestured toward Mack—"looks like a lot of fun."

Leslie left, and Camille and Mack sat silently for a few minutes. Mack's laughter broke the silence.

"That was pretty entertaining to watch. She clearly enjoys seeing you squirm."

"I'll get even," Camille said, taking a long sip of her cocktail.

"I'm sure you will." Mack looked for the bartender, who seemed to have stepped away. "I can ask them to box up this food. We don't have to stay."

Camille sighed deeply. She wasn't sure if it was the cocktails or Leslie's antics, but she started to laugh and began to relax. "No, we should stay and enjoy the food. Leslie needs to win occasionally." She lifted her hair off her neck and turned toward Mack. "I forgot how hot Alabama gets. How much you can feel the heat. It just sticks to your skin."

Mack nodded. "I know. When I first came back after California, it took me a few months to reacclimate. You'll get your Alabama tolerance back in no time."

"Do you miss California?"

"Yes and no. I loved living there. I loved my work, but when my dad got sick, none of that mattered. I wanted to be back here with him and my mom."

"Why didn't you go back . . . after?"

"After he died?"

"Yes."

"It gets easier, you know. To say that someone you loved died and not feel physical pain when you say the words."

"I know. At least, I think I know. Some days it's easier, and then I feel bad about that. Like it shouldn't ever be easier."

"I get that." They sat for a few minutes. Camille didn't want to talk about Ben, but Mack's reaction surprised her. It was nice to have someone hear you and not try to fix you.

Camille sipped her drink and said, "So why didn't you go back to California?"

"I thought I was going to. That was always the plan. I took a year's leave of absence from the university. I taught ecology in California. I thought I'd go back to teaching, but Dad's illness was . . ." Mack searched for the words. "It changed me. Changed what I wanted, what I needed in life. After he died, I couldn't imagine leaving."

"Do you like it now? Life here?"

"Yeah, it's a good life. Not the life I thought I wanted. As a kid, if you had told me I'd be back running Dad's fishing business, I would have thought you'd lost your mind. But I like what I'm building with the community of people down here. I like caring about this place and being a part of it. I don't have some grand life plan; this just feels right."

"I've had a grand life plan since birth."

"I can tell."

"I have zero plans right now."

"You say that like it's a bad thing."

"Isn't it?"

"Nah. Plan too much and you miss the good stuff."

"Like what?"

"Like meeting a stunning redhead that you can't stop thinking about."

"Mack, I'm not stunning."

He laughed. "There isn't a single person in this bar that hasn't been eyeing you. You're stunning."

"I don't feel stunning. I feel . . ." Camille searched for the word. "I feel lost."

"I think that's okay. I think we all have to feel lost in order to figure out where we're supposed to be."

Camille wasn't sure how Mack did it, but his words had such a soothing effect. She smiled and relaxed into her drink, enjoying the moment.

Eating dinner with the seafood supplier for the restaurant had its perks. The chef kept sending over extra bites and things for Mack and Camille to try. It was clear the entire restaurant was charmed by Mack; the waitresses all stopped by for a quick chat. He had an easygoing manner that seemed to attract everyone. He had inside jokes, remembered past interactions, and asked for updates. It was like having dinner with the mayor. Despite all the interruptions, he made Camille feel like the focus. He introduced her to everyone, explaining the jokes if they weren't readily apparent, suggesting things they might have in common. At some point in the night, his hand landed on top of hers, and she let it stay there. They sat, bodies touching in the most remote way, and it was hard for Camille to focus on anything except the feel of Mack's rough palm on top of her hand.

They shared the fried oysters for an appetizer, which were served with a chowchow chili sauce. The rich, crisp fried oysters paired perfectly with the tang from the pickles in the chowchow and the sweet heat of the chili sauce. Camille devoured the blackened grouper with charred green beans and a lemon aioli. It turned out Mack's usual order was a steak and baked potato. "I eat so much fish. I need a break sometime," he explained when Camille laughed.

They fell into an easy banter throughout dinner. She found herself mentioning Ben a few times—things they had done, things Ben had liked. Mack listened. He didn't balk and he didn't try to avoid those conversations. Camille often worried about how uncomfortable everyone seemed whenever the topic of Ben came up, so Camille tried to avoid it. But trying to avoid talking about Ben put Camille on edge. The way Mack seemed to accept Ben as part of the conversation made Camille relax. His ease made her freer to feel and not worry. It was a novel way to be for Camille.

Shortly after they ordered their appetizer, the bartender sent over a bottle of white wine. Camille made a joke, saying she hoped it wasn't a local wine. Mack agreed. "Alabama is not conducive to making wine out of anything other than muscadines." The wine was perfect with the oysters and the grouper. It had a crisp granite start with a lemony finish. After each bite and each sip, Camille felt herself enjoying the evening more and more.

Mack told Camille more about his life in California, and they traded stories about their teenage antics growing up by the bay. Mack was a few years older than Camille, but they had some mutual acquaintances.

"How come you've never been married?" Camille asked, then immediately apologized. "I'm not usually so blunt."

"Yes, you are. I like that about you. Besides, it's a fair question. Especially here, where everyone seems to get married while they're still babies." Mack took a bite of his steak,

chewing slowly before continuing. "I almost did get married.
I was with someone for five years. She was a vet in San Diego.
Then I came back, and, well, it didn't work anymore. Alabama
isn't everyone's cup of tea."

"That is a very true statement."

"We had built a life in California, and then, suddenly, I
was asking her to make a huge change in those plans. I can't
blame her for not wanting to stay here."

"And it wasn't enough for you to want to go back to
California?"

"Sometimes geography gives you answers to things that
you didn't even know were problems."

Camille thought about Mack's statement and how true it
was. Since she had come back to Alabama, she had realized so
much about her life in DC, her career, her relationship with
Willa, the inertia of their routine that she never would have
questioned, that she never would have had the time to question. Pulling them out of that life and putting them in Alabama had shined a spotlight on her former life. There were so
many things that she didn't miss, and even more that she knew
had to be fixed. A brave teenager had left Alabama with ideas
of how she was going to conquer the world. And somehow she
had returned home seventeen years later realizing that there
had been no grand conquest, only a slow descent into doing
exactly what everybody around her expected.

She took a long sip of her wine and then looked across the
bar at Mack.

"How come you aren't drinking the wine?"

"Well, I'm not much of a wine guy, so I stopped after my
first beer. But it has been fun watching you."

Camille put her hand over her mouth. "I can't believe
I've drunk half a bottle by myself. And I had a shot and two

cocktails. I'm drunk. I'm really drunk." Camille started moving her mouth slowly and gesturing with her hands, trying to see if she could shake out the alcohol. "I can't remember the last time I drank this much."

Camille had been so wrapped up in talking to Mack and enjoying the evening that she hadn't been paying attention to the bartender refilling her glass or keeping track of her drinks.

"I think you're due a night or two of not thinking."

"Well, since I'm drunk, I can get away with asking the questions I really want to know the answers to."

"I can't wait to hear this," Mack said, leaning back on the barstool. "Is it about my hair care routine? Women always want to know."

Camille snorted. "No. I want to know how can you afford Preston Crane. It's one of the top firms in the country, and I know what those firms charge. It's what I charge, and I can't even afford my own rates."

Mack smirked. "Been doing some digging, I see."

"I'm a naturally curious person. There's no way a fisherman can afford Preston Crane. There's no way a college professor can afford Preston Crane."

"What else did your Google searches say about my background?"

"I couldn't find anything more." As soon as she said it, Camille put her hand over her mouth.

"It's okay to admit you've been Googling me."

"I haven't." Camille looked sideways. "Okay, maybe I Googled you a little. Alabama can be boring. I needed to fill the time."

"There is nothing boring about an Alabama with you in it, Camille."

"I know you don't smuggle cocaine in your fish, so where does this money come from?"

"That's the latest gossip? That's good." Mack shrugged. "The money comes from me. Plus, I've got some connections with Preston Crane. They owe me some favors, so I get a good deal."

"How did you get that kind of money?"

"The old-fashioned way."

"Prostitution?"

"No." Mack smiled as he said, "You're funny when you're drunk. I made my money through blind luck."

"The lottery?"

Mack was enjoying himself. "No, in college, I was working with a group of friends on our senior thesis, running a bus on old cooking oil from the cafeteria. This was long before biofuels became mainstream. Our project worked, we turned it into something more; now that something more is a pretty big company in California, selling biofuel to trucking companies. I figured out early that the corporate life wasn't for me, so I sold my interest when I was twenty-five. My college buddies are still running the company. They use Preston Crane for all their legal work."

"So, you're rich?" Camille's eyes grew wide in shock at her own question. "I'm sorry, I am very drunk, and that was very rude."

Mack chuckled. "It's okay. I'm not rich. I'm very, very comfortable and very, very lucky."

"So why are you running a fish shop?"

Mack shrugged. "Because I like it."

They finished their dinner, both laughing at Camille's drunken antics. Camille wasn't a messy drunk; she was an effusive drunk. Everything was amazing. Everyone was so kind.

The food was the best she had ever eaten. The waitress was the best waitress. And finally, Mack was the best date Camille had had in months. Then she started giggling and said, "You're the only date I've had in months. But still, the best."

Camille turned her head sideways and asked, "Wait, is this a date?"

"Two single people, eating dinner together. Looks like a date to me."

Camille's eyes widened. "I'm single." In her drunken state, she was both surprised and amused by her statement.

Mack paid the check and walked Camille out to his truck. It was an idyllic Alabama summer night. Fireflies danced in the distance, the bay waters lapped against the shore, and a gentle breeze blew across Camille's arms.

Mack walked Camille to the passenger side and leaned around, opening the door. His arm was around her waist, and Camille leaned into his body.

Camille put her hands on his chest and looked up into his eyes. He was a full head taller than her. Camille cocked her head upward and asked, "Mack, do you want to kiss me?"

Mack reached down and cupped his hand around her chin. "Camille, I've been thinking about kissing you since the moment you walked into my shop."

"Well, are you going to do it or not?"

Mack kicked the dirt. "I am not going to kiss you. As much as I'd like to. I'm going to drive you home and carry your drunken body inside your parents' home and hope to escape without being harmed by your father."

"Probably a good plan." Camille smirked. "Are you going to keep thinking about kissing me?"

"Probably, as long as you don't throw up in my truck."

"I rarely vomit." Camille leaned against the truck door and looked up into the dark sky. "Mack, I've been thinking about kissing you. And that scares me."

"I'm not scary," Mack said, stepping closer.

"Yes, you are. You make my head constantly swirl, and I catch myself thinking about you and the things you say and the way you walk into a room. I think about you and your ridiculous body and how it would feel to have you hold me and touch me—"

Mack shook his head before cutting Camille off, one final step erasing the space between their bodies. He pulled Camille against his chest and wrapped his arms around her narrow hips. He leaned down and gently brushed his lips across hers, bringing his hands up into her hair. She leaned in farther, parting her lips, but he pulled back and whispered, "I think I better get you home."

"Well, you're no fun," Camille said, as she climbed into the truck.

"I know it," Mack said, climbing behind the wheel.

As they drove down the road to Camille's parents' house, "Sweet Home Alabama" played on the radio. Camille started humming along, and then found herself belting out all the words. She was completely off-key and enthusiastic. Mack couldn't stop laughing. She continued serenading him for the rest of the ride home.

When Mack pulled into the entrance to Camille's parents' house, Camille said, "That show was for free. In exchange for the ride, kind sir." She opened the car door and immediately fell onto the ground, laughing hysterically.

Mack walked around to find Camille lying on the driveway looking up at the stars. "I fell," she deadpanned.

"I see that. Somehow you got drunker on the ride home. You didn't puke on me. For that I am thankful." Mack scooped her up and carried her to the front steps.

Marion walked onto the porch. Camille had started singing again. This time it was "Friends in Low Places" by Garth Brooks. It wasn't clear whether the singing had woken Marion or if she'd been waiting around, just like she had all those nights when Camille was a teenager.

Marion looked at Camille draped across Mack's arms, her head lolling backward and her feet dancing in the air. "What happened to her?" Marion asked.

"I got drunk as a skunk, Mom. That's what happened."

"Oh, Lord. Well, hand her over," Marion said, shaking her head. Mack tried to transition Camille, but she started squirming and very ungracefully flopped onto the porch.

"Oh, you two are ridiculous. I can walk up to my room," she said as Mack helped her stand. "And don't worry, Mom. He wouldn't even kiss me. Said I'm too drunk, which is probably true. I hate it when men are right and I am wrong."

Camille walked inside and elaborately closed the door as quietly as she could.

"Well, this is a flashback to high school," Marion clucked.

Mack laughed. "I can only imagine what a teenage Camille was like."

"She kept us on our toes, that's for sure. Probably always will. She and her daughter are the most interesting, most joyful, most stress-inducing part of my life."

"I can certainly understand that." Mack and Marion were quiet. The cicadas were chirping, but otherwise there wasn't even the sound of a breath between them.

"What was she like in high school?" Mack asked tentatively.

"Fire. Camille was living, breathing fire. She looked it, she acted it. Her father and I figured she'd either carve a path of destruction or set the world ablaze." Marion had a far-off look before she turned to Mack and said, "I appreciate you bringing her home."

"Yes, of course."

Mack stood in front of Marion, not sure what to say next, whether there was any more to even say. Marion decided for them both when she turned and walked inside.

Camille was lying across the couch, her heels kicked off, humming happily as she heard Mack's truck drive away. It was rare to recognize a feeling when it was happening, but somewhere between the appetizers and the entrees, Camille recognized that this was a happy night. One of the first in a very long time.

Marion cleared her throat and Camille sat upright, then slumped again.

"We need to have a discussion. A discussion without little ears listening." Marion's face was tight, her eyes filled with exhaustion.

Camille sighed. "Okay. What do you want to discuss?"

"This relationship," Marion said, waving her hand dismissively, "with Mack Phillips. What exactly is going on?"

"We had dinner. It's Leslie's fault. That's it."

"It is so problematic, Camille."

Camille groaned, quickly sobering from her mother's criticism. "I know it isn't ideal with the lawsuit."

"I'm talking about more than the lawsuit."

"What then?"

"Do you really think Mack is the ideal person to be bringing around Willa? Is that the type of father figure you imagine?"

Camille recoiled. "Ben is the father figure. There is no imagining anyone else. I had dinner with a man. I had a good time. Why can't it be as simple as that?"

"Because when you are a mother, nothing is ever simple again."

"It was simple until you came into this discussion."

"What is your plan for the future? Do you think you could have a life with someone like Mack? A person who flits around from project to project, brings lawsuits, stages protests of good, solid businesses? A person who cares more about winning than the people he hurts in the process? Is that the person you imagine a future with, Camille?"

"No one is making plans for the future. And you have the wrong idea about Mack. There is so much more to him."

"I have plenty of information about Mack. This is about you. Why aren't you making plans? What is going to happen at the end of the summer? You're going to go back to Washington, DC, and what? Hire a live-in nanny to take care of Willa? She's lost one parent. Are you going to have her raised by a stranger? We both know what kind of hours that job of yours requires. How are you going to do that without Ben?"

Camille stared at the ceiling, trying to gather the words to respond to her mother. "I went out one night, and you are using this as a referendum on my parenting?"

Marion nodded. "Yes. I don't see you thinking about these issues. I cannot understand how you think it is appropriate to date a man like Mack Phillips. When are you going to put your daughter first? She needs stability. That man is reckless."

"Well, tell me, then, what should I be doing? You seem to have thought this through. What is best for me and Willa?"

"You and I both know it's better for you to stay here in Alabama. You should be building a life here, finding a job that will allow you to spend more time with Willa, looking for a partner interested in supporting you, creating a stable environment for Willa."

"That is quite the agenda." Camille shook her head. "Was there a specific person you had in mind?"

"Camille, you don't have to be disrespectful, but since you asked, yes. Someone like Griffin; that's a partner. He has supported this family in ways you can't imagine. Helping us with this lawsuit, holding my hand while I cry about the stress this has put on your father, checking in on us at night, on the weekends. He is a good man. I can't imagine why you have been setting him aside for someone that has brought so much pain to our family."

"Mack has not brought pain to our family. Trident did that."

Marion shook her head. "Your father puts on a good face, but this lawsuit has tied him in knots. He's taking on extra projects, looking over the books constantly. He should be scaling back his business, but instead he's so worried about what's going to happen that he's scraping for every project he can find. Plus he feels so bad about what happened that he's spending weekends on the river, volunteering for cleanup projects. You've been so wrapped up in yourself you haven't seen the pain we feel."

"I'm sorry my husband died and I got wrapped up in myself," Camille said, throwing Marion's words back at her.

"Your sarcasm is unappreciated."

"So is your advice." Camille's voice broke as she looked away. "I feel awful about the lawsuit. I've been trying everything I can think of to help Dad. I don't understand why you can't see that, why you're always so critical. Why can't you be supportive? Why can't you trust that I will figure out what's best for Willa and me?"

Marion opened her mouth to respond, but Camille cut her off. "I worry about going back to my job, what it will be like for Willa, what it will be like for me. I don't know what I'm going to do next, and it terrifies me. I don't need you to point this out. I don't need you sitting here throwing sand on the one night of fun I've had in months. Sometimes I wish you would leave me alone."

Camille stood up and walked toward the stairs. She turned to her mother and said, "I don't have the energy to fight you anymore. Good night, Mother."

Camille crept upstairs and crawled into her bed, curling on her side, reaching for the empty space beside her.

24

LESLIE BREEZED INTO THE house, her eyes sparkling as she announced, "I'm on my way to church, but I wanted to stop by and check on Cam."

"Over here," Camille groaned. She was slumped across two of the kitchen barstools, unable to open either eye fully. Marion was washing dishes as Sam sat in the corner, sipping coffee and reading the paper.

"How are you feeling?" Leslie asked.

"Like death," Camille said, unable to raise her head.

"You girls must have had a good night," Sam chuckled. "You were due one of those, Cammy. Why don't I grab you a soda and some aspirin? That always does the trick."

Sam walked upstairs, and Camille looked over at her mother. Marion's steely glance told Camille everything she needed to know. For whatever reason, Marion hadn't mentioned who had brought Camille home.

Camille swallowed as she turned toward Leslie and asked, "Why are you going to church on a Saturday?"

"It's vacation Bible school. I'm doing a craft project with the girls."

"Why just the girls?" Camille asked, squinting.

"Girls do crafts, boys play sports."

Camille started to shake her head, but the motion was too painful. "There is so much wrong with that statement."

Leslie waved her hand dismissively. "Oh, please. We don't force them; that's what they choose."

"I'm too hungover to debate. Can you speak softer? My head is pounding."

Marion clucked. "You think it's pounding now. Just wait until Willa turns off the cartoons and you have to converse with your daughter. That child has two volumes, off and sonic boom."

"I'm well aware," Camille said, lowering her head back onto the stool.

On cue, Willa walked into the kitchen, describing the latest undersea adventures on the cartoon she had been watching.

Sam walked in, plopping a Coke can and two aspirin in front of Camille. Camille whispered, "Dad, please make her stop talking."

Sam raised his eyebrows. "I'm not Moses. I can't part the rivers, and I can't make your daughter stop talking." He turned to Willa and scooped her into his arms. "But I can take my favorite crew member on an adventure. How about we go pick up some biscuits for your momma?"

Willa nodded her head and followed Sam out the door as he said, "Someone needs some grease to soak up the good time she had last night."

Once Camille heard her father's truck start, she bit her lip before saying, "Dad is in a good mood. You didn't mention anything to him?"

Marion shook her head. "No. I don't tell your father everything, especially things that are going to hurt him. I'm hoping you're putting an end to this behavior."

Camille sighed. "I'm certainly putting an end to the cocktail consumption."

Marion pursed her lips. "Leslie, you talk some sense into her. I'm going for a walk." A few moments later there was a forceful door slam.

"She didn't look happy," Leslie whispered.

"No, she's not happy with anything. The fact that Mack drove me home was not good." Camille pointed at Leslie. "And that is all your fault."

Leslie held up her hand. "I didn't realize hurricane Marion was brewing. I just thought you'd enjoy yourself."

"I did enjoy myself. Which makes this more complicated, and my mother even madder."

Leslie sat down, a gleam in her eye, and asked, "What happened after I left?"

"I drank too much. I stayed and ate dinner with my parents' sworn enemy, and then I tried to kiss him." Camille slumped back on the counter, then sat up abruptly and said, "And I sang. Twice. I'm never leaving this house again."

Leslie started laughing. "You sang? You have the *worst* voice."

"I know."

"Putting aside your mortification and your mother's anger, how do you feel about it? About the night with Mack?"

Camille squeezed her eyes shut and sat quietly. She spoke softly as she said, "I feel guilty."

"Because of Ben?" Leslie gently asked.

Camille nodded. "Ben, the lawsuit, my mother. I feel guilty about it all. How can I laugh and have a good time when Ben is dead?"

Leslie reached out and grabbed her friend's hand. "Camille, sometimes we have emotions that fight against each other.

There's no winner. You have to let them settle in. Your happy may be swirled with other feelings too. It will work itself out, but you can't stop laughing because you're afraid of the guilt."

Camille sat in silence. She felt like a teenager again, soaking in Leslie's wise advice.

Leslie asked, "What exactly was Marion upset about? It can't be one dinner with Mack Phillips."

Camille sighed. "It is and it isn't. She thinks I should be making plans, figuring out exactly how I'm going to manage my life, raising Willa, and the fact that I had dinner with Mack suggests very poor judgment. She'd be a lot happier if I was having dinner with Griffin and opening a law office down the street."

"And what do you think?"

"She's not wrong. That's the problem with our fights. They always hurt more because every painful thing she tells me has a lining of truth," Camille said.

"Griffin is also a very tasty treat. You don't want to sample him?"

"Leslie, please stop referring to men as treats."

"I can't help it. I'm living vicariously through you."

"We've been over this. There is nothing to envy here." Camille gestured to her disheveled hair and oversized T-shirt.

"Let's say you did everything Marion wanted. You dated Griffin. You moved to Alabama. Is that the life you want?"

"I have no idea." Camille sighed. "All I want right now is for this headache to go away."

Leslie picked up her bag and gave Camille a quick hug as she said, "The biscuits should help. Be open to the possibilities for the rest."

Camille wasn't sure if she could do that, but she thought maybe she should try.

25

"WOULD YOU LIKE TO go on a date?" Camille blurted out as Griffin took a sip of his coffee.

Griffin looked up, a mixture of shock and amusement across his face. "Umm . . . yeah. I'd like that."

Camille nodded her head nervously. "Great. Tonight?"

"That works," Griffin said.

"Okay. I'll pick you up at seven. There's a place I've been wanting to go all summer."

"Sounds great, Camille. I'll be ready." There was a deep smirk on Griffin's face as he turned back to his work.

Camille walked out of Griffin's office, closed the door, and immediately slumped against the wall. The whole interaction had taken approximately forty seconds, and Camille was relieved it was over. She'd done it. She'd asked a man out on a date and hadn't passed out in the process.

For days, her mother's words had played on repeat, a commercial jingle she couldn't shake. Camille wanted to move forward. She wanted to find happiness in life, even though it was a life without Ben. She wasn't sure what she needed to do, so she figured taking her mother's advice, trying it on for size, was a good thing to do in the meantime.

Thoughts of Mack still flew into Camille's head. She'd remember how his body felt pressed against her own, the way he'd made her laugh with his stories of the river and the characters that inhabited it. But she pushed those thoughts away quickly. She couldn't hurt her father. She saw the strain across her father's face; the way Sam nervously called Griffin's office every morning to ask if the judge had decided; the way he thumbed through the company ledger at night, eventually shoving it into the side of his easy chair. She listened to her mother and thought about the needs of the people she loved and tried not to think about whether those aligned with her own.

By the time Camille pulled up to Griffin's house that evening, the heat was starting to break. August in Alabama could be stifling, but Camille loved the early evenings, when the breeze pushed through the curtain of humidity and brought cooling relief. She was ready to have a good time. Dating was fun, or at least it had been fun at one time, and Camille wanted to find the fun again.

Camille knocked on the bright-red door of Griffin's townhouse, and he opened it immediately.

They looked at each other and laughed. Griffin said, "One of us needs to change."

Camille was wearing a green tank top and simple black shorts and sneakers. Griffin had on a navy blazer and khaki pants.

"I guess I should have given you a little more detail about my plans for tonight," Camille said.

"No problem. Give me five minutes. You can wait on the couch. Want a drink?"

"No," Camille said, too quickly.

Camille sat on Griffin's couch and looked around his house. There wasn't much hanging on the walls, and the furniture was mostly shades of brown and beige, but it was comfortable. It was nice, just like him.

Griffin came out of his bedroom a few minutes later dressed in a golf polo and shorts. It was probably the most casual thing he owned. He looked like a businessman with an hour to kill on a work trip, trying very hard to relax.

"Better?" Griffin asked.

"Perfect," Camille replied.

"Are you sure you don't want to have a drink here first?"

"Nope. I can't wait to get this night started," Camille said, itching to get in the car and drive Griffin to their destination.

"Neither can I," Griffin replied, smiling.

Once Camille was behind the wheel, Griffin peppered her with questions about where they were going, but she shook her head. "It will be more fun to surprise you when we get there."

They discussed the case and Griffin's law practice. It was always easy to be around Griffin. They had a lot in common, and there was comfort in their shared language, their shared experiences.

As they pulled into the parking lot, Griffin shot Camille a sideways glance. "This is where you wanted to go on our first date?" he asked.

"I have been dying to go here all summer."

"And you didn't want to take Willa?"

"She's not tall enough for the fun ones," Camille said, pulling Griffin's hand toward the entrance of the largest amusement park on the Gulf Coast. "I love roller coasters."

The amusement park was filled with mostly teenagers and a few families with kids. Camille bought wristbands and then headed straight to the back of the park for the big roller coasters. Griffin jogged to keep up.

The roller coaster operator got such a kick out of Camille that he let her stay in her seat, front left, for three trips in a row. She kept laughing and screaming. Griffin had to jump off after the second round. His head was still spinning when she exited and said, "Let's do the Tilt-a-Whirl. I love those too!"

Griffin might have thought he was in shape, but there was no keeping up with Camille. She bounced from ride to ride. She was like a kid in a candy store. After the Tilt-a-Whirl, she wanted to do the Double Shot, a free-fall ride where Griffin noted that he was surprised more people didn't piss themselves. Then she wanted to do the roller coaster just a few more times.

They took a break for hot dogs and slushies, finding an empty bench where they sat to eat their dinner. Griffin sat close to Camille, not quite touching her, but leaving so little space that the heat from his body brushed against Camille's arm.

Camille said, "Thank you, Griffin. I know this isn't what you had in mind when you agreed to a date."

"Not that I have any complaints, but what changed your mind about the date? You surprised me."

Camille thought for a moment before she said, "I realized I was ready for fun again."

Griffin looked around the amusement park and smiled. "Well, this has been a good surprise. Life should be full of fun."

Camille stopped, sipping her slushy slowly. "Why isn't it? When you're a kid, everything is fun. Even the mundane is fun. Willa gets excited when I throw the warm laundry on top of her. What happens that sucks the fun out of life?"

"When did it stop for you?"

Camille thought for a moment. "It feels wrong to say the fun stopped. I think somewhere along the way, I put the stuff

I was *supposed* to do before the fun. I made sure the grocery shopping was done before I'd sit down to play a game with Willa. We put off trips because we were saving for a bigger house. I figured there would be more time to have fun, until there wasn't. There wasn't any time left."

Griffin nodded his head.

"I'm sorry. I shouldn't talk about Ben."

"It's okay," Griffin said.

Camille looked around the amusement park. "Ben had motion sickness. He couldn't even take the train to New York—too much shaking. We never came to places like this, and I love roller coasters."

"You mentioned that once or twice," Griffin said, finishing his hot dog.

Camille smiled. "I haven't done this in probably ten years. I don't know why I didn't come by myself. Why did I stop doing something I like?"

"When you care about someone, you make sacrifices," Griffin said. "This dinner is certainly a sacrifice on my part."

Camille looked at Griffin, embarrassment creeping across her face. "You hate hot dogs?"

"I'm tired of eating meals with you on a bench. When you mentioned a date, I thought we'd finally be able to sit across a table. Next time," Griffin said, wrapping an arm around Camille's shoulders.

Camille leaned back, resting her head on Griffin's shoulder. "I like talking to you. It's easy, and not many things feel easy right now."

"That's because you keep waiting in line to hurl your body in circles."

Camille laughed and asked, "What do you want to do next? Tilt-a-Whirl again?"

"You're crazy. We just ate."

Camille held up her hands. "Okay, your choice."

Griffin thought for a moment and then pointed up to the center of the amusement park. "I want to ride the Ferris wheel."

Camille frowned. "That's not very exciting."

"You are correct. But maybe we'll get stuck at the top," Griffin said, raising his eyebrows.

Camille bit her lower lip, then reached out her hand and held Griffin's. "Okay. I'll give it a try."

They walked together toward the Ferris wheel, and Camille said, "But after this nice ride, I want some excitement."

Griffin laughed and said, "You got it."

♦ 26 ♦

CAMILLE THREW ON HER swimsuit and went outside, searching for Willa. She saw Marion first, sitting in the shade reading a book. Marion looked up briefly, smiling.

Camille had experienced a fair amount of silence from Marion this summer, especially after the date with Mack. Marion was an expert at the silent treatment, expressing her disappointment through steely glances and judgmental huffs. But over the last week, Marion had softened, thawing the silence with nods of agreement, even a few compliments, especially whenever Camille mentioned seeing Griffin. Camille felt a mix of relief and discomfort. No matter how old she was, how many things she accomplished, Camille still wanted her mother's approval. But she wasn't sure if the life Marion wanted was the life Camille needed.

Camille scanned the yard and found Willa sitting at the edge, her toes lined up with the first board on the dock. Camille sat next to her daughter, nudged Willa's side, and asked, "Do you have your bathing suit on underneath that dress Nana gave you?"

Willa nodded vigorously, her eyes sparkling.

"Great," Camille said. "Throw the dress over in the bush and let's go swim."

Willa popped up, flinging the dress off as fast as she could manage.

"Cannon balls off the end of the pier?" Camille asked.

"Race you!" Willa squealed as she took off. Camille ran to meet her daughter and held her hand as they jumped into the cool water.

When Sam got home, he found his daughter and grand-daughter swimming in the bay, choreographing a synchronous water dance with increasingly ridiculous and elaborate moves. He smiled as he heard their laughter carrying over the water.

He brought two towels to the end of the dock and said, "Griffin called. He's stopping by. He has some news about the case."

Camille hopped out of the water, wrapping the towel around her body.

"Good news? Bad news?" Camille asked.

"He didn't say," Sam said. "He should be here in about ten minutes. I'm sorry to break up the performance."

"That's okay," Camille said, lifting Willa out of the water. "We'll work on our dance routine tomorrow. Right, Willa?"

Willa wrapped the towel around her shoulders like a cape and asked, "Why is Griffin allowed to come over and Mack isn't? I like Mack better."

Sam raised his eyebrows and walked back toward the house. Camille grabbed Willa's hand and spoke gently. "I know you like Mack, but he did some things that made Nana and Gramps mad. That's why he can't come to the house."

"Did he do something bad?" Willa asked.

"No," Camille said, shaking her head slowly.

"Then why can't he come over?" Willa pleaded.

"It's complicated," Camille sighed, walking inside.

Willa looked up at Camille and said, "You always say things are complicated when you don't want to explain the answer."

Camille said, "Sometimes there isn't an answer. There isn't always good and bad. There's a lot in between."

Willa rolled her eyes, completely unsatisfied with Camille's explanation. "I'm going to play with my fishermen dolls," Willa said as she marched upstairs.

Camille didn't have the answers Willa needed. She couldn't explain how someone protecting the bay she loved was also hurting the people she loved. She couldn't explain how good intentions and simple mistakes could lead to trouble. She couldn't explain all the complicated emotions she felt toward Mack. The lawsuit muddled the lines of right and wrong, love and hate.

Camille quickly threw a dress over her bathing suit, nervously wringing the water out of her hair as she heard Griffin's car pull up to the house. She'd seen Griffin several times in the week since their date at the amusement park. They continued to dance between friendship and something more, their hugs longer, the brushes of their hands more frequent as they discussed the case and plans for dinner. He never pushed, he never rushed. Camille smiled in the mirror, excited to see him, hopeful for his news, still uncertain about her feelings.

Marion and Sam opened the door together, barely even greeting Griffin before pinging him with questions about the lawsuit. Camille took one look at Griffin's face and knew his answers weren't going to be what they wanted to hear.

Griffin walked over and gave Camille a hug, looking at her for a beat too long before pulling back.

"Good to see you, Griffin," Camille said. "Why don't we all sit, and you can fill us in."

Griffin sat on the couch, the nervous energy filling the room. Sam broke the silence when he asked, "The judge? Did he rule on our motion?"

Griffin shook his head. "No, not yet. It's not unusual for it to take this long, especially in the summer. But I'll be honest, it's not a great sign either. If he were going to dismiss you, he'd want to do that as soon as possible, so you wouldn't waste your time getting ready for the lawsuit. The settlement conference is scheduled for next week. All the parties have to be there, so we should know something before then."

"One more week of waiting." Sam exhaled.

"Maybe not," Griffin said, reaching into his briefcase. "That's what I wanted to talk to you about."

Camille joined Griffin on the couch, watching as her father's eyes fell and her mother's hands fidgeted.

"Trident's lawyers called me," Griffin said. "They have a proposal."

Griffin started spreading papers across the coffee table, arranging them in neat piles and flipping through his notebook. He was stalling, Camille thought.

Griffin cleared his throat. "Trident is willing to drop their claim against you. That means you'd be out of the lawsuit."

"In exchange for what?" Camille asked.

Griffin swallowed and said, "In exchange for Sam's cooperation."

Marion looked back and forth between Griffin and Sam before she smiled, threw up her hands, and said, "What a relief. Griffin, this is wonderful."

"I think so," Griffin said. "We don't know how the judge is going to rule, and none of us want this to go to trial." Griffin looked over to Sam and said, "This is the best solution."

Marion blew out a puff of air and said, "I feel like I can breathe again. Let's pop the champagne!"

No one moved. No one stood up to join Marion in celebration. Camille cleared her throat and asked, "What exactly do they want, Griffin?"

Griffin reached for his papers and said, "Standard stuff. They'd want Sam to testify, explain that the plan was to have wooded homesites. Any damage caused in the clearing process would have been remedied through the replanting."

"They want me to lie," Sam said.

"Not lie," Griffin shook his head. "They'll argue that Mack Phillips and the Fish River residents jumped the gun with this lawsuit; any harm that was caused in the clearing process was allowed, was planned for, and was going to be fixed. Mr. Phillips is really the problem, filing this lawsuit and forcing the construction to stop when you could have been moving forward, replanting and cleaning up like you'd planned all along."

"Well, that sounds reasonable to me," Marion said. "What's the problem, Sam?"

Sam looked over to his wife and shook his head. "That's not the way it happened."

Marion grabbed her husband's hand. "It's details. We could put all of this behind us."

Sam looked at Camille. She was reading over Griffin's shoulder, reviewing his notes from the call with Trident, detailing the cooperation they expected from Sam in exchange for dropping the lawsuit.

Sam asked, "Cammy, what do you think?"

Camille looked into her father's eyes. She knew he was a good man, a good man who had made a mistake. Griffin was giving them a way to get out of the lawsuit, to save her father's business, and to save her parents' future. She wanted to nod her head, to give him the freedom to make this choice, but she couldn't do it. She couldn't put aside the churning in her stomach telling her that this was wrong.

Camille spoke softly as she asked, "Could you do that? Could you stand up in court and tell that story?"

Marion said, "Of course he could. Like Griffin said, it's not a lie. Trident would have fixed this. Your father would have fixed this, but Mack rushed in and filed this lawsuit and ruined our lives."

"Nobody's life is ruined," Sam said.

Griffin interjected. "Sam, I'm going to level with you. This lawsuit could mean financial ruin for you and Marion. Trident will fight this to the end. They won't admit liability, not when every developer in the Southeast is standing behind them, knowing that one win for the plaintiffs could mean liability for all of them. They've got the money to fight. You don't. You need to take this offer. It's your best bet."

Sam looked from his wife to his daughter. "I thought Trident was decent; that's why I went into business with them. We all make mistakes. Decent people fix their mistakes."

"Exactly," Griffin said. "Trident made a mistake in the clearing. They planned on fixing the site, but the lawsuit held that up. That's all they want you to say."

Marion nodded her head and said, "Yes," reaching out to squeeze Sam's hand.

Camille looked down. She couldn't make eye contact with anyone. She could see how this would play out in court. Her father's testimony would be a powerful argument in Trident's favor. It was a smart move on Trident's part. It might have been their strategy all along—to bring Sam into the lawsuit to create pressure to force his cooperation. Griffin wasn't wrong—it was her father's best bet—but it didn't feel right either.

When Camille looked up, her father was staring forward. His eyes had an intensity Camille hadn't seen before.

Sam turned toward Griffin and said, "No. Tell them no."

Marion's chin started trembling. "Sam, think about this."

"Marion, it wasn't a mistake," Sam said quietly. "They knew what they were doing. They'll do it again. I'm not going to lie in a court. I'm not going to spin some story that excuses what they did."

"Sam, you don't have a choice," Griffin said. "Your conduct is tied to theirs. If you don't defend them, you have no defense. You can't afford this loss. You can't afford this fight."

Camille quickly said, "We'll figure out a way."

"There are no other options," Griffin said. He turned to Sam and said, "If you lose the motion to dismiss, you have no other options. Trident made it clear that this offer expires today. They're not going to wait around and see how the judge rules. I know this is a difficult decision, Sam. I get that. But you're going to have to make this hard choice."

Sam closed his eyes and leaned back in his chair as Marion began pacing the room.

Griffin turned toward Camille, draping his arm on the back of the couch as he said, "Camille, you know I'm right. You should be helping him understand."

Marion quickly added, "Sam, this is crazy. We could put this whole nightmare behind us. Listen to Griffin."

Camille stood up and walked over to her father. He reached up and grabbed her hand. He looked into her eyes and said, "Cammy, you tell me what to do."

Camille smiled as she said, "Do the right thing. That's what you always told me."

Sam gave Camille a half smile. He nodded his head and stood. "Griffin, tell Trident no. We'll take our chances with the judge, and if that doesn't work, well . . ."

Camille looked at her father. Sam swallowed hard as he continued, "If that doesn't work, then I'll handle it."

Marion shook her head, her silent shield resumed, shooting blame at Camille.

Griffin started gathering his papers. "Sam, I'm advising you to reconsider. If you can't follow my advice, I'm not sure I'm the best person to represent you."

Sam nodded. "I understand."

Marion shook her head, her eyes pleading with Sam. "No. We need Griffin. We had a hard enough time finding a lawyer."

Sam shoved his hands in his pockets. "Marion, I'm not doing this," he said, heading outside.

Marion watched him go. Before following him, she turned around and said, "I'm sorry, Griffin. I'll talk to him. I'm sure we can work this out."

Marion followed Sam, expressing pointless pleas. Sam had made up his mind. Camille knew that no matter what Marion said, her father would stand his ground.

Griffin was packing his bag, shoving papers into a folder, when Camille asked, "What are you doing?"

Griffin sighed. "Camille, I sacrificed a lot to take on this case. By representing your dad, I cut myself off from all the business that local developers send to law firms. I lost work to help your dad, but it's clear he doesn't want my help. If he's not going to listen to me, he needs to find another lawyer."

"I understand it would be easier if Dad would agree to Trident's terms, but you can't quit because of one disagreement."

"I'm not quitting. My job is to advise your father. He's not following my advice. Makes my job kind of pointless."

"No, it makes your job a little harder," Camille said.

"Do you realize how ridiculous this is? Your father could be out of the lawsuit. But he won't do it. Because he feels guilty? Because his idealistic daughter is giving him hope that doesn't exist?" Griffin pointed at Camille. "You could convince him to do this, but you won't do it. Because of whatever is going on with Mack Phillips."

"Griffin, what are you talking about? There's nothing going on with Mack Phillips."

"I'm not a fool, Camille. I've heard you talk about him, about this lawsuit, like he's some savior of the watershed. I don't know what's going on, but there's something. I can't figure out why you care more about him than your parents."

"I don't care more about him. I care about this place," Camille said, gesturing toward the bay. "I want to find a way, a way to protect this water and protect my father. Letting Trident win isn't the way."

Griffin held up his hands. "It's pointless. Trident must win for your father to win. I'm done waiting for you to come to your senses. You need to be practical."

"What do you mean you're done waiting?"

Griffin tilted his head sideways, staring into Camille's eyes as he asked, "Do you like me?"

Camille's eyes widened. "Is this about us or about the lawsuit?"

Griffin shook his head. "It's about all of it. Either you want a relationship or you don't. Either you want to end this lawsuit or you don't."

"I want to end the lawsuit, but not if it means my father has to put aside his integrity and his values to get there. And I don't know about a relationship, Griffin. I need time. I thought you understood that."

"It's been months. If you wanted this, you'd know by now. If your dad trusted me, he'd settle this. I don't want clients that don't trust me, and I don't want to convince a woman to like me."

Camille swallowed hard and gave a small nod of her head.

"Okay, then." Griffin curtly nodded and snapped his bag closed. "Good bye, Camille," he said, pulling the front door firmly shut behind him.

Camille watched Griffin drive away, wondering if she'd done the right thing.

She found her parents sitting together on the back porch swing, silently moving in rhythm with the waves. When she joined them, Marion looked up and said, "I'm going to check on Willa. You two can discuss how you're going to get us out of this mess, since no one wants to listen to me."

Marion walked away, and Camille sighed. "She's mad at me again."

Sam shrugged. "No, not you. Me. I'll work this out with your mother."

Camille sat down next to her father. "Griffin left."

"Is he still our lawyer?" Sam asked.

Camille shook her head. "I don't think your interests are aligned anymore."

"What about you two?" Sam asked, eyebrows raised.

"No. Our interests are not aligned either."

"So we both got dumped?"

"Yep."

Sam chuckled and asked, "Know any good lawyers?"

"We'll find someone," Camille said. "Until then, I'll take over the case."

Sam shook his head. "No. You're here to focus on yourself, on Willa. Not some crazy lawsuit."

Camille patted his arm. "I'll be temporary counsel, at least. Could be the shortest case I've ever had. The judge might dismiss you. By next week, we could be celebrating."

"Yep," Sam said, not convincing either one of them.

Camille was silent, looking out over the water, hoping she was right. Hoping that she hadn't made a mistake in pushing her father to follow his gut instead of being practical. She could hear Griffin's words, Marion's protests, and her hope started fading, worry taking over.

✦ 27 ✦

THE NEXT FEW DAYS were a flurry of tasks, filing paperwork with the court so that Camille could replace Griffin. All the exchanges with Griffin were terse, full of business without any emotion. It was clear that Griffin was done with the case and done with Camille.

Camille tried to maintain a routine, taking Willa on as many adventures as possible, even if it was simple trips to the playground while Camille worked. As Camille and Willa were leaving the playground one afternoon, Camille saw a poster out of the corner of her eye. It was for Mack's festival. Camille knew the festival was coming up; it had been something Willa had been looking forward to all summer. Camille walked toward the poster, thinking the festival was exactly the type of distraction she needed.

The poster listed the vendors, showcasing the artisan bakers and crafters and sellers on the Eastern Shore. Camille smiled, thinking about all the small, passionate businesses in her hometown. At the bottom of the poster, in bold red letters, was the word *Canceled*.

Camille stopped, Willa's hand pulling her toward the car. Camille wasn't sure what had happened, why the festival that

Mack had been working on all summer would suddenly be canceled. Even though she'd spent the last week mentally pushing him away, trying to focus on preparing for the settlement conference, just like that, Mack was back in her thoughts.

Camille dropped Willa off at her parents' house and told Marion she needed to run an errand. She knew she shouldn't, but she couldn't stop herself from driving to Billy's Seafood. She needed to talk to Mack, to find out what had happened to the festival. She also needed to tell him that she was representing her father, mostly to prepare herself. She wasn't sure how she would feel seeing him again, and she couldn't be an unsure lawyer, especially not when her father was her client.

She pulled into Billy's parking lot, searching for Mack's truck. It was a quiet weekday afternoon, and the usually busy marina was calm. When she walked into the store, there was a gentle-looking woman in her late sixties behind the counter. She was reading a book on coastal birds, which she promptly set down as she greeted Camille with a soft, "Good afternoon."

"Hi," Camille said. "I was looking for Mack. Is he around?"

"No, he's not in today. Is there something I could help you with?"

Camille shook her head. "No. I was hoping to talk to him about the festival."

The woman frowned. "Unfortunately, the festival is canceled."

"I know. I wanted to ask him what happened."

"Are you a vendor?" the woman asked.

"No, I'm a . . ." Camille searched for a word that would describe the complicated relationship she had with Mack. "I'm a friend. I wanted to check on him."

"Oh, I see," the woman said. She stared at Camille, her eyes narrowing and then softening. "You're the woman he's mentioned. The one with the daughter?" The woman walked out from behind the counter and stood in front of Camille. She gestured as she said, "He said you had red hair."

Camille bit her lip. "Mack mentioned me?"

The woman smiled. "Yes. I have my ways of extracting information out of that boy. I'm Faye. I'm Mack's mother."

Camille extended her hand, shaking Faye's, as she said, "It's nice to meet you." Faye was petite, with shortly cropped silver hair and bright-green eyes that matched her son's.

"He's at his house. It's on the Fish River," Mack's mother said as she grabbed a piece of paper and began writing down Mack's address. "Maybe you can cheer him up."

"I'm not sure about that," Camille said, looking at the floor.

Faye shrugged. "He always smiles when he mentions you." She walked back behind the counter and said, "Bring your daughter by next time. I hear she loves oysters. I'd like to see that." She picked up her book and went back to reading.

Camille walked through the parking lot, staring at the address. Before she could stop herself, she plugged it into her GPS and started driving the few miles down the road.

Camille could see the heat coming off the road, shimmering waves on asphalt. She watched the address numbers increasing, the entrance to each house more amusing than the last, with brightly painted signs bearing names like *Pier Pleasure* and *Latitude Adjustment* dotting the road. The entrance to Mack's house was different. There was a simple wooden sign with his address and a neatly kept sand path bordered by pine straw.

Camille drove down Mack's driveway, meandering through the tall pines. The driveway ended, and she searched for his home, almost missing it. Tucked into the trees, hidden, was a wooden structure. She got out of her car and stared. Lots of houses on the river were built on stilts because of flooding, but this was different. This was a grown-up tree house. Mack had built a home beside an old oak, wrapping it in extensive decks that tucked into the tree's large limbs. The house was made of cedar shingles that had weathered and blended into the tree's bark. There was a wide staircase that led up into the tree, taking you into his home, hidden in the branches. She saw strings of lights woven into the limbs and immediately thought that she'd love to see the house at night, to watch the sun set over the river while the house twinkled.

She stood at the foot of the stairs, uncertain about being in this place, nervous about seeing Mack. She hadn't seen or heard from him since the night at the Wash House.

She was walking up the steps when she heard cracking wood. She turned and followed the sound toward the river.

She found Mack standing next to a fallen tree, hauling limbs that had been cut and chopping them in neat piles of firewood. He was covered in dirt and sawdust and sweat. His body never stopped moving, lifting one log after another, raising the ax above his head, his muscles pulling as he brought the ax down, splitting more wood than any one person could need, especially in the summertime.

Camille cleared her throat, and Mack looked up.

"Camille. What are you doing here?" he asked.

"I wanted to talk. I stopped by Billy's, and your mom gave me your address."

Mack nodded his head, smiling. "Of course she did."

"You aren't working today?" Camille asked.

"No. I'm not good company today. Needed to be alone," he said as he trudged over to grab another log.

Camille watched him move back and forth. He was usually so calm, so gentle, but she could see the anger pulling across his face.

"I can leave you alone," she said. "I just wanted to know what happened with the festival."

Mack swung his ax again, breaking a log in two and moving the pieces aside. Camille started walking away, but Mack's voice stopped her. "It got canceled."

"I know," Camille said, turning around. "Why did you cancel, Mack?"

"I didn't have much choice. Just about everybody dropped out."

"Why? Everybody was so excited."

Mack put down the ax, lifting the bottom of his shirt to wipe the sweat off his forehead. His stomach was tanned and hard, and Camille stared for a moment too long before looking away, feeling herself turn red.

Mack was gazing off toward the river. "I could use something to drink. Let's go up to the house, and I'll try to explain."

Camille followed Mack, who was uncharacteristically quiet, as he marched up the steps to his house. He walked inside to a room surrounded by windows and poured himself a glass of water from the pitcher in the fridge.

Camille looked around. The furniture was modern, simple and clean, but there were antique oil paintings hanging on the walls and worn Turkish rugs covering the wooden floors. Everywhere you looked, there was green flooding in from the windows.

"There's a breeze on the top deck. Want to go up with me?" Mack asked.

Camille nodded. Mack grabbed her hand and led her up a narrow staircase in the center of the house. Camille could feel his large hand wrapped around hers, warm and secure, as she followed him up the creaking wooden stairs. At the top, Mack opened a door, and Camille was blinded with light. From the top deck, you could see the river flowing into Weeks Bay, birds soaring above and boats motoring upriver. Mack walked to the edge of the deck. Leaning on the railing, he said, "Everything seems calmer up here."

"It's unbelievable," Camille said, taking in the deck with teak loungers surrounding an outdoor fireplace and one of the best views of the river she'd seen. "How long have you lived here?"

"I've had the land for a while. I bought it right after I sold my interest in the company. I built the house when I moved back."

"It looks like it was meant to be here."

"That was the idea. Build something comfortable but save as much of the land as I could." Mack pointed toward the river. "See that spot over there, where the bay bends into the river, all of those reeds peeking out?"

Camille nodded.

"There was this species of crawfish that experts had been tracking for decades. Its population kept declining. Eventually, the Fish and Wildlife Service said it was extinct. The ecology community was worried. We always worry when a species disappears. But it turns out it wasn't gone. There were a few living right over there. A bunch of crawfish experts came down and found more living in the creeks that shoot off the river. It was living here all along, and no one knew."

"I had no idea there are crawfish experts," Camille said, smirking.

The corners of Mack's mouth turned up. "Yep. They're a wild bunch."

They smiled at each other, then Mack shook his head as he said, "This place is forgotten, neglected, but it's full of unique creatures. We don't even know how rich these waters are, how full of life. When we kill it, it's impossible to measure the damage."

Camille reached out and laid her fingers on top of his. She saw his passion. She understood. She said, "That's what you're protecting. That's why you're fighting."

Mack nodded. "I'm trying. Not doing a very good job of it."

"What do you mean?"

"Trident. I don't know if I can take them on. This festival thing is . . ." Mack looked down as he trailed off.

Camille asked, "What does Trident have to do with the festival?"

Mack blew out a steady stream of air as he started walking around the deck. "I can afford to lose a little business. These other places, the small farms, the businesses operating out of their garages—they can't afford a hit like this."

"But wouldn't the festival help their business? I don't understand."

"The festival would help. That was the whole point of it. But Trident is blackballing these small shops to every major hotel and restaurant chain on the Gulf Coast. That kills their business."

"What do you mean? What did Trident do?"

Mack slowly shook his head in disgust. "I had a few contracts with some of the beach hotels that got pulled last month. I didn't think much about it. Then the other vendors started mentioning lost jobs; restaurants stopped buying their products; hotels said they didn't need any more stock for the gift shops. It was small at first, but then it became clearer. Eventually, all the vendors were told if they kept associating with me, they'd lose their contracts."

"How do you know it was Trident?" Camille asked.

"I had a chat with a friend at the Wash House. They were the only restaurant still buying my fish. He told me Trident approached them, threatened all kinds of things. The guys at the Wash House have been operating for decades. They've got more connections than Trident, so they weren't worried."

"Why would the other businesses worry? What kind of power does Trident have?"

"Trident is connected to every construction crew, every developer up and down the panhandle. You know what it's like after a storm—all these businesses need contractors immediately, so they can repair any damage and reopen. Trident comes in and tells them they'll be at the bottom of the list, have no access to crews. That would even put the big hotels and restaurants under." Mack turned toward the edge of the deck, gripping the railing, the muscles in his arms quivering.

Camille stood next to him. "Why would Trident do that? Why would they care about the festival?"

"They want to scare me, punish me for bringing this lawsuit. If they lose, it will impact their entire business. Following the environmental regulations cuts into profits, and none of the regulators in this state have ever stopped them. If these citizen suits work, the local developers will have to make changes."

"Is that what you want? To put Trident out of business?"

"No." Mack sighed. "Maybe. I get that we have to build, but I want it done in a way that respects our surroundings instead of hurts them."

"Like this place," Camille said, gesturing at Mack's home.

"Yeah."

"I understand," Camille said. "I think what you're doing is working. Trident is worried." Camille thought about Trident's offer to her father. She knew they were getting more and more desperate, and the trial hadn't even started. She didn't want her father anywhere near this fight. "I wish more homes were built like this, but the community needs jobs. Alabama needs the money and growth that these developers bring."

"The jobs are temporary. The damage is permanent."

"We're on opposite sides of this, Mack. Because of my father. I understand what you're doing, but I'm going to have to fight it."

"Why you?" Mack asked. "This is Trident's fight, and I'm sorry your father is wrapped up in it, but that still doesn't have to involve you."

"Yes, it does. He's my father. And now I'm also his lawyer."

Mack looked up quickly.

Camille nodded her head. "It's another reason why I wanted to see you today. I needed to tell you before the settlement conference."

"Well, I guess that's good news," Mack said as he smiled.

"How is that possibly good news?" Camille felt his eyes on her body.

"I've got something to look forward to. I've only imagined what you would look like in one of those business suits. Looks like I'm going to get to see the real thing tomorrow."

"Mack, don't joke. This whole situation is a mess." Camille sighed. "Nothing about this is easy."

"I'm not interested in easy." Mack said, approaching Camille.

She swallowed hard and asked, "What are you interested in?"

"I'm interested in you." Mack slid a hand around Camille's waist and pulled her body against his. He brought his mouth down hard on top of hers. There was so much urgency on both sides. Everything Camille had been holding back, for weeks, for months, since the first time she'd seen Mack smiling, came erupting to the surface. Camille's arms wrapped tightly around Mack's neck, lifting her up on her toes as his lips continued moving over hers.

Mack slid his hands lower, past Camille's hips. She instinctively wrapped her legs around his body as he pressed her against the railing. She found herself breathless at the feeling of his hands on her body, his lips moving from her mouth to the crook of her neck.

Camille dug her fingers into his back and squeezed her legs tighter around his waist. Mack whispered, "Camille, you're driving me mad."

Camille lost all restraint, wanting to feel every inch of his hard body. Mack moved one hand upward, his rough palm teasing her torso. He wrapped his hand in the tangle of her hair and crushed his mouth against hers again. She let out a moan as he nipped at her bottom lip.

Mack slowly pulled back, looking into Camille's hot, hazy eyes that were now a steely blue. Camille wasn't sure what he was going to do next, but she was breathless waiting to find out. Mack slowly let Camille's body slide down against his until her feet were back on the ground. He kissed her again, this time slowly, gently, and left his hands cupping her face.

She moved a hand onto his chest. He clasped her other hand, entwining their fingers.

Camille shook her head. "I don't know what's wrong with me."

A slow grin crept across Mack's face. "Nothing wrong from where I'm standing."

"We're in the middle of a lawsuit. I have a child at home, parents who have everything to lose, and I'm standing here kissing you." She pointed a finger at him. "You are impacting my good judgment."

"Well, only seems fair, because you're impacting a lot of me." He raised his eyebrows and smirked.

"I have to go," Camille said.

"I know," Mack said, leaning back against the railing.

"Good bye, Mack."

"See you around, Camille."

Camille walked slowly down the stairs and out of Mack's house toward her car. She sat for a moment, letting the engine run and cooling off the car, cooling off herself. She glanced down at her phone and saw a notification from the court.

She opened the message slowly, taking a deep breath as she began reading the judge's order. She read the words over and over, eventually slumping against the steering wheel. They'd lost the motion to dismiss. Her father was still in the lawsuit.

Camille drove away as the reality set in; to save her father, she had to fight Mack. She had to forget whatever had just happened between the two of them and focus on what mattered—protecting her family.

28

CAMILLE COULD FEEL HER nerves building as she walked into the conference room. She hadn't slept much the night before. She'd stayed up late with her father, preparing for the meeting and weighing their strategies. Settlement conferences were mostly a formality, mandated by the judge. Camille and Sam had decided that their best strategy was to use the conference to gather information and try to distance themselves from Trident as much as possible.

Camille looked around the room, and her palms started to sweat. Trident's lawyers were there, an army of environmental and insurance defense counsel, as well as a few of Trident's top executives. It was an intimidating group. The dozen men in suits were lined up along the far wall. Camille took a deep breath before walking down the line and introducing herself as Sam's counsel. Camille and Sam sat, waiting silently for the meeting to start. There was no small talk with Trident, no coordination before the plaintiffs arrived. Camille looked at her father, who was twisting and untwisting a paper clip, occupying his hands so he could avoid eye contact with everyone else in the room.

A few minutes later, Mack walked in. Camille had to bite back a smile. The entire room was in business suits and Mack looked like he had just stepped off his boat. He had sunglasses pushed up on top of his head, a T-shirt, and shorts. Not even a lawsuit could make him into something he wasn't.

He was accompanied by one lawyer, and Mack laughed when he saw Trident's army standing before him.

"We're outnumbered, Chuck," Mack said, holding up his hands in mock surrender. The man standing next to Mack was Chuck Billings, Mack's lawyer from Preston Crane. Chuck was a well-respected litigator, the head of Preston Crane's Seattle office. Camille found herself inadvertently sitting straighter knowing Chuck was in the room. Camille had done her research, and she knew he was one of the best lawyers Mack could have at his side.

Chuck shrugged his shoulders. "Not the first time, Mack."

Trident's lead lawyer stepped forward, eyeing Mack's attire with a judgmental glance before he turned to Chuck and said, "We were surprised you flew in from Seattle for this conference."

Chuck put an arm around Mack's shoulders as he said, "Well, Mack promised to take me fishing, so I figured I could afford a few days out of the office. Nice to meet all of you in person. Those videoconferences are always so formal."

The pleasantries stopped there, and Trident's legal team resumed their stoic expressions, sitting quickly and shuffling papers back and forth.

Mack and Chuck walked toward Camille and her father. They introduced themselves, and as everyone was getting settled, Mack whispered in Camille's ear, "You look even better in that suit than I imagined."

Camille shot him a look, the same look she reserved for Willa when she was negotiating bedtime, and Mack replied with a sheepish grin.

"You couldn't find a suit?" Camille asked, eyebrows raised.

"Nah. Don't own one. Told you the corporate life wasn't for me," Mack said, sitting.

Trident's lead lawyer, Sean Banks, began introducing his team and then kicked off the meeting. "As everyone knows, the judge requires settlement conferences so that parties can agree on as many issues as possible before bringing them before the court. The judge has outlined a series of tasks—first and foremost, discussing a settlement on the merits to avoid litigation. I know I speak for everyone in this room when I say that we all hope to avoid any waste of the court's resources and that settlement is in everyone's best interests."

Camille stopped herself from rolling her eyes. It was laughable that any of these parties wanted to settle. They wanted to punish the other side as much as possible. Camille knew the judge was going to receive an unsatisfactory report.

Mr. Banks continued, "This lawsuit is completely without merit. Trident Development received a permit for the clearing of the land along the Fish River. Neither the local authorities nor the federal authorities have brought any action against Trident. The small group of citizens represented by Mr. Mack Phillips are clearly wasting the court's resources and harming Trident by bringing this frivolous claim."

Chuck put his hands behind his head, leaned back, and said, "You may have had a permit for clearing the land, but that permit doesn't allow you to fill the river with mud. You violated the water quality standards, plain and simple. But please, argue that you had a permit. We can all use a good laugh once in a while."

Camille was impressed. Chuck easily dismissed one of Trident's strongest arguments while avoiding the other more difficult issue. Citizens were allowed to sue, but the fact that the government hadn't brought an action against Trident made the case more difficult for Mack, especially in a place like Alabama, where juries were suspicious of any individual acting like they knew better than the government.

The Trident team started whispering back and forth. A young lawyer grabbed a folder of papers and pulled out a sheet to pass down the table.

Mr. Banks said, "There has been a history of poor water quality along the Fish River, long before Trident purchased any property. The levels have been elevated off and on for years. Wastewater, upstream damage, even Mother Nature herself; it's hard to know the true culprit. There was a storm right around the time that you allege Trident caused this damage that likely led to much of the sediment in the water. It will be very difficult for you to prove that Trident's actions caused the violation."

Chuck looked around the room, nodding his head, and then said, "Yes, that sure will be difficult, won't it, Mack?"

"Yep," Mack said. "We should probably give up, Chuck. Should we go fishing now?"

They both started to stand, but Chuck grabbed Mack's arm as he said, "But wait, what about the photographs?" They sat together, nodding their heads with dramatic exaggeration.

"Let's dismiss with the theatrics," Mr. Banks said. "If there is evidence you would like to discuss, let's do that like the professionals we are."

Sam whispered into Camille's ear, asking, "What photographs?"

Camille turned toward her father and whispered back, "I don't know. There aren't any photographs in evidence, just the soil and water samples."

Chuck sighed as he continued, "We certainly don't have to do this, but I'm feeling generous. How about you, Mack?"

"I'm a very generous person," Mack said, raising his eyebrows at Camille.

It was frustrating how much Mack and Chuck were enjoying themselves, and yet Camille couldn't stop watching them. She leaned forward, eager to see whatever evidence they were going to reveal.

Chuck pulled a folder of photographs out of his briefcase and started passing copies across the table. "These are photographs of the river abutting the construction site from September and early October of last year. It's a beautiful site."

Everyone looked through the pictures, seeing little difference from photo to photo. There were dozens in the stack.

Chuck pulled out another folder and passed those copies across the table. He started laying photographs across the conference room table, slapping one down harder than the next. "This is the day before the clearing. This is the day after. This is the week after. The month after." The line of pictures got worse and worse, aerial shots showing the mud seeping out of the construction site and flowing into the river. Compared to the shots from September, the river had changed colors completely.

As everyone in the room stared at the photographs, Chuck casually walked toward the window, hands in his pockets, relaxed. "You see, expert reports and water samples can get confusing for juries. But photographs? Images like these stick in people's heads."

Trident's CEO stood up, pointing his finger at Mack. "You were setting us up. You were planning this lawsuit all along."

Mack was leaning back in his chair, his arms casually crossed against his chest. He spoke softly but clearly. "No, I was watching. That's all. That's my home. My home you filled up with mud."

"This is entrapment," Trident's CEO yelled across the room.

"Now that's a mighty big word," Chuck said, sitting next to Mack. "My client here happened to take some pictures, some pictures from his own backyard. Nothing illegal about that. The only violations I see are the ones your company made in destroying this beautiful river."

Trident's CEO was stalking the conference room like a predator. Mr. Banks put his hand on his client's shoulder and said, "We will challenge the authenticity of these pictures. Colors, images can be manipulated. Mr. Phillips clearly had a litigious agenda months before Trident set foot on the Fish River. Juries won't look kindly on that either. These photographs don't concern me in the least."

Camille looked over at her father, who was staring at the pictures with a sorrowful intensity. Sam's voice began shaking as he spoke. "They sure as hell concern me."

Trident's CEO narrowed his eyes at Sam and said, "I'd be careful if I were you, Sam. Don't forget which side of this lawsuit you're on."

Sam turned to Mack. "I knew it was bad, but I didn't know the extent. I guess I didn't want to know. How do we even begin to repair this damage?"

Mr. Banks interjected, "We do not repair this damage, because this is not the responsibility of Trident or its partner. Ms. Taylor, please advise your client to be careful with his words."

Camille looked at her father, who was still intently focused on the photographs. She said, "I think you should be advising your own client to be more careful. Trident's lack of care is the reason why all of us are sitting around this table today."

"Ms. Taylor, you are new to this case and perhaps you are forgetting which side you are representing, but your client is also being sued for alleged damage to the river," Mr. Banks said, with a shake of his head.

"I'm very aware who I represent and our position. Samuel Graves continues to argue that any harm to the river was caused by the actions of Trident and Trident alone. Should Mr. Graves have any legal liability, that liability is minimal," Camille said.

Mr. Banks scoffed as he said, "The judge didn't agree with that argument."

Camille stood her ground, speaking clearly and with authority. "We will not defend Trident's actions, only our financial responsibility for those actions."

Chuck nodded toward Camille and then turned to Mr. Banks as he said, "Your own codefendant knows your arguments are pointless. Want to test out any other strategies? Or should we start working through the court's checklist of what we're supposed to accomplish today?"

"It is very clear that nothing is going to get accomplished today. Trident will never admit liability for any alleged harm to the Fish River," Trident's CEO said.

Mack stared at Trident's CEO. "You destroyed the river. I don't care how long it takes. I won't stop until you fix it. Until you realize you can't treat this place as a dumping ground."

Mr. Banks looked back and forth between the two men, Mack and Trident's CEO staring at each other with a heated intensity. There was anger bubbling, and they were both working hard to restrain its escape.

Chuck cleared his throat. "I think this might be a good time for a break. Let's all take fifteen minutes, then we can work through the scheduling issues. Settlement on the merits is not going to happen today."

Trident's lawyers quickly gathered their files and moved to a conference room across the hall, strategizing like they were preparing for battle.

Camille sat next to her father. His hands were shaking as he continued looking through Mack's photographs.

Sam turned to Mack. "How do we fix this? Can it be fixed?"

Mack paused, considering his words carefully. "No. It will never be same. The amount of mud that flowed into the river is more than would have flowed in two hundred years under natural conditions. At least that's what my experts tell me. We can't fix all the damage, but we can fix some of it."

Sam looked at Mack. "Then let's do that. You two talk and figure out a way for me to start being a part of the solution instead of the problem."

Camille saw her father's hands were still shaking as he stood up. "I'm going to get some fresh air, Cammy. I'll meet you back in here." Camille put her hand over her father's, trying to reassure him.

"Okay, Dad." The room cleared. Mack's lawyer stepped out to take a call. Camille walked over to the window, knowing Mack was the only person left in the room, feeling his presence vibrate on her skin.

"You okay?" Mack asked.

"Yeah. These things are always tedious," Camille said, closing her eyes.

"But not all settlement conferences involve your father. How are you holding up?" Mack rubbed the small of her back, and Camille relaxed into his hand before jerking her eyes open and taking a protective step backward.

"Honestly. I'm worried. I feel like he's aged years in the last few months. The stress of lawsuits . . . I'm used to it, he's not. It's a lot for someone his age. I think he's been avoiding the site, avoiding the damage to protect himself. Today was difficult for him to see."

"It didn't seem to impact the Trident team at all," Mack said, shaking his head. "I don't know what it will take to convince those guys."

"Money. That's what it will take," Camille said. "I'm just worried about how much more harm the river will have to take."

"I know," Mack said. "Every day this lawsuit drags on is another day that more mud fills the water. The construction site is frozen; Trident won't remedy anything as long as the lawsuit is pending."

Camille nodded. "Yes, but that hurts them more than you. They can't sell a single lot, can't build a single home while the lawsuit is pending. Their investment is frozen."

Mack nodded back. "If we settle, they'll do it again. It won't punish them the way they need to be punished."

Camille looked into his eyes. "What do you want more? To punish them, or to protect the river?" She turned as Chuck walked back into the room. "I'm going to leave you two to chat. I could use some fresh air too," she said, and headed outside to find her father, intent on providing him with some reassurance that everything would work out, reassurance she needed too.

Camille found her father sitting on a bench outside the office building. He was still twisting the paper clip as he patted the open seat. Camille sat next to her father and leaned her head on his shoulder.

Sam said, "I'm glad you're in there next to me. Thank you, Cammy."

"We will figure this out, Dad."

Sam shrugged his shoulders and joked, "What would I have done in retirement anyway? Driven your mother crazy, probably. I'll keep working. I'll do whatever it takes to make this right."

"I love you, Dad."

"Love you too," Sam said, hugging his daughter close.

A few minutes later, one of the junior lawyers on Trident's team walked over, and Camille and Sam stood abruptly. The lawyer said, "The plaintiffs have asked for a longer break. We will resume at two PM."

Camille asked, "Why? What's happening?"

The Trident lawyer shrugged. "They asked to set up a videoconference and said they'd need more time. That's all I know," he said as he walked away.

Sam wrapped his arm around Camille's shoulders and said, "Should we grab some lunch?"

"I don't have much of an appetite," Camille said.

"Well, I do, and I'm not sitting on this bench for two hours. I need a muffuletta sandwich from Pete's."

"Do they still have those beignets for dessert?" Camille asked.

"Not much of an appetite, huh?"

"I can always eat beignets."

It turned out fried dough and powdered sugar were the perfect distraction from a tense settlement negotiation. By the time Sam and Camille got back to the office building, they'd tried to put the tension of the morning behind them.

As they walked into the conference room, they realized they were the only ones in a good mood. The Trident team

THE RIVER RUNS SOUTH 267

seemed particularly annoyed by the extended break. The joviality between Mack and Chuck that had been present all morning had been erased. Everyone was serious, and Camille and Sam took their seats at the table with a feeling of dread.

"Now that all the parties are present," Mr. Banks said. "We can resume. Should we begin with discussing the schedule for discovery?"

"Not yet," Chuck said. "We'd like to revisit settlement on the merits."

"We are done with your theatrics," Mr. Banks said. "We made that clear before the break. Whatever you have up your sleeve is of no interest to us. You can file your evidence with the court."

Chuck sighed as he said, "If I were you, I'd listen for once." He looked across the table, the look of a seasoned litigator that achieved its purpose. The room was silent.

Chuck continued, "Against my advice, my client would like to offer terms of settlement. Very generous terms of settlement. As you know, if we were to win this lawsuit, Trident's costs would be significant. We could seek financial penalties, fees for compliance and monitoring, reimbursement of all costs associated with the enforcement, including the expert fees and legal fees. This is a very expensive mess you created." Chuck stared at Trident's CEO.

Chuck passed a piece of paper across the table to Mr. Banks and then handed another to Camille. "These are the steps our experts have said are necessary to repair the damage caused by Trident, including estimates of the costs. Obviously, the slope into the river will need to be stabilized, new grading of the land, and the area will have to be replanted. You'll see the total at the bottom, including the cost of future monitoring."

Trident's team immediately swept into action. Camille knew they likely had a file of their own, from other experts with other line items, their estimation of the cost to mitigate the damage they'd caused.

"We are willing to drop the lawsuit if these steps are taken," Chuck said. "Don't show me a report that says you can get away with less. This list is what you must do if you want this lawsuit to go away so that you can resume building your lovely riverfront community. You have one hour to consider our offer, and then it expires." Chuck stood to leave, but Mack grabbed his arm.

Mack said, "Tell them the other requirement, Chuck."

Chuck looked over at Camille and Sam, shaking his head. Camille was stunned. She had been listening to Chuck's offer, paralyzed with confusion. She couldn't have predicted any of this, and she had no idea what was coming next.

"Mr. Phillips and the other plaintiffs want to ensure that the remedy cost is assumed by Trident and Trident alone. Samuel Graves Landscape is welcome to volunteer their time and services, but they're not obligated to pay anything to fix this damage. Trident pays for it all or no deal," Chuck said.

Chuck tapped Mack on the shoulder and said, "Let's give them the room to discuss. I need to get something to eat."

The Trident team immediately started whispering, a flurry of action with papers being passed back and forth, heads shaking and nodding in equal enthusiasm.

Sam turned to Camille and asked, "What just happened?"

Camille shrugged her shoulders. "I don't know. I've never seen anything like this."

Mr. Banks cleared his throat and said, "Ms. Taylor, Mr. Graves, can you please give us the room? Apparently we have a tight timeline and need to discuss this offer privately with our client."

Camille and Sam nodded their heads and quickly walked outside.

Camille saw Mack and Chuck walking toward Mack's truck. Mack turned, gesturing to Chuck that he needed a minute as he approached Camille. Sam held back and Camille joined Mack.

"What happened back there?" Camille asked.

"Hopefully, the right thing," Mack said. "We'll see if they accept."

"They'd be fools not to," Camille said. "Why would you do that?" she asked. "If this goes to trial, you could win. You proved that this morning."

Mack nodded. "Maybe. But I care more about the river than winning. I care about this community." He pointed toward Camille's father. "This wasn't about hurting good people. I can't lose sight of that just because I want to punish Trident." Mack rubbed the back of his neck. "It's a long game. I should have done this earlier. You helped me see that today. Trident knows we're watching now; hopefully, they'll think twice before doing something like this again. If not, I'll catch them."

Chuck yelled across the parking lot, "Mack, I'm starving. Let's go."

Mack shook his head and smiled at Camille. "I'll see you in an hour."

Sam joined Camille as they watched Mack drive away. "So, what do we do now?" Sam asked.

"We wait," Camille said.

Toward the end of the hour, Camille and Sam headed back into the conference room. It was a hard group to read, and Camille searched their faces for any indication of what they had decided.

They could hear Mack's and Chuck's laughter before they even entered the room. As soon as they opened the door, Mr. Banks stood. All eyes focused on the Trident side of the table and their announcement.

Mr. Banks picked up a piece of paper and opened his mouth, but Chuck interrupted. "Don't try to negotiate line items, Banks. It's a yes or a no. We've wasted enough time already."

Mr. Banks looked over to his client, who gave a subtle nod of his head before crossing his arms.

Mr. Banks said, "We accept your terms. I'll have my associate draft the settlement agreement."

Chuck sighed. "Well, that's it, then." He reached out and shook Mr. Banks's hand. Camille looked over to Mack, unable to read his face, to discern whether he was regretful or relived.

Trident's CEO walked out of the room without exchanging any words with anyone. The rest of the team lingered, discussing the logistics.

Mr. Banks cleared his throat. "Mr. Graves, I believe you are free to go. This lawsuit is no longer any of your concern."

Camille and Sam stood and walked slowly out of the room. Before she left, Camille looked back at Mack, who gave her a subtle nod of his head and a half smile before turning back to the conference room table.

Once they were outside, Sam turned to his daughter, their eyes widening before they fell into each other with hugs and laughter.

Sam said, "Cammy, I can't believe it. Is it over? Is this nightmare really over?"

"For you, yes," Camille said. "It's over, Dad."

She looked at her father, his face so full of joy, his lip quivering as the happy tears flowed after so much stress and worry. "Let's go home," Sam said.

Camille and Sam drove in stunned silence. When they got home, Marion was nervously sweeping the front porch, waiting for them to return.

Sam couldn't contain his excitement. He spun his wife in a circle as he said, "It's over, Marion. It's over."

Sam spent the next hour relaying the events of the day. Marion wavered between tears and laughter, eventually popping a bottle of champagne and settling into Sam's arms. Willa was oblivious to the released tension, happily doing cartwheels across the lawn.

Marion said, "I still can't believe it. All of this worry, for months. It's finally lifted."

"I know, Mom," Camille said. "I hate that I brought this on you two."

"Camille, what are you talking about?" Sam said.

"If you hadn't been with me in DC, none of this would have happened. It was my fault. I'm just glad it's over."

Sam leaned forward, staring intently at Camille. "None of this was your fault. But it's thanks to you that it's all over. You saved us."

"No, that was Mack," Camille said, her mind wandering.

Marion swallowed as she said, "I misjudged him. I owe him an apology."

Camille smiled at her mother, knowing that she was quick to judge, quick to forgive, and quick to apologize. That was her mother.

"There's somewhere I need to go," Camille said. "I'll be back in a few hours. Is that okay?"

Sam walked toward his daughter, put his hand on top of hers, and said, "Tell him I said thanks."

"I will," Camille replied.

She drove straight to Mack's house, turning down his driveway, dizzy from all that had happened since she'd been there the day before.

She parked her car and looked up to see Mack standing at the top of the steps. He walked down slowly and met Camille, pulling her into a tight hug.

She exhaled in his arms, feeling their warm strength and comfort wrap around her body. She looked up as he bent toward her face, kissing her softly, holding her tightly, both of them afraid to let go after so much waiting. They didn't exchange words. There was nothing to say. They could finally stand together without any lawsuit, without any guilt, without any regrets between them. They stood together as the sun set over the Fish River.

29

CAMILLE STOOD IN FRONT of the stove while Willa peppered her with questions.

"So, we sit, and eat on a blanket, and listen to music? What kind of music?"

"Ummm . . . tonight is show tunes," Camille said. "Those old movies that Nana likes to watch where people burst into song, except there won't be anyone singing."

"Momma, this sounds awful," Willa said, her lip protruding.

"I agree. Pops in the Park may be more of an adult-focused evening, but there are lots of good things for you, like this dinner I'm packing that we get to eat with our hands, on the ground, which I know you love. Plus most of the kids end up playing tag and hide-and-seek, so there will be lots of other bored kids your age that want to play."

Willa sighed deeply and said, "Okay. I guess I'll go. But I need to pack my flashlight in case the hide-and-seek game gets intense."

Camille kissed Willa on top of her head. "That is an excellent idea. Thank you for being such a good sport. Nana is really looking forward to this."

"Sometimes we have to do things for family that we don't want to do, but we do it anyway because we love them, right, Momma?"

"Yes. Although I'm kind of looking forward to this. I like a good picnic."

"I like that part too. You are probably looking forward to seeing other grown-ups, right?"

"Yes," Camille said. It had been a week since her father had been dismissed from the lawsuit, and she'd seen Mack almost every night, usually after Willa was in bed. Tonight would be their first time together with her family. She knew her parents had softened to Mack and she knew Willa was crazy about him, but she was still nervous about the evening.

"Mack will be there tonight," Camille said. "Is that okay?"

Willa nodded her head enthusiastically. "I'm going to pack Go Fish too. He'll probably like to play that game."

Camille smiled as Willa ran off. She continued packing the picnic dinner. Pops in the Park was one of her favorite traditions. The park on the bluff overlooking the bay held monthly concerts, and the whole town showed up. The music changed every month, and over the years the picnics had become more and more elaborate. Most families treated it like a tailgate, setting up elaborate chair arrangements, competing over more extravagant dinner spreads.

Marion packed a separate bag with an old quilt, cloth napkins, silverware, and plates. Camille always thought it was ridiculous to have a picnic with real plates. The rest of the world made reasonable choices, like using something disposable when you were eating dinner in a park. But not Marion Graves. She always insisted on making things as nice as possible.

Sam was in charge of the chairs. He had upgraded their beach chairs to reclining models with attached side tables. Marion had insisted they were worth the investment because the typical beach chair only had a cupholder, and those didn't work for wineglasses. Camille knew there was no point in explaining to her mother that most people didn't drink out of a wineglass at the beach. At some point, Sam must have bought a miniature version of the beach chairs for Willa. Or maybe they'd always had it, hoping she and Camille would eventually come for a visit. Camille tried not to beat herself up about the fact that they had only come down here after Ben died. They were here now, and Willa was blossoming with the love of her grandparents.

Sam was packing the car as Camille's phone rang. She answered it, barely registering the DC area code.

"Hello," Camille said.

"Camille, it's Duncan Hatch. Did I catch you at a bad time? I was hoping to chat with you for a few minutes."

Camille walked around the back of the house, searching for a private spot to take the call. It was almost September. She should have expected Duncan's call, but it still caught her off guard. Camille immediately cleared her throat and smoothed her dress, somehow trying to impress a voice on the other end of the phone. It was ridiculous, but a hard habit to break. Camille had spent so many years trying to impress Duncan, wondering what he thought about her hours, her client originations, the feedback she received from clients and associates. She shook her head, trying to gather herself.

Duncan said, "I hope you've had a nice summer with your parents. How's the weather?"

"Hot," Camille said. "Is everything okay?" She wasn't used to small talk with Duncan Hatch.

"Oh yes, I just want to catch up."

Camille hesitated, then said, "Duncan, I've never known you to take any meeting without a specific agenda. Want to give me a preview of this one?"

He chuckled. "You were always direct. Your clients love that, you know," Duncan continued, fumbling his words in a way that put Camille at ease. He sounded nervous, which was a nice reversal.

"The firm wants you to take all the time you need," Duncan said. "But we wanted to let you know about an opportunity. It's up to you, of course. The client has asked for you specifically. We explained that you're on leave, but they want you. It turns out, most of your clients just want you. It has not been an easy process finding suitable replacements for your cases, Camille. You're not an easy person to replace."

Camille was taken aback. She hadn't expected to hear from Duncan, and she certainly hadn't expected this kind of news. "Well, that's nice to hear," Camille said.

Duncan told her about the assignment. It was the type of client Camille had always wanted to work with—developing a cutting-edge program with substantial resources. A dream job, really. She should have been thrilled.

Duncan outlined a timeline for her return, at full partner status, with a base compensation increase to accommodate the anticipated workload. A year ago, if Duncan had told her about this client and the raise, she would have run home to tell Ben the good news. They would have opened a bottle of champagne and celebrated. But now all Camille could think about was Willa. How would she travel and do all the site visits at the client's international offices? She would have to hire a live-in nanny. This job would require long hours; there was no way to have a part-time position with an assignment like this. Duncan mentioned that there was a pipeline of work that could flow from it. For a junior partner, there was nothing better than hearing that you had a steady flow of client-facing assignments. Camille's mind spun as she considered the logistics, the schedules, the constant state of juggling. Her heart raced at the possibility.

She told Duncan she needed a day or two to think about it. They made plans to speak on the phone by the end of the week and said their good-byes.

Camille made a mental pros-and-cons list as she walked to the car.

"Who was that?" Marion asked.

"It was nothing," Camille said, wanting to avoid any discussion of the conversation, especially with her mother. When Marion raised her eyebrows, Camille whispered, "We can talk about it later. We don't want to be late."

Marion and Sam exchanged glances but didn't push further. Camille sat in the back seat next to Willa, her mind running in circles.

They drove into town and lucked out, finding a parking spot near the park. There were already dozens of families setting up. Marion started complaining right away. "Sam, I told you we needed to get here earlier. I do not want to end up by those tall grasses. You know the mosquitoes are awful over there."

"Marion, I'm aware of the mosquito situation. I packed the citronella candles and the bug spray." Sam gestured across the park. "Look, we're fine. Our usual spot is waiting for us."

Camille and Willa hung back, letting Sam and Marion handle the setup, since it was clearly a task they took seriously.

Willa tugged on Camille's hand. "Momma, I don't see many kids here. I see a lot of old people."

Camille scanned the crowd and agreed with her daughter. "I'm sure they're on their way." Camille hoped that was true; otherwise, it was going to be a long evening for Willa.

Camille picked up the picnic basket, and they started walking across the park to the spot her parents had picked. Camille felt a hand on her back. She turned around to see Mack.

"Want some help carrying that?" he asked.

Willa squealed, "Mack! I'm so happy you're here! I didn't think any of my friends would be here tonight. This place is full of old people like Nana and Gramps."

"Willa, please don't call Nana old. She might get her feelings hurt."

"But why, Momma? She is old. It's just a fact."

Mack chuckled. Then he turned and looked at Camille.

She was wearing a white linen dress with thin straps and tortoiseshell buttons down the front. An outdoor picnic at the end of the summer in Alabama limited clothing options, and the dress was the coolest item Camille could think of besides her bathing suit. Her hair was thrown up in a messy pile on top of her head, rogue strands escaping to soak up the early evening humidity.

Mack gave her a quick kiss on the cheek and said, "You look beautiful."

Willa quickly chimed in, "She does look beautiful. She even took a shower again!"

Camille blushed. "Don't give away all of my beauty secrets, Willa."

"Should we join your parents?" Mack asked.

Camille nodded. "Are you sure you're ready for this?"

Mack nodded back, reaching out to touch Camille's face, weaving his fingers into her hair before releasing her. "Yes, Camille, I'm ready."

Willa looked up and asked, "Mack, do you know how to play Go Fish? I brought cards. We can eat, and then play, and then you can tell me about your fishing boat, and then maybe Mom will give us dessert."

Having a conversation with a six-year-old was like getting pelted in a game of dodgeball, but Mack took it in stride. He looked down at Willa and said, "That sounds like an excellent plan."

"I'm so happy you're finally having dinner with us," Willa declared. She grabbed Mack's hand. Mack gave her a broad smile as they walked across the park.

Camille's heart hitched slightly, seeing Willa holding a man's hand—the hand of a man who wasn't Ben. Seeing the way Mack was so open and accepting of Willa and the way Willa reached out for him. Camille felt a swirl of discomfort and hope, and let the two emotions sit next to each other as she walked toward her parents.

Marion and Sam were bickering over chair placement when Willa plopped in the middle of the blanket.

"Nana, Gramps, look who's here!" Willa said.

Marion and Sam looked up and saw Mack standing at the edge of the blanket. He waved subtly and said, "Hi, Mr. and Mrs. Graves. How are you guys doing this evening?"

Marion stopped, unprepared and unsure, but Sam nodded his head and stepped forward, shaking Mack's hand.

"I owe you a great deal of thanks, young man," Sam said, emotion creaking out of his voice.

"No, sir," Mack said. "No thanks needed. It was the right thing to do. The right thing for the river."

Marion walked over and wrapped Mack in a giant hug. "You have no idea what you have done for us. Thank you so much."

Sam cleared his throat. "Well, grab a seat, Mack. Camille's fixed enough food for a football team. How's the fishing these days?"

Camille exhaled. She saw the respect in her father's eyes, the forgiveness, the gratitude. She saw her mother trying to gather herself from the uncharacteristic display of emotion. Camille looked from her parents to Mack and smiled, hopeful for their new beginning.

Mack said, "The fishing is excellent. No jubilee yet, but we've had some good catches recently."

"What's a jubilee?" Willa asked.

Sam smiled. "I'll let the professional explain that one. It's a pretty special happening in these parts."

Mack took a deep breath, looking relieved to have the assignment as a distraction from the introduction to Camille's parents. He plopped down on the blanket next to Willa and started explaining. "Jubilee is something that only happens right here, in this spot along Mobile Bay, between Point Clear and Daphne. Some years, if we're lucky, we might have two jubilees, but usually it happens once a summer."

"What happens?" Willa impatiently asked.

"I'm getting to it," Mack said. "Early in the morning, while most people are asleep, all the fish and shrimp and crabs in the whole bay start swimming right for the bank. They swim ashore, and you can walk out with a bucket and scoop it full of fish. Some people will fill up their whole truck with fish from a good jubilee."

"If everyone is asleep when this happens, how do you catch any fish?" Willa asked.

"Oh, everyone is on the lookout for a jubilee. The fishermen, the weathermen, the local news will even guess when the jubilee is coming. When the fish start swimming up, the phones go crazy and everyone calls everyone they know."

Camille smiled, remembering all the years when her parents would pull her out of bed and they would wade into the water in their pajamas to scoop up fish and shrimp.

"Why do the fish do that?" Will asked.

Sam chimed in, "Because they know that Fairhope, Alabama, is the most special place in the world, and all the fish in the ocean want to come visit."

"Gramps, that's a silly answer. I want the science answer."

Camille raised her eyebrows at her father, who continued to be surprised by his precocious granddaughter.

Mack was equally impressed and excited. "Well, Willa, it turns out that I happen to have lots of information on the science answer. Jubilee is something I have been interested in since I was your age. In fact, it was one of the things that made me want to study animals and the ocean."

"I thought you owned a fish shop," Willa said.

"Well, I do, but I also spent a lot of years studying and learning everything I could about how creatures live in the oceans. Then I taught some college students what I learned."

"Really?" Marion asked.

Mack nodded and continued explaining the jubilee to Willa, patiently answering all her questions about weather conditions and how those impacted the oxygen in the bay, forcing the fish to the surface.

Camille looked over to her mother, who was quietly watching Mack. Camille whispered, "He's not what you thought, is he?"

Marion shook her head. "No. He is full of surprises."

Camille started unpacking the food. She'd made fried chicken with quick-pickled cucumbers, a potato salad with capers and Dijon mustard, and a kale salad with bacon, golden raisins, and the herbed goat cheese from Elberta. Camille had spent the morning making homemade cheese crackers with Willa for snacking. For dessert, she had packed mason jars of banana pudding, topping each jar with homemade whipped cream. Camille pulled out a juice box for Willa and a bottle of wine. The town seemed to turn a blind eye to the liquor laws on the night of Pops in the Park.

Once everyone had a plate and started digging into the dinner, Camille relaxed.

"The food is excellent, Camille. Willa was right; you are an amazing chef." Mack patted her hand. The gesture did not go unnoticed by Marion, who smiled.

After they finished eating, Sam rubbed Marion's knee and said, "We should go say hello to the neighbors, shouldn't we?"

"Yes, we should," Marion said, reaching for her husband's hand.

Willa pulled out her cards and played Go Fish for approximately three minutes before her attention span waned and she found kids her age and begged to play with them. Camille agreed and found herself alone on the picnic blanket with Mack.

Mack reached over and put his hand on top of Camille's, weaving his fingers into hers. It sent a bolt of electricity through her skin. Even this simple gesture had the ability to set off all her senses. Suddenly, the space between their shoulders seemed to evaporate. She couldn't stop staring at the way his wavy hair peeked out from the edges of his baseball cap. She could even smell the fresh soap from his faded blue T-shirt. *He must wash his clothes in Gain*, she thought, her mind wandering from laundry detergent to what the shirt would look like off his body. She bit her lip before coming back to her senses. It was a dangerous thing to be outside in a public park, surrounded by people, including your parents and your daughter, having thoughts like that about the man sitting next to you.

The band was starting to warm up as the sun set. It was a beautiful summer night, and Camille leaned back, enjoying the quiet for a few moments. She looked around the park. Her parents were chatting happily with their friends, more relaxed than Camille had seen them all summer. Leslie and her family should arrive soon, joining them for the picnic. Mack waved as groups passed by, providing a running commentary on his customers and fishing buddies. Willa was squealing with laughter as she played chase with a group of children.

Camille leaned in and kissed Mack quickly, but it was enough to suck her breath away. "I have to make a quick phone call. Is that okay?"

"Oh, sure. I'll just be here enjoying this music," Mack said, with only a hint of sarcasm.

Camille laughed as she walked toward the bluff. It was a quiet spot. The sun was leaving streaks of pinks and purples across the sky. Camille looked out over the water, knowing that no place would ever feel as good as home.

Camille dialed Duncan's number and got his voice mail. She said the things she was supposed to say, thanking him for the opportunity. Then she said the only thing that mattered: "I quit."

❖ 30 ❖

A year later

CAMILLE STEPPED OFF THE plane, happy to be home. As she and Willa loaded their luggage in the car, Camille called her mother. They'd only been gone two weeks, but Camille knew Marion was eager to see Willa.

Willa had spent two weeks being showered with love by Ben's parents. They alternated trips, Camille and Willa traveling to DC, Ben's parents visiting them in Fairhope. When Camille had first told them about her plans to move, tears were shed on both sides, but they'd found a way to make it work, to keep their connection.

Seeing Ben's parents was always full of emotion, but at the end of this visit, Ben's mother had squeezed Camille tightly and said, "You look good. It's so nice to see you like this. Ben would be proud of you."

Camille didn't miss Ben any less, but she'd found new things to love. Things that surrounded her grief so that the pain felt smaller.

Camille drove down Mobile Street, past her parents' bay cottage, and turned onto Fig Avenue. The neighborhood, nicknamed the "fruit and nut district" by locals, was one of Camille's favorites. She pulled into the driveway to find her parents waiting in the front yard. The two-story bungalow had been built in the forties. It needed work. It was one of the few older homes on the street that hadn't been renovated, but that was what Camille loved. Paint, sweat, and an updated bathroom were all in the plans, but for now, it was everything she needed.

Camille and Willa had moved in months ago, but they still didn't have much furniture and Camille wasn't sure if she was ever going to convince Willa to sleep in a bed again, she was having so much fun with the mattress on the floor. There was work ahead and decorating, but every time Camille saw the house, it felt perfect. Willa had picked the bedroom upstairs that looked out over the backyard. She wanted to paint her room like a rainbow, and Camille was still working on that negotiation.

Camille parked the car and joined her parents in the front yard. Willa ran over to hug her grandparents, quickly rattling off all the miniscule details about her weeks away.

Marion grabbed Willa's hand, and they walked to the back patio, laughing and giggling all the way.

Sam helped Camille unpack the car as he asked, "How was the trip?"

"Good. Exhausting, but good."

"We'll let you rest. Your mother just had to see Willa for a few minutes," Sam said. He shouted across the yard. "Marion, you said this would be a quick hello."

Marion and Willa rejoined Camille and Sam, still hugging each other tightly.

"Playdate at the playground tomorrow?" Marion asked Willa. Willa nodded.

"We'll let you guys get settled," Marion said. "We missed you both."

"We missed you too," Camille said, meaning it.

She smiled. Her relationship with her mother was far from perfect, but there was less fighting now. Fewer tears. They had realized that accepting each other was much easier than the constant criticism. They were both trying, and Sam was thrilled by the cease-fire. It turned out he was right: they had more in common than they'd thought. They were opposite sides of the same coin. Camille and her mother had been hosting monthly dinner parties, Camille handling the cooking and Marion handling all the decor. They made an excellent team when they stayed in their own lanes.

After her parents left and Camille finished unpacking their bags, she joined Willa outside, digging in her favorite pile of dirt. Camille heard the familiar rumbling of a truck and looked up to see Mack pulling into her driveway.

"Looks like we have another member of the welcome crew," Camille said.

"Mack!" Willa squealed.

Mack hopped out of his truck, his arms full of grocery bags. "I figured you two might be hungry. How do you feel about burgers on the grill?"

"Sounds perfect," Camille said.

Mack listened patiently as Willa described her adventures in DC. They grilled and ate and laughed, Camille feeling her body ache with how much she had missed Mack over the last few weeks. Willa escaped cleanup duty by claiming there was something she had to go do in her room.

As Mack picked up the last of the plates, he asked Camille, "So how do you feel? Was it hard being back?"

"Every trip gets a little easier. There were a lot of good memories in DC, but I like making good memories here more."

Mack picked up his beer. "To new plans."

Camille took a sip of her beer. "I can't believe it. This is . . ."

"Exactly where you are supposed to be," Mack said confidently.

"I guess it is."

Mack set his beer down and gave Camille a sideways glance. "Not to talk shop, but how did the meetings on the Hill go?"

Camille rolled her eyes. "You always want to talk shop."

He held up his hands in surrender. "I can't help it if I'm invested in my girlfriend's career."

Camille walked over to Mack and sat in his lap, wrapping her arms around his neck. She described her meetings with the EPA and the legislators. Over the past year, Camille had set up a practice in Fairhope, monitoring the rivers, watching for polluters, and suing when necessary. She knew the lawsuits were only one part of the solution; legislative reform was critical for real change. She was proud of her work, playing a small role in pushing the state forward in the direction it so badly needed to move.

There was an energy and excitement to her days. Willa loved tagging along, meeting with homeowners, advocacy groups, small businesses, everyone in the growing community of people who wanted to protect Alabama's rivers. It was the beginning of a long fight. Mack had been right about that, but Camille knew it was a fight she was meant to lead.

"It feels like we're moving in the right direction," Camille said. "It feels right."

Mack cocked his head to the side. "You know what also feels right?"

"What?"

"This," he said, wrapping his arm around Camille's waist and kissing her slowly.

Camille raised her eyebrows. "Willa is having a sleepover at my parents' house on Saturday."

"Does that mean we get to have a sleepover on Saturday?"

"Yes." Camille looked into Mack's eyes and smiled. "You know something else that feels right?"

"What?"

Camille bit her bottom lip and then smiled at Mack before saying, "Loving you."

Mack took a sip of his beer, nodding his head slowly. "Yep, I'm sure it does. You are one lucky woman."

"You are incredibly confident for a man who has been telling me he loves me for months. I thought this would be some bigger moment. The first time I say it to you."

"First time you said it with words. You've made me feel loved for a while now." He kissed her cheek and said, "See you Saturday night. I'll bring some grouper to grill."

"I'll make pancakes on Sunday."

"I guess that makes me the lucky one." He winked and then waved to Willa, who was peeking out her bedroom window as he hopped into his truck.

Camille was in love with a man who drove her mad in all the best possible ways.

The windows were open, the early fall breeze cooling the rooms. Camille could hear Willa playing a wildly imaginative game of battling frogs and snakes. At least Camille hoped it was imaginative.

Camille walked around the back of her house. It was hers, just hers. It was a mess, full of weeds and vines. She could envision what she wanted—a couple of beds near the house, some space for Willa to dig. Her dad would help her, but it would be hers.

She walked to the back and started working, pulling down the vines, smelling the honeysuckle, and smiling.

ACKNOWLEDGMENTS

I ALWAYS WANTED TO write, but with a legal career and three children, I didn't think it was a dream within possibility. Cue the pandemic. Like many families with young children, we struggled and ultimately pivoted. I paused my legal career while I stayed at home with our children and found myself stealing moments to write this story. At a time of personal and global upheaval, writing this book was a complete joy, bringing hope into a confusing time.

The story on my computer never would have become the book in your hands without the help of so many wonderful people.

My agent, Dani Segelbaum, took a chance on a writer in her giant slush pile and kicked off this adventure. I'm grateful for her faith in my second act and her steady advice in my most neurotic moments.

My editor, Faith Black Ross, fell in love with these characters and changed my life. Faith's smart edits elevated this book. The Alcove Press team, including Madeline Rathle, Dulce Botello, and Rebecca Nelson, were so patient with a debut author, embracing ideas and lifting them beyond my wildest dreams. It's a privilege to work with such kind and thoughtful professionals.

My early readers, Joelle Babula, Jessica Stevens, and Jo Ann Mathews, provided gentle encouragement and insightful feedback. I forced drafts upon my family, Sandy Crittenden, Bonnie Volk, and Cindy Chandler as well as Marilyn Knowles and the Blue Ridge Book Club. Julie Gilchrist read, edited, discussed characters, and brainstormed plot while we wrangled children on hiking trails. I'm so grateful for the generosity of these women. This book exists and is better because of their involvement.

Meagan Fitzsimmons, Jennifer Miller, Maria Fehretdinov, and Sara Colangelo are the best law school friends an ex-lawyer could ever ask for. Thank you for your support, laughter, text chains, skincare recommendations, and annual getaways. Our friendship is a lifeline in my worst and best times. I hope our husbands get on board with the retirement commune we've planned.

The Loudoun County Public Library never suspended my account even though I always checked out too many books and requested even more obscure ones to borrow.

Kacey Musgraves's music was my writing soundtrack, transporting me into this story, even when I was squeezing in writing sessions during toddler naptimes.

Ben Raines's work, in particular *Saving America's Amazon,* provided a compelling portrait of Alabama's river systems, their natural splendor, and the unfortunate threats to their survival.

I spent the best summers of my childhood in Fairhope, Alabama. Even though it's an impossible task, I tried to capture a sliver of this town's magic and how much it means to my family.

My mom, Pam Laning, and my sister, Meredith Kimener, were my first readers and biggest cheerleaders, even when those early drafts weren't exactly cheer-worthy. My mom has always made me feel both loved and accepted, and I can only hope to have the same kind of relationship with my daughter. Meredith may be my younger sister, but she's my wisest confidant and I treasure her friendship.

My children, Isabel, Henry, and Leo, make me laugh, give me joy, and bring purpose to my life. Many times, I look across the room and can't believe I'm fortunate enough to be a part of our family.

Lastly, boundless gratitude to my husband, Jeff Ingram. After fifteen years of marriage, I know words of affirmation aren't your love language, so I'll leave it at this. Thank you for everything. Every day. Every moment together. I'm the luckiest